JAMES SCOTT

BYRNSIDE

IT'S ABOUT IMPOSSIBLE CRIME

ISBN: 979-8-218-68817-2

Special Thanks to:

Gary Nathan, Jaimie-Lee Wise, Gigi Pandian, Matt Willis-Jones, and Gabriele Crescenzi

Cover Design by:

James Scott Byrnside

Dedicated to:

MacKinlay Kantor
and
William Spier

CONTENTS

1.

SILENT STEPS OF MURDER

Whispering Pines was mostly dark. The residents were out patronizing the speakeasies in eager anticipation of the year's final celebration. At Navy Pier, rows of mortar tubes were loaded with aerial shells and rockets. In less than three hours, they would be launched into the cold, starless sky, exploding into webs of multicolored spangles. Their brief existence was destined to be syncopated to the drunken chorus of 'Auld Lang Syne.

It was New Year's Eve and Chicago was ready to bid farewell to 1927.

Private detective Rowan Manory and his assistant Walter Williams weren't planning on working very long that night. The only item on their agenda was verifying a witness statement—a routine follow-up on a finished case. The task wouldn't take long. A good thing—the detectives were looking forward to celebrating at their favorite watering hole, the Brown Bear Bar.

The snowfall that night was meager. It had nearly stopped when the detectives turned onto Manning Street.

Rowan looked up at the lamppost. One final snowflake pirouetted weightlessly in the beam of light. A thin layer of snow dust covered the ground.

At that moment, Chicago was a serene and magical place, quieted and wrapped in pristine purity.

Rowan stopped to take in the image. "It is beautiful, is it not, Williams?"

"It'll look a better after a few beers. Speaking of that—why can't we do this tomorrow, old boy? The witness isn't even important to the ca—"

A scream reverberated in the night.

"Murder!"

The sound lingered like the haunted notes of a jazz saxophone. Rowan and Walter peered down the street in search of its origin.

"Did you hear that?" asked Walter.

"Of course. How could I not?"

"Did he say…murder?"

"I believe he did."

Again, the cry rang out—a desperate, haunted voice slicing through the night.

"Murder!"

"I definitely heard it that time."

The detectives rushed toward the sound. They passed several apartment buildings before spotting a turbulent beam of light bobbing and weaving in sync with the frenzied dash of its holder. The figure holding the flashlight screamed for a third and final time.

"Murder!"

"Stop shouting," said Rowan, approaching the man cautiously. "What's happened?" The light shined directly into Rowan's eyes, burning his retinas. He slapped it away. "Damn you!"

The man holding the flashlight blurted out breathlessly, Listen here, you— My God. Is that you, Mr. Manory? What in blazes are you doing here?"

Rowan snatched the flashlight from the man and turned it toward him. "How did you know my name?"

The navy-blue wool overcoat and the badge on the peaked cap left no doubt that he was a cop. From under the cap, a curl of orange hair reached out, defiantly burning against his gaunt, pale face. His blank gaze and wide eyes suggested shock.

"Everybody knows you, sir. You're the most famous detective in the world."

"I fear the world is too vast a place for your statement to

be truthful. I appreciate the compliment nevertheless. I am indeed Rowan Manory. This is my assistant, Walter Williams. What's your name, son?"

"Quinn, James Quinn."

"Let's have it, Officer Quinn. What happened?"

"There's been a murder."

"Yes, we gathered that from your conspicuous announcement. Where is the victim?"

He pointed at the apartment building behind him. "She's in there."

"Who is the she?"

"I don't know her name. She lives…lived in the rear apartment on the ground floor of the building. Shot and…and stabbed."

"Do you have a working theory?"

"Pardon?"

"What do you think happened, my good man?"

"Robbery gone bad would be my best guess. I think the woman caught a thief red-handed and he musta gone berserk. She was shot once but…" A look of disgust swept over him. "He stabbed her in the face more than a few times. That's why I came running out screaming. There's a callbox on Turlington Road. I was headed there to call it in."

"Fleeing madly from the crime scene and screaming the word *murder* probably wasn't the best tactic."

"No, I guess not."

"Better to secure the location and use the phone inside the apartment, yes?"

Quinn exhaled a few frosty breaths before stuttering an answer. "I'm sorry, sir. I've never seen a dead body before. It's awful."

"How long have you been on the job?"

"Two weeks."

Rowan's tone softened. "No need to apologize. We will simply limit mistakes going forward." He turned to Walter. "Take a walk around the building. See what you can find."

Walter nodded. "Right, boss."

Rowan directed his attention back to Quinn. "Breathe, officer. In through the nose, out through the mouth."

"I'm fine. Just in shock, I think."

"Tell me how you came upon the scene. Slowly."

Quinn obeyed, addressing Rowan the way he would a shellshocked infantryman. "I was walking my beat, blocks 173-180. I was in front of this building when I heard a loud crash from inside. I didn't know what it was, but it sounded…dangerous, like a skirmish. I ran straight to the side door."

"Was it open?"

"Huh?"

"The side door—was it open?"

"Yes. I stepped inside the vestibule. The door to the rear apartment was also open. The woman's body is on the living room floor. She's lying face up. There's a gunshot to the chest and cuts all over her face."

"Do you think the crash you heard could have been the gunshot?"

He shook his head. "There's a blanket next to the body with a hole burned through the center. I figured the killer used it to muffle the sound of the gunshot. I'm pretty sure the crash I heard was from a mirror at the back of the apartment. It's smashed in half. The glass is over the floor. It looks like there was a fight."

Walter came running up the left side of the building. "No footprints other than Quinn's. The right walkway has a garden, but no door. The entrance to the vestibule is on the left and there's a back door from the rear apartment that leads to the back yard. It looks to me like there are four apartments in total, two on the ground floor and two upstairs."

Rowan rolled himself a tidy cigarette and lit it. "That's odd. Most low-rise apartment buildings have the common entrance on the right side. This must be an older building. Did you have a look into the vestibule?"

"A quick one. There's a staircase and the two doors to the

apartments on either side. The rear apartment was open. I didn't stick my head in, but I could see the body through the kitchen doorway into the living room.

"Very good. Officer Quinn?"

"Yes."

"Take us to the body."

Quinn gulped. "Okay, Mr. Manory." He began to walk forward until Rowan stopped him.

"You'd better have your gun at the ready, Quinn. Just in case."

"Oh, right." With a shaky hand, he pulled the gun from his holster.

Rowan and Walter stared quizzically at the firearm. The standard revolver given to beat cops was a Colt Positive 38, but that was not the revolver in Quinn's hand. Rather, it was a well-worn Smith & Wesson Model 10. The finish was a mottled grey with pitting on the barrel and a cracked grip.

Walter cleared his throat. "That's an interesting weapon you've got there. Is that what the force issues these days?"

Quinn forced a chuckle. "Mine got stolen a week ago. I didn't want to report it, so I got this at Windy City Pawnbrokers. I've never shot a gun outside of the pistol range." He stared uneasily at the revolver. "I've never had any reason to."

Policeman was the one occupation that any Irishman could latch on to, regardless of age or experience. Walter sympathized with Quinn who probably took this job as a last resort. If he ever found himself in a shootout, Quinn would be a dead man. He certainly didn't have any experience securing a crime scene.

Walter had spent two years in the war. He knew exactly what to do. "I'll take the lead if you want."

Quinn offered him the gun without hesitation.

Walter declined. "No, thanks. That pea-shooter would blow my thumb clean off. I'll take your bully though."

The officer gave Walter his club and the investigation began.

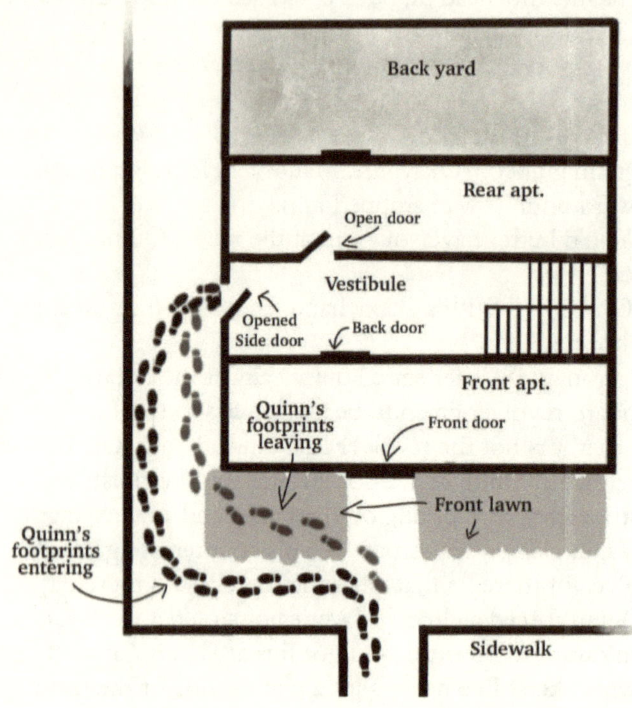

The kitchen's worn linoleum floor and cracked, cream-colored walls were a testament to the passage of time. A wooden table with peeling paint sat in the center of the room, flanked by mismatched chairs. A block of knives sat on the countertop, its top slot empty where the largest blade should have been—and the missing knife was nowhere in sight.

It wasn't the worst kitchen Rowan Manory had ever stepped in, but his inclination about the building's age had been on the money. This was most likely one of the older buildings in Whispering Pines.

A doorway led from the kitchen to the largest area in the apartment, the living room. It was here that a fight had most likely occurred. Against the wall, a battered dresser stood with its doors slightly ajar. Glossy issues of Photoplay and Vogue lay crumpled over the floor and a kaleidoscope of shattered powders, smudged lipsticks, and broken compacts were scattered around a crushed makeup kit.

Dust outlined shapes on the surface of the dresser, suggesting that many items had recently been removed. The edge of the dresser had small amounts of blood spatter as did the corner of the wall.

A hell of a fight.

A threadbare couch dominated the middle area of the room. Its fabric was a muted shade of brown that likely once resembled a warmer hue. The rear door to the back yard stood at the far end. Next to that hung a wall-mounted mirror shattered into shards of reflective glass. Half of it defiantly clung to the wall while the rest lay piled on the floor in jagged pieces.

The glass curio cabinet on the right-side wall stood out, oddly pristine amid the room's chaos. Filled with a collection of photos, globes, and crystal knickknacks, the curio obviously represented the victim's more treasured possessions. It appeared to be completely undisturbed.

One of the more curious features in the room was a pile of three items in the center. At the base rested a slightly tarnished jewelry box, followed by a worn shoebox in the middle, and crowning the stack, a radio with a patina that suggested years of use. These items, arranged haphazardly, told Rowan much about the evening's unfortunate order of events.

So did the corpse.

Though the scene was just as gruesome as Quinn had described, Rowan felt no trepidation. He had witnessed so many dead bodies in his career that his only reaction upon seeing a new one was to read it. Hovering above the bloody woman's face, he took his time to make a note of all the details.

She was tall and lithe. Her dark hair and smooth, fair skin were now stained red. She was dressed to the nines in a flowy, burnt-sienna evening gown layered with a sage-green skirt. A red spinel necklace lay bunched up at the bottom of her bloody throat and rings of sterling silver graced her fingers.

Both her clothing and jewelry suggested a very different evening than the sort she experienced.

At her right wrist was a pale imprint. Even against the backdrop of her wan flesh, the lighter-hued mark stood out like a ghostly whisper. It suggested that she had habitually worn a watch or bracelet that was no longer there.

Walter returned from the bedroom with an envelope and a card. "The victim is Veronica Hart, a burlesque dancer at the Uptown Theatre." He poked the brim of his fedora. "A damned shame."

As Rowan announced the injuries, Walter wrote them in his trusty notebook.

"I make out six stab wounds to the face. No other visible cuts to the body. The single gunshot is centered roughly between her breasts. Though there is no stippling, the blanket that Quinn mentioned is only a few feet away. No doubt she was shot at close range with the blanket as a muffler. In fact, I can see some fibers in the injury which match the blanket. There is tearing at the dress's shoulders and sleeves. Her nails are cracked and tinged with blood. Miss Hart put up quite a fight."

Walter looked up from his notebook. "Bless her. I hope she got the son of a bitch good."

Rowan pointed to her right arm. "This was a remarkable scuffle. Note the bite marks."

"Bite marks. Jesus. What sort of scum bites a woman?"

"There is one on the bottom of the bicep and one on the underside of the forearm close to the elbow. Both are quite small, only one or two teeth wide."

"That's interesting. Are we looking for a guy with a small

mouth?"

"No, Williams. We are not." Rowan took a long drag of his cigarette before crushing it under his shoe.

The puzzle reveals itself, piece by piece. The lack of knife wounds on the body, the fact the knife was taken from this very kitchen, these bizarre bite marks—it creates a very specific picture of what has happened here tonight.

Quinn, who had been sent to the front apartment to call the police, appeared in the kitchen doorway. "There's a unit on the way with a crime scene analyst just like you asked."

Rowan nodded. "Well done, officer."

"The woman who lives in the front apartment is named Mrs. Kozlowski. She owns the building. Do you want to speak with her?"

"I do. Wait five minutes, then send her in."

"What should I do after that?"

"Stand guard out front. Don't let any curious citizens engage with the crime scene. When the officers arrive, tell them to conduct a thorough search of the building and get a statement from the tenants as to their whereabouts this evening. I want to know if they saw or heard anything strange. The officers are to be on the lookout for any fresh wounds or bruising. There was a nasty fight here tonight and I think our killer won't be in peak physical condition. Have you got all that?"

"Yes, Mr. Manory." He glanced at Veronica Hart's corpse—just a flicker—before hurrying from the room, his stride catching for half a second on the threshold.

Walter joined Rowan next to the body. "So, if the killer isn't found in one of the other apartments, that would pretty much wrap up the case, yeah?"

Rowan furrowed his brow. "How do you mean?"

"Well, it would be obvious. There aren't any other footprints leading out of the apartment besides Quinn's. If the killer isn't here…" He waited for Rowan to agree with him, but the detective said nothing. "Do I have to spell it out for you? If the killer isn't here, that means Quinn is the killer. He looks like a guilty man to me. Did you see the way he looked at her just now?"

Rowan shook his head. "Officer Quinn did not murder Miss Hart. He's an innocent man, and I'd ask you to stop casting ridiculous aspersions regarding his character. What you perceive as guilt is very much disgust for the violence inflicted upon her. If the rest of the force held as much revulsion for violence as Officer Quinn, I dare say the city would be better off."

"So, you think the killer is inside the building?"

"I do not know, Williams. That's why I'll wait for the police to search the apartments."

Walter cast a suspicious side glance at his boss. Rowan was always onto the solution well before Walter had developed his first incorrect theory. This particular instance of ignorance seemed especially feigned.

"Are you sure you don't know. It sounds an awful lot like you know exactly what happened, and you're just waiting for me to make an even bigger fool of myself than I already have."

Rowan let the suggestion lie. "Let's have a quick look at these stacked items. I find them to most intriguing."

With a handkerchief wrapped around his hand, Rowan lifted the radio off the top of the pile. "This is an Atwater Kent, one of the more common models of radio." Rowan opened the shoe case revealing a set of scuffed, low-heeled pumps. "Do you recognize the brand?"

"Those are Mary Janes."

He replaced the lid and lifted the case. His eyes widened. "Hello." At the corner of the jewelry box was a small trace of blood. "Now that is an interesting clue."

"It is?"

"Definitely." He looked over the radio and shoe case again. "No blood on the other two. Just this one."

Walter nodded along as if he too had become fascinated by the clue.

Inside was a mishmash of rings and pendants bunched

around several bracelets. Rowan chose the one he thought looked the fanciest, a sterling and moonstone link bracelet. He read aloud the engraving on the inside.

"Nag pines for Nagiana. In lust, Marty."

"I don't get it."

Rowan smirked. "They are snakes. The giver of this gift is a fan of Kipling. And a fan of sobriquets. He's also a pervert."

"I still don't get it."

"I will explain it to you later." Rowan pulled a few more bracelets. Each was engraved with a different name along with an endearing note. "It would appear that Miss Hart had plenty of suitors, some wealthier than others." Rowan re-stacked the items to their original positions and rolled himself a cigarette.

"What's our next move, boss?"

"I have an important job for you, Williams. In fact, it is of the *utmost* importance."

"Consider it done. What do you need?"

"I want you to walk Manning Street for two blocks in either direction and count how many buildings have a vestibule on the right side, how many have one on the left side, and how many have one in the front. When you are finished, come back and report your findings."

"But…why? Why would the structures of the surrounding buildings have anything to do with this murder?"

Rowan patted Walter's shoulder. "The *utmost* importance."

"Are you angry with me?"

"No."

"Are you just giving me busy work as a brush off?"

"If you don't hurry, I'll be forced to hire an assistant who doesn't ask silly questions. Now go."

Walter inched toward the door. At one point, he turned around forcefully as if he were about to protest, but his confusion kept him silent. He left the apartment without lodging a single complaint.

Rowan moved on to the curio. In each picture frame,

Veronica was in a ritzy-looking club with her arms draped over an important looking man. One of the photos caught his attention.

My God! If my eyes do not deceive me, that is Martin Santillo. He was an alderman. Hanged himself last year. At least, that was the opinion of the investigators.

Nearly all the spaces between the framed photos were filled with trinkets—tiny crystal ballerinas, a ceramic set of Airedales, a glass egg—too many to categorize on the fly.

There was, however, one glaringly empty space on the shelf.

Once again, the dust patterns revealed to the detective that something had been removed. This time, it was a circular object.

Rowan bent down next to the shards of mirror at the back of the room. Within the shattered glass were tiny miniature buildings coated in a dusting of artificial snow. He quickly surmised that a snow globe had been taken from the curio and thrown into the mirror.

Why?

Before Rowan could come up with an answer, a nasal voice came from the kitchen doorway.

"Oh, God! Ronnie!"

There stood Miss Kozlowski, staggering while standing and leaning on the wall for support. In her sixties, she had a ruddy face and an alcoholic's breath. The long bushy hair framing her head resembled a pair of curious, furry ears. An over-sized, olive-green robe hung from her shoulders, paired with a faded red silk scarf. Lipstick had been applied to excess, smeared past the contours of her lips the way a child disobeyed the lines of a coloring book. Tall, brassy, and loaded—she was a spectacle.

"He butchered you." She sobbed.

"Who is he?" asked Rowan.

"Whatdya mean? The sunnuvva bitch who did this."

"I see. Are you the owner of the building?"

She nodded. "Myra Kozlowski. And I know who you are.

I've seen you in the paper. It's because of you that Brent woman and her baby got murdered."

(Note this is in reference to the Tommy Brent murders the previous year. A case Rowan famously botched.)

"Don't believe everything you read in the papers, Miss Kozlowski." He spat the words at her angrily, but, upon seeing her flinch, lightened his tone. "They are in the business of sensationalizing tragedy." He pointed to the body. "Is this Veronica Hart?"

"Yes."

"She was your tenant?"

Myra looked at the corpse and nodded. "Look at what he did to her face."

"Was there anyone who had cause to harm Miss Hart?"

"She wasn't the smartest girl on the block. She coulda made some fella jealous. Plenty of them came around to see her."

"I noticed. Her jewelry box was full of bracelets. I assume they were gifts from different…suitors."

"That was her favorite jewelry. She always asked for a bracelet. Bless her soul. She used to be a star at a fancy burlesque joint, rubbing shoulders with big shots. She had rich boyfriends lined up. That's what she told me anyway." She hiccoughed. "Lately, things got rough for her. Lost her job and started working at some not-so-swanky places. I reckon some of the new guys she was with were shady characters. Poor Ronnie."

"Did you hear anything strange noises from this apartment tonight?"

"I've been asleep all night."

"You didn't hear the mirror shatter?"

She shook her head quickly.

Normally, Rowan would question such an assertion, but it was reasonable for a drunk like Myra sleep through some noise. Still, Rowan had to make sure. "Would you remove your scarf?"

She raised a hand to her neck. "My scarf?"

Rowan didn't budge. "Yes. Remove your scarf. Please."

She obeyed, untwirling the silken accessory with all the enthusiasm of a prisoner walking to his execution. Her neck was indeed bright red, but it was not from a fight. It was obvious the woman suffered from some skin condition and this, accompanied with the sagging bit of turkey flesh hanging from her neck, told Rowan that she had put on the scarf in order to hide her embarrassment rather than any evidence of murder.

"And now could you roll your sleeves."

She huffed in protest, but did the action. Again, there was nothing to indicate she'd been in a fight.

"Thank you, Miss Kozlowski. Tell me, how long was Miss Hart your tenant?"

"Three months."

"Did she pay her rent on time?"

"Oh, yeah. She still had fellas who would throw her some rubes, and she was smart enough to squirrel away some nuts. Ronnie never wanted for money."

"Do you have any names for these fellas with the rubes?"

"No, but…" She leaned forward, looking carefully at a specific place on the corpse. "No, I don't."

"What were you looking at just now?"

"Her wrists. Like I told you, johns would buy her a bracelet 'cause that was her favorite thing to wear. And she always asked the guy to have it engraved cause she was sentimental like that. I thought you could have looked at the engraving and gotten the name of the man she was supposed to meet, but—"

A twinkle came to Rowan's eye. "But she is not wearing a bracelet."

"No."

He considered that fact as he puffed away at the wispy bent end of his cigarette.

Fascinating.

Miss Kozlowski was uncomfortable with the silence. "Do you need anything else from me?"

"Only one more thing." He pointed upward. "Two apartments upstairs as well?"

She nodded. " The Fredricks live in the rear apartment, Annie and Andre. They're older than me. The front apartment is rented by a younger couple named Edwards, but I'm sure they're out for New Years Eve and all." Her eyes drifted back to the body, and her countenance grew sour. "Such a cruel way to go. Maybe somebody got jealous. It's the only reason to do that to her face."

"Miss Kozlowski, that is a fine deduction. I think that'll be all for now."

She stumbled out of the room.

When the police arrived on the scene, they were accompanied by no less than Sergeant Delbert Grady. Why Grady was bothering with this mundane murder, Rowan didn't know. Veronica Hart didn't seem like the sort of very important corpse that would attract his attention.

At 45, Grady carried the weight of years on his broad shoulders, his once-dark hair surrendering to an unforgiving shade of grey.

"What brings you here, Grady?"

He scratched his head. "Teamsters got rowdy at the South Canal Union Hall—someone fired a pistol in the air and half the crowd dove for cover. One guy lost a finger, but nobody's dead. I had to put out the fire." The gravelly timbre of his voice betrayed no emotion. Grady may as well have been talking about buttering his bread. "On the way back, we got a call about a murder. When I heard you were here, I got curious." He nodded at the body. "Who is she?"

"Veronica Hart."

"What's so special about Veronica Hart that the great Rowan Manory gets himself involved?"

"I was in the neighborhood…just like you were. Your officer needed help."

"And you're being a good Samaritan. Is that the story?"

"That's right."

"And I suppose you've already solved this little murder?"

"I have a decent idea about what's happened."

"Of course, you do. Let's hear it."

Rowan shrugged. "I think your crime scene analyst will have no problem gathering the necessary facts. This murder is as obvious as a neon sign in the dark."

"My crime scene analyst is busy with a more important case. It's New Years Eve and we're stretched thin. If you're willing to help out, I ain't gonna say no."

One of the cops entered the apartment to announce their findings. "The front apartment is empty. The couple in the back are both practically deaf, and they're both elderly. There's no way they were involved in this. The killer isn't here."

"What do you say, kid? You gonna help us or not?"

Rowan considered the idea for a moment before shrugging his shoulders in compliance. "All right." He turned to the curio and took hold of a snow globe about as big as the one that had been smashed into the mirror."

Grady squinted at him. "What are you up to?"

With all his might, Rowan heaved the globe against the remaining half of the glass. The mirror gave way with a cascading shatter, splitting apart in jagged veins. The globe burst open on impact, scattering water, glitter, and porcelain ruins across the floor.

"Jesus H. Christ!" screamed Grady

"I don't know this neighborhood very well, said Rowan calmly. "Is there a good place to eat?"

Walter knew Rowan had a penchant for finding hidden clues in the oddest places, but he couldn't imagine any possible connection between the neighboring buildings and the murder of Veronica Hart.

As he trudged back toward the crime scene, he spotted Officer Quinn standing on the sidewalk.

"What's doing Quinn?"

The officer blew on his chilled hands. "I'm not sure. They

must have found something by now." He winced. "She sure looked awful, didn't she?"

"I don't mean to offend you, but it could be you're in the wrong line of work."

He laughed. "It's that obvious, huh? I had to take this job. The Loop and every pier over Lake Michigan are NINA. All of Chicago is NINA. I've got two choices: get shot or blow out my back with a shovel. If I die, at least my wife will be taken care of."

Walter noticed the wedding band on Quinn's finger. "Any kids?"

He nodded absently. "One so far. A baby girl."

"Quit."

"What?"

"The police force is a pipeline for orphans. Now you take a guy like me. I'm never going to get married. This is perfect for a guy like me. Or like Manory, he—" Walter grew silent at the sight of his boss walking toward them.

"Isn't that right boss?"

"Isn't what right?" asked Rowan.

"I was just telling Quinn here that he needs to quite, find himself another way to earn a living."

Rowan grinned at Quinn. "Never listen to Williams. It will only cause you trouble." He lit a cigarette. "Tell me, boys, while you were out here did you see or hear anything strange?" He looked from one to the other with an expectant expression on his face.

They answered in calm unison. "No?"

"Never mind then. Have you finished your survey, Williams?"

Walter dutifully took out his notebook. "There are twenty-two apartment buildings in a two-block radius. Once you reach Palmer it's all residential houses. Of the apartment buildings, fifteen have a center vestibule and six have one on the right. Veronica's building is the only one with the entrance on the left side."

"Just as I suspected. This building is older and I seriously doubt Miss Kozlowski is interested in renovation of any kind." He turned to Quinn. "Officer Quinn, I'd like to thank you kindly for your assistance. You have proven instrumental in solving the case."

"I didn't do bupkiss. I think your partner might be right about me."

"Come now, officer. Every case brings with it a chance for improvement. Now, if you'll excuse us, we're off for a cheeseburger and some coffee."

"We are?" asked Walter.

It was only a few blocks to the nearby BG Sandwich Shop which, to Rowan's chagrin, did not serve burgers past eight o'clock. He settled for a Reuben and a cup of black coffee. By the time he finished establishing the important facts of the case for Walter to compile in his notebook, the sandwich was gone and he was puffing on his third cigarette.

"So, my friend, what do the facts in this case tell us?"

Walter took a deep breath. "You're not going to like my opinion."

"Only if it is nonsense. I rarely like it when you opine nonsense."

"Despite what you said earlier, the facts seem to point to Quinn shooting and stabbing Veronica Hart. Quinn's footprints tell a very clear story."

"I agree. They tell us a crystal-clear story. This clarity, however, has seemed to evade your understanding. Officer Quinn is incompetent, yes. A fool, undoubtedly. But he is not a murderer."

"That doesn't leave us with many suspects, does it? The couple upstairs couldn't have done it, the other couple weren't home, and you cleared Miss Kozlowski. If none of the four people who were anywhere near the body during the time of the shooting are the killer, then who is? And how in God's name did he escape?"

"The killer's identity and method of escape can be found

by accumulating the details in that notebook and building a faithful reconstruction of the truth through rigorous concatenation. Let's start with simplicity. What do you know to be likely?"

Walter thought about it for a moment. "Veronica Hart came home to a burglary. The killer had already begun to stack the items he wanted when she came through the door. He probably thought it would be easy to overpower a dame, but some of them can fight, by God. That's not outrageous for a cabaret girl. Those types know how to defend themselves. You don't hang around the people that Veronica did without knowing how to handle yourself. She scratched him good, probably got a few licks in. That made him angry and he pulled out the knife. When he finished cutting her up, bang, he popped her in the chest."

"What of the blood I found on the jewelry box?"

"Spatter from the gunshot."

"But the jewelry box was on the bottom of the stack. There was no blood on the radio or the shoe case. How did the blood travel to the bottom of the pile."

"Because…" Walter paused. He looked up from his notes. "You know what? That's a good question."

"I contend that all three items of the stacked items were on the dresser when Veronica was murdered. They were removed and stacked afterward."

"That may very well be, but it doesn't eliminate the possibility that this was meant to be a robbery. A good thief knows what he wants to steal."

Rowan smiled. "And what would he want to steal?"

"Huh?"

'What would a good thief want to steal? A shoebox containing old worn shoes? A busted-up radio?"

"No, I guess not."

"I know what I would steal—the pendant on her neck, the rings on her fingers, hell, besides the bracelets, none of the jewelry in the box was worth much. And the very first thing I'd do is clear out the crystal on the curio shelves. You might even say that I would have done none of the things our thief did."

"That's a fair point. But—"

"But nonsense. The timing of events is antithetical toward your *theory*."

"Why'd you say the word *theory* all sarcastic like that?"

"The killer shot Veronica, then stacked up the items on the floor. The only reason to do it in this order is to make it look like a robbery gone wrong. And it worked. Both you and Quinn accepted it without question. With this in mind, what happened next?"

"I suppose he smashed the mirror for reasons unknown."

"Not yet. There is the matter of the knife. I told you there were no knife wounds on her arms. What does that indicate?"

Realization overtook Walter's face. "Oh, yeah. The stabbing was all post-mortem, otherwise she would have had defensive wounds. The first cut may have surprised her, but she would have tried to block the others. There would be wounds all over her arms. Stab me once, shame on you. Stab me twice…" His eyes widened. "Unless she was tied up, then—"

"There were no ligature marks on her wrists."

"You checked?"

"Of course I checked."

"Hmmm. You know what, Manory? This wasn't a robbery at all. I don't know how you could you have come to that conclusion. Rather silly of you."

"My dear Williams, investigation is not simply about the facts. Psychology plays an enormous part. There is a burning question, begging to be asked, and, for some incomprehensible reason, you are ignoring it."

"All right, but don't get mad at me if it's the wrong question." He cleared his throat. "Why did the killer stab a corpse six or so times in the face?"

"Exactly."

Walter let out a sigh of relief. "That was a lot of pressure."

"It takes a tremendous amount of effort to stick a knife into flesh and pull it out once. After the sixth time, she was probably exhausted."

Walter narrowed his eyes. "What do you mean she?"

"No doubt about it, the killer is female."

"Wait, wait, wait. How do you know that?"

"The bite to the arm tells me it was a woman."

"Which bite?"

"There was only one."

"No, no." Walter flipped a page in his notebook. "See, I'm not crazy. You said there were two tiny bites, one on the right bicep and another one on the right forearm. Both were close to the elbow."

"I said no such thing. I told you there were two bite marks, not two bites."

"How is that any different?"

"Extend your right arm."

Walter obeyed.

"Bend your elbow."

"Okay, but I don't see…oh." He looked in astonishment at the newly-formed nook between his forearm and bicep. The scene played out in his head. "She had the killer in a headlock! The killer bit her arm to get out of it. That's why there were two bitemarks and that's why they were so tiny. The only teeth that can grab hold of the skin from that position are the…uh…"

"Cuspids."

"Sure." He slapped the table. "Holy shit!"

"Do you know any woman that would put a man in a headlock?"

Walter smiled. "My mother?"

"Williams, this is not the time for jokes."

"I'm sorry."

"Even a tough broad, as you would refer to Veronica Hart, doesn't put a man in a headlock. And it's quite rare for a man to bite during a fight, certainly during a fight with a woman. As you asked earlier, what sort of scum bites a woman? If we combine this with the wounds to Veronica's face, what does this tell us psychologically?"

"The killer was angry. Could be jealousy. Yeah, it's the wife of some john that Veronica was seeing. That makes sense. Okay, so the killer goes to her apartment with the intention of killing her."

"No."

"God damn it, can't you lie to me and tell me I'm right just one time."

"If the killer had intended to murder Veronica, why would she not simply shoot her. Why the fight? It seems to me the killer went there with the intention of discussing something with Veronica. Perhaps, she wanted to convince her to cease all sexual activity with her husband. When Veronica responded in the negative, a fight ensued. The gun was the last resort. The killer stacked three items to fake a robbery and throw off the police."

"What about the globe and the mirror?"

Rowan checked his pocket watch. "It is nearly 11:40. Come, I will explain it on the way."

"On the way where?"

"To the killer's home, of course."

"Do we need to catch a cab?"

Rowan shook his head. "We can walk."

The detectives walked in silence. They passed Nagle into Portage Park, where the median income dropped every time you crossed the street. The brick townhouses were spalled, cracked, and bulged; a few looked like modern ruins.

It was only when they entered this dilapidated neighborhood that Rowan continued his lecture.

"Look at your diagram of the building once more. Do you notice anything funny about the footprints?"

"I'm not the greatest artist in the world, if that's what you mean."

"I refer to their location, Williams. What is funny about their location?"

Walter studied the picture.

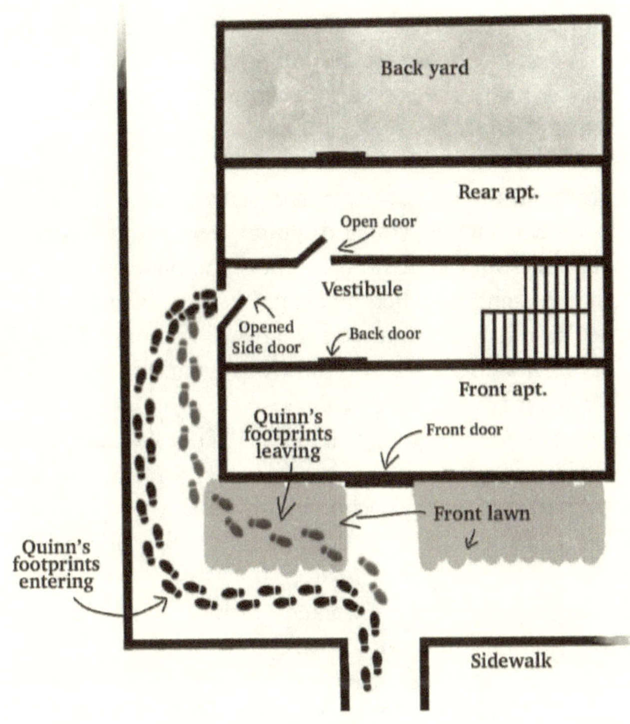

"Nothing funny at all. He walks to the door and enters. Then he leaves."

"How did Quinn know?"

"How did he know what?"

"That the entrance was on the left. You looked at every apartment building on the block. None of them have an entrance on the left side. At the very least, he should have walked to the right and shined his flashlight to look for a door, but no, his steps are directly to the left without a single one out of place."

"That means…that means…"

Rowan nodded. "Say it."

"That means Quinn had been to Veronica's apartment before."

"I came to precisely the same conclusion. Of course, it was necessary to prove that Quinn did not run to the left because he heard the smash of the mirror through the opened side door. So, I tested him."

"How?"

"I smashed the rest of the mirror with a snow globe. When I went outside, you and Quinn were standing on the sidewalk in front of the house—the same place where Quinn was standing when he claims to have heard the mirror shatter. When I asked if he heard anything, he said he hadn't. That's how I know Quinn was lying. He couldn't have heard it from the sidewalk."

Walter stared at him, mouth agape. "That's so smart."

"And if you need further proof, look at the way Quinn approached the house. Was he in a hurry?"

"How can I tell that from looking at the footprints?"

"Did he take the quickest route?"

Walter gasped. "No! He walked on the concrete walkway."

"How polite of him not to walk over the grass. If I heard a violent crash and suspected something nefarious was happening, I would not hesitate to cut across the lawn. You'll notice that Quinn had no such reservation when he left the crime scene. He ran right over the lawn because that was the quickest route."

"Then…then who smashed the mirror? And when?"

Rowan stopped walking when they reached a worn-down townhouse. "Let us put ourselves in officer Quinn's shoes. He arrived at the apartment building at 2240 Manning Street, fully intent to spend quality time with his mistress."

"Our tax dollars pay for that."

"He found both doors open and Veronica Hart lying dead on the floor. He must have been shocked."

"Yeah."

"Quinn had to report the murder, but explaining why he was in Veronica's apartment was going to prove quite difficult. He could not use the excuse of the gunshot because of the presence of the blanket, but the idea of a loud noise was one he liked. He made it by smashing the mirror. Then, screaming bloody murder, he ran from the building. And whom should he run into?"

Walter grinned. "Us."

Rowan shook his head. "Me."

"You."

"Chicago's finest detective. Though I must confess, there was another bit of misfortune that befell Mr. Quinn. The snow proved the murderer never left—unless, of course, she had gone much earlier."

Walter turned toward the townhouse. "And where are we now?"

"This is the extremely humble abode of Officer Quinn and his wife."

"Do you mean the wife is the killer?"

Rowan held out his arms. "Was that so difficult, Williams?"

"It was extraordinarily difficult. It would have taken me weeks to figure it out without your help."

"I like to think you would have accidentally backed into the solution after a mere few days."

"Wait a minute. Do we have proof she was the one?"

Rowan pointed down the sidewalk. "I believe Grady is delivering it to us now. That's why we stopped for food, to give him a chance to collect the evidence."

It was indeed Grady, clopping around the corner with several officers in tow. He looked and sounded untypically joyful. "Kid, you are something else. Every hunch you had was spot on."

Rowan remained resolute. "Where did you find the weapons."

"In two garbage containers on the way here, just like you said."

"No, I mean what were the names of the streets?"

"Who gives a shit. You're done, Manory. We'll take it from here."

"With all due respect, I'm the one who solved the murder. I'd like to finish the job by obtain a written confession from the killer. Now, on what streets were the garbage containers located?"

"She dropped the knife in a bin on Taylor. Then, she dropped the Positive on Cunningham."

"Knife on Taylor, gun on Cunningham. I've got it." He was about to turn up the walkway when he remembered something. "Oh, did Quinn have the bracelet?"

Grady answered by plucking the bracelet from his trench coat pocket and handing it to Rowan. "He snatched it off the dead broad's wrist. What a scumbag. Anything else?"

"No. Williams and I will call out to you when she is ready to confess."

The thin layer of snow had hardened into a brittle sheet of ice. The detectives stepped carefully over the icy walkway to the house.

"Do you think Mrs. Quinn will put up a fight?" asked Walter.

"No. This cat's claws are surely dulled at this point. Nevertheless, I want you near the door. Keep your eyes on any drawers which might contain knives. Don't let her make coffee."

He took a deep breath and rapped at the door. "Mrs. Quinn." He knocked and called out again. Mrs. Quinn!"

"Who is it?"

Walter whispered. "She sounds Polish, doesn't she?"

"I'm Detective Rowan Manory. I have news about your husband."

"James!" She screeched his name like a wailing banshee.

"Yes. Please let us in."

The chain rattled and the door pulled open. "Where is James?"

Upon seeing Mrs. Quinn, Rowan understood immediately

why this woman, as Irish as they come, sounded Polish. A stiff jaw and a split bottom lip had lessened the movement of her mouth. The result sounded uncannily like a Polish accent.

My goodness. Veronica did a number on you, didn't she?

One of her eyes was a blue drop in a sea of white. The other had been painted red and rancid black by burst blood vessels. Her face carried an impressionistic collection of scratches going this way and that.

Rowan pretended not to notice. "Mrs. Quinn, may we come in? The weather is most disagreeable."

She welcomed them into the kitchen nervously, scrunching up sections of her blue and white checkered frock. The kitchen table was splintered with four mismatched chairs of different sizes, just like Veronica's kitchen. A taupe muslin weave covered the back wall, poorly hiding a patchwork of damp and faded blotches.

Rowan sat without asking. He laid a paper on the table and pinched some tobacco on top of it. "Won't you sit down, Mrs. Quinn"

"Do you want coffee?"

Walter pulled a chair. "Have a seat, Mrs. Quinn."

She hovered behind the chair, hands fluttering uselessly at her sides, as if she'd forgotten how to sit. "What happened to my husband? Is he all right?"

Instead of answering, Rowan carefully rolled a tight cigarette. He struck a match and took one of his long, thoughtful drags before blowing a bitter, blue cloud into the room. "You do not have much time, Mrs. Quinn. You need to sit down and talk with me."

She curled onto the chair with her eyes magnetically glued to the floor. "Okay, I'm sitting. Tell me what happened to James?"

Again, Rowan chose to ignore her question. "Very soon, the police are going to come into this room and arrest you."

"Why?"

Rowan regarded her with a look that blended

disappointment and disbelief. His brows knit together, forming a creased line of concern on his forehead as he maintained an unwavering gaze. With a subtle shake of his head, he said, "We are way past that, Mrs. Quinn. That is not even a conversation worth having."

"I don't understand." Her immobile jaw failed to hide the growing desperation in her voice.

"In a city like Chicago, someone is always watching. The wino in the alley on Taylor Street sees you toss the bloody knife into the garbage. On Cunningham, an old woman is looking out her window when you throw away the gun. Even on a night like tonight, someone is watching. We have those weapons now; the gun you stole from your husband and the knife you took from Veronica Hart's kitchen. The one you used to disfigure her after her death."

"I would never do that."

"That is what murderers always say. Those of us who break the fifth commandment cannot imagine ourselves acting so reprehensibly. I would never do that. I *could* never do that. The truth is that no matter how fully formed your ego, there is always room for the savage. The mind is a willing traitor of your humanity. You find yourself covered with blood and you don't even know exactly how it happened. In the throes of murder, your mind gives itself completely to your mad, newly-formed notions of the world. Reality becomes a wild sleep, both exciting and calming within the calamity of things. But all dreams must end." Rowan leaned forward. "This is over."

She protested once more, but something had changed. Her voice was suddenly devoid of passion, the words droning out apathetically. "I've been home all night. I was with the baby. I would never…"

"You can embarrass yourself, but no one will believe you. The past cannot be undone. The future, however, has yet to be written. If you choose to deny what you did, the story of your future will be the murder of Veronica Hart, a beautiful woman brutally murdered by a failed wife. Such a narrative will not be in your favor, and you will lose your life to a massive prison sentence."

"Why can't I talk with my husband? He'll know what to do."

Without missing a beat, Rowan placed the bracelet on the table. "This is what he bought her, Mrs. Quinn. When was the last time he spent any money on you, his wife? Hell, a man who puts his family in a home like this ought to be saving up for something better. Instead, he's buying gifts for a tramp. Cheap gifts—this is easily the worst bracelet in Veronica's vast collection—but I bet you would consider it to be a lot of money. How much formula would it have bought? How many pairs of shoes? This is the man you think will help you now? Seriously, Mrs. Quinn?"

Her eyes turned to the bracelet and she finally broke down. "I…I…" She sobbed.

Rowan handed her his handkerchief and patiently waited for her to compose herself. When her sniffling had abated, he continued. "There exists an alternative narrative in which this crime becomes focused on you, a good, faithful woman who would do anything to keep her family together. A woman who went to see her husband's mistress with every intention of ending the affair peacefully. You only brought the gun for self-defense. That much is obvious. If you had wanted to murder Veronica Hart, you would have done so straight away. Instead, you tried to talk to her. Veronica was insane, violent, a dangerous woman. The murder was a last resort. She had attacked you. We know she put you in a headlock. Had you not defended yourself, who knows what might have happened."

Once again, something changed within Mrs. Quinn. She had gone from confusion to panic and was now displaying something which might be called clarity. "What about the stab wounds? They'll know. They'll know I did them after she was dead because I wanted her to be ugly."

Rowan scoffed. "Nothing but the residue of the passion you had for your family. The press likes a fighter, someone who will not give up easily. And if that person is a new mother…" He whistled long and slow. "That's a hell of a story. Chicago's best public defender is Clarence Darrow. You may recall the Feldstein case. A woman shot her husband and his mistress in her own bed. She's a free woman today because of Darrow. In fact, she served less than three months. And she didn't even have a baby to elicit sympathy."

Walter chimed in. "After your face heals, Darrow will take you to the beauty parlor and doll you up real nice before you go in front of the cameras."

"That's right. He'll craft your image for the press—that's what he does. You will be a wronged woman seeking absolution for the sin of loving her family too much."

Mrs. Quinn finally looked away from the bracelet. "How long will I be in prison?"

"That we cannot promise. No one can say how the cards will fall with certainty. Your best chance is to take responsibility for what you've done. That is the only way for you to control the narrative."

A baby's sharp cry called out from another room, breaking the tension that had built up in the kitchen. Mrs. Quinn's eyes turned moist once again. "My Maeve."

At this, Rowan showed no pity. He leaned back with all the confidence of a man who had every fact backing him up. "The choice is yours. If you say nothing, the overwhelming evidence will put you away for years. You won't see Maeve again until about the year 1970. And I seriously doubt you will last that long in prison. There are no old women in prison. Do you think that your daughter will even want to see you? Imagine what her life will be like? The orphanage will be her home. Things will not go well for Maeve Quinn and she will blame you for everything." He shrugged. "Or you can be released from prison while Maeve is still a child. I would guess the worst-case scenario to be ten years, but I highly doubt it will be that long. Regardless of the exact number of years, you will still have a relationship with the girl and she will have the possibility of leading a fulfilling life."

Her focus faltered. This was the pivot every interrogation reached—the moment when the suspect, having edged close to the truth, suddenly feels the weight of what that truth will cost. For a heartbeat, they believe they can still claw their way back to safety, still spin the lie that saves them. Denial flares up like a last defense.

Rowan sensed it. She was entertaining one last mad attempt to deny the murder. He wouldn't let it happen. He clasped her hands and looked into her mismatched eyes.

"Little did you know when you woke up this morning that today would be the most important day of your life. I don't know how to make it any clearer to you. Right now, you decide. Which story will be told? Which life are you going to live? You can choose life or death, but you must choose now."

The room remained quiet and still for several moments. Rowan held his breath the entire time.

Her shoulders slumped. Her good eye went dead. She nodded. "Okay." Her eyes welled with tears. "Okay."

"Good." He opened the door. "She's ready."

There was a flurry of activity in the kitchen. One officer explained to Mrs. Quinn that she was under arrest and her confession was completely voluntary while another began wordlessly taking her fingerprints.

Walter left the residence. Rowan followed him, but stopped at the door on his way out.

"Mrs. Quinn?"

"Yes?" She sobbed.

"You have made the correct decision."

He turned around just as the first crack of fireworks split the air. Bursts of light spilled through the open door—blue, then red, then white—flickering across the kitchen walls behind him. He didn't look back.

1927 was finished.

2.

WHERE THERE'S SMOKE, THERE'S PAZUZU

Many of Rowan Manory's cases began with the shrill ring of the telephone. The case of the Pazuzu Curse was no exception.

Riiiiing.

Rowan checked his pocket watch. "10:00. I thought we might just make it to lunch without a phone call today."

Walter shook his head. "I knew we weren't going to be that lucky." He answered. "Good afternoon. This is Walter Williams speaking. How may I—" He took his legs off the desk and sat up straight in his chair. "Who is this?" His expression shifted to one of alarm.

"What's wrong, Williams?"

Walter slid the telephone toward him. "It's for you, old boy. He won't give his name, but he says it's a matter of life or death."

Rowan nestled the receiver against his ear. "This is Manory."

The man's voice was calm but insistent. *"My dear Mr. Manory, I wish to bring to your attention a terrible murder that will soon take place."*

"Oh?" Rowan listened intently. Over the line, he could make out the tail end of a faint, hollow ringing sound. It remained for a moment as a dull resonance before fading into the mild static of the telephone. *Was that a bell?*

The caller loudly cleared his throat. *"Are you there, detective?"*

"Of course, I'm just grabbing a pencil." He snapped his fingers and Walter handed him one. "Do you know who is going to be murdered?"

"Burt Parnell."

Rowan jotted down the name. "I don't know this man."

"You'll meet him soon enough. Mr. Parnell is going to be murdered in the most horrible way imaginable. His body will be torn apart. Then, it will be set on fire. His head will be cut off and his entrails spilled onto the floor. It's going to be a bloody mess. There will be no suspects...at least none that are human. I would give you more information, but it would be better if you discovered the truth for yourself."

"How do you know all this?"

The man gave a chuckle. *"If I told you that, you'd probably be able to ascertain my identity."*

"It sounds as if your voice is muffled. Are you speaking through a cloth?"

"Very perceptive, detective."

"Why telephone me? Why not the police?"

"Because I want the very best detective working the case. I know you'll accept. Solving Mr. Parnell's murder would bolster your reputation as Chicago's preeminent sleuth. Mind you, failure will be the outcome. You can say you gave it the old college try at the very least."

"You don't think I'll be able to solve it?"

"There will be nothing to solve. This murder will be a completely supernatural affair."

"I have investigated many murders. The solution always lies within the bounds of reality."

"Not this time, Mr. Manory. Hopefully, you are honest enough to report the truth to the press. I will be a very happy man when I read a full account of your failure in the newspaper."

"Why is that important to you?"

"I didn't telephone to answer your questions. I'm giving you information. Mr. Parnell has an office on the third floor of Pinnacle Place. You'll have no trouble contacting him—his office is on Harrison, directly across from the candy factory."

"I did not catch your name, Mister...?"

"Goodbye, detective."

“Shit.” Rowan hung up the phone and turned his notes toward Walter. “Do you know Burt Parnell?”

“Never heard of him, but I know Pinnacle Place. It’s one of those shared office spaces.”

“Shared office—what’s that?”

“If someone’s running a private business or if a company doesn’t have a set place, they can rent office space in that building. A lot of private attorneys work directly out of Pinnacle Place. Why? Is this Parnell fella going to be murdered there?”

“He is going to be murdered, butchered, and set on fire.”

“Talk about overdoing it.”

“Indeed. Get me Pinnacle Place on the telephone.”

Walter placed the call, then passed the receiver back to Rowan.

“This is Cityscape Retail and Management, Pinnacle Place division. Alan Figgins speaking. With whom shall I connect you?”

“I’d like to speak to Burt Parnell, please.”

“Just a moment.” The phone rang for a while before Alan returned to the line. *“I’m sorry, sir. He doesn’t seem to be answering. Hold the line a moment. I’ll knock on his door.”* There was a longer pause. Finally, Alan returned. *“Sir?”*

“Yes?”

“He still isn’t answering. I’m terribly sorry about this. Would you care to leave a message?”

“Could he have stepped out for a moment?”

“I’m afraid that’s impossible. I saw him enter his office this morning and his door is in view of my desk. He hasn’t left that room.”

Rowan slammed the transmitter back into its cradle. “Let’s go, Williams.”

The detectives hurried outside into the brisk, spring air. Rowan flagged a cab with the ease of someone who did this far too often. He tossed a crisp five-dollar bill at the cabbie. “Pinnacle Place, and make it fast.” The driver’s eyes lit up as he pocketed the cash. “You got it, pal.”

The cab lurched into a sharp U-turn, causing Walter to clutch the headrest.

"Why do you think the caller wants you involved?"

"He wants a respected investigator to verify his wild claims. There's no one in Chicago better than me."

"Why does he want them verified?"

"Difficult to say. My initial thought is that the caller might be the leader of some crackpot religion or perhaps a seer or psychic. It's an old con. He claims to foresee some terrible supernatural event – a murder, in this case. He gathers his followers or his clients, feeds them visions of death, destruction, whatever fits his narrative. Then, when the time is right, he orchestrates the crime himself, but makes it look like something beyond human means is the culprit. His true targets, already primed to believe in his mystical powers, read in the newspapers that even the great Rowan Manory cannot explain these gruesome murders. Now more than ever, they believe he can foresee death. After that, they'll swallow anything he says and pay for the privilege of hearing it."

"How would he manage to kill somebody that way in a busy building like Pinnacle Place? In broad daylight?"

"That's a question that can only be solved after examining the crime scene. I—"

The taxi screeched to a halt on Harrison, trapped by a massive crowd overtaking the street and sidewalk. All the faces were turned upward, eyes wide and fixed on the billowing smoke pouring from a third-floor window of Pinnacle Place. The fumes were thick and solid black, snaking down the building's side and coming to a crawl like venomous fog. All the while, the vague smell of burning chemicals lingered in the air along with the distant wail of an oncoming siren.

"What's burning up there?" asked Walter as they exited the cab. "It smells a little like sulfur, doesn't it?"

As they shoved their way through the crowd, the blare of approaching sirens engulfed them, shrill and rising from four speeding police cars. A deeper, thunderous wail announced the firetruck at the center. Red lights flashed, casting an eerie glow over the scene as all five vehicles thundered down the street, closing in fast.

The squad's teamwork was impressive in its efficiency. While the police created a lane to the building, a team of six firefighters jumped off the truck with a hose and quickly affixed it to a nearby hydrant. The firetruck continued forward until it was directly in front of the building where the remaining firefighters grabbed the essentials—smoke masks, tool sacks, and axes—before rushing through the front door. All the while, the police worked to establish a fifty-foot perimeter to keep civilians at a safe distance.

Rowan recognized the escort squad commander. Officer Len Parker was a badge polisher and a holster warmer at the station who had been making lanes for firetrucks and ambulances for the better part of ten years. Rowan crossed paths with him on occasion, but this was the first time he had cause to seek him out. He moved to the edge of the perimeter and cupped his hands around his mouth.

"Parker! Hey, Parker!"

Officer Parker's eyes lit up when he saw the detectives. He motioned for his men to let them through.

"Well, I'll be damned. Rowan Manory and Walter Williams! What's doing, boys? I haven't seen you two in a coon's age."

Rowan motioned toward the building, "What is the emergency?"

Parker tilted his head like a bulldog. "What do you think, Manory? It's a goddamned fire. Didn't you hear the sirens? I thought you was the best detective in the city. It don't take Sherlock Holmes to see what's happening here this morning."

"Who called in the fire?"

"I don't ask questions. I just clear the way. You know what I mean? If I had to guess, I'd say it must have been someone from the building."

"Doubtful."

Parker's face twisted in bewilderment. "How's that?"

"Why hasn't the heat detector been activated? Where are the occupants? Shouldn't they be exiting the building?"

His eyes went blank for a moment before he laughed and shook his head. "Those sound like the problems of a man being paid much more than I am."

As if on cue, the building's heat detector rang out.

Parker stuck his tongue between a big gap in his teeth. "There's your damned alarm, detective—just like you asked. And looky here—the occupants you was just talking about."

Rowan nodded as a surge of people poured from the building's exits, scattering in all directions.

The firefighters on the ground aimed the hose at the open window. The force of the water shattered the remaining pane, sending shards of glass and a torrent of water into the smoke-filled room. Thick, dark smoke billowed out in a dense, liquid-like wave, swirling into the sky. After a few seconds of pressure, the hose was shut off. One of the firemen raised a bullhorn to his mouth. "Alright, boys, axe that door!" Through the window came the sound of sharp cracks—splintering wood.

Rowan, ever composed, rolled a cigarette and lit it, puffing slowly as he waited for word on what lay inside the burning room. He didn't have to wait very long.

While stragglers continued to flee the exits, a lone fireman soon emerged through the front door. His mask was off, revealing a soot-smeared face twisted in raw terror. He crossed the lot toward Parker and leaned in, whispering something low and urgent.

The officer stepped back, to examine the man's expression. He seemed in desperate search of some sign of exaggeration or a cruel joke. When he saw there was none, Parker looked around helplessly until his eyes met Rowan's. He shuffled his fat frame a few feet toward him.

"We need your help, Manory."

"A murder?"

"How did you know?"

"Who is the victim?"

"We can't tell. He was in the room that was on fire and the door was locked…and…and…"

"Yes?"

"His damned head was cut off. The body was—"

"Disemboweled?"

"What does that mean?"

"It means to slash or tear the abdomen so that the internal organs protrude."

"Then, yes. He was disemboweled."

"Was there anyone else in the room?"

He took off his hat in awe. "That's the other part that don't make no sense. The room was empty!"

Sergeant Grady was barely two days into his vacation on Mackinac Island when he got the phone call. He wasn't very happy about it.

"Listen to me carefully, Manory. I'm back in one week. If you don't have this business wrapped up by then, I'll kick your fat ass. Understand?"

"Does this mean I am in charge of the investigation?"

"What do you think, numbskull?"

"Thank you?"

Click.

Rowan's first order of business was establishing the morning's events.

1. The fire was reported anonymously at 10:04. The caller said only four words before hanging up the phone: *Pinnacle Place, fire, quick.*

2. Emergency services and police arrived at 10:18.
    a. Six firefighters stayed outside.
    b. Seven were stationed on the third floor.
    c. Eight moved throughout the other five floors in order to evacuate the building. Both staircases were used for evacuation.

3. When the signal was given, the door to the office was axed open and the firefighters entered the room. One of them tripped over an object. He picked it up and held it close to his mask. To his absolute horror, he found himself holding a severed head. As the smoke dissipated, the charred body sitting in the chair became visible as did the entrails underneath the desk. The room was thoroughly searched, but no one other than the victim was found inside.

Rowan saw the corpse before it was taken away. The body was burnt to a crisp, but the head was in decent shape. It was positively identified as Burt Parnell with the help of photographs. By all available accounts, Parnell was a respected and successful investment banker who, though he enjoyed a loose affiliation with Harborview Investments, preferred to operate independently whenever possible. How he came to be in his current state and why somebody wanted him that way were the questions at hand.

Because the fire marshal had to inspect the room before anyone else could have a look, the detectives were forced to begin with witness testimony.

Walter flipped to a blank page in his notepad. "Who's up first?"

"The front desk operator—Figgins."

Alan Figgins quietly sipped coffee from a ceramic cup. His creamy blonde hair was meticulously chiseled at the edges, and a subtle hint of citrus cologne lingered about him. His respectful demeanor didn't match the traces of inherent impishness present in his long, carefully-groomed face. Had Burt Parnell not been slaughtered that morning, Alan would have certainly been delivering well-placed bon mots for the detectives' enjoyment. That's the impression Rowan had anyway.

Alan recognized Rowan's voice. "You're the chap who

telephoned this morning?"

"My apologies for not saying goodbye. This is my assistant, Walter Williams. We're handling the investigation into Burt Parnell's murder and we need to ask you a few questions."

Alan wiped his upper lip with a thick handkerchief. "I can't believe I'm discussing murder on a Friday morning." He glanced across the hall at the remaining jagged shards of Parnell's door. "Honestly, there's not much I can help you with. I'm as dumbfounded as everyone else."

"Yes, well, considering the proximity of your desk to the crime scene, your testimony is paramount to the case. What time did Mr. Parnell arrive this morning?"

"Roughly 9:00 a.m. He entered from this stairwell." Alan pointed to the door next to his desk. "I greeted him. He nodded in return before walking straight to his office. He used his key to open the door. That was the last time I saw him. No one could have slipped in or out of that room. I was either at my desk or in the hall all morning. I might also add that no one other than Mr. Parnell has a key to that office."

Rowan scoffed. "That isn't terribly interesting."

Alan furrowed his brow. "Really?"

"The doors to all of the offices have metal warded locks. They are cheap and easy to pick. Anyone with the vaguest hint of locksmithing experience could have broken into Mr. Parnell's office and locked the door from the inside."

"How troubling. I had no idea they were so ineffective."

Rowan paused to roll a cigarette, handling the tobacco with the calm precision expected of someone who had done it a thousand times. He licked the edge of the paper, sealing it with a quick swipe of his tongue. A match flared to life. He puffed at the cigarette a few times before taking a long, deliberate drag. The smoke created a thin veil between himself and his interrogatee.

Alan seemed unnerved by the silence. "Do you…do you have any other questions for me, detective?"

"I'm having trouble wrapping my head around a certain aspect, Mr. Figgins. This emergency was reported at 10:04—by whom, no one seems to know. The firemen arrived at 10:18 with all sirens blazing, and yet, not a single soul from any of the building's five floors evacuated during those fourteen minutes."

Alan rolled his shoulders into a confused hunch. "I didn't know there was a fire. It isn't surprising that no one else did either."

Rowan pointed across the hall without taking his eyes off Alan. "You didn't know there was a fire in the office directly across from your desk…less than fifty feet away? Is that correct?"

"It sounds ridiculous, I know, but as God is my witness, I never heard or saw any indication of a fire."

"What about the sulfurous odor in the air? Surely you could smell it inside the building."

"There was an odor coming from the room, yes, but I have smelled something similar coming from his office from time to time. Believe it or not, it often smelled much worse. Of course, I never inquired about it; it was Mr. Parnell's business, and it's my job to make the occupant happy, not the other way around."

"What about those other occupants? Did they ever complain about the odor?"

"Some did. Through trial and error, I discovered that eucalyptus oil and tap water nullified the stench quite effectively." He lifted a perfume atomizer from under his desk. "You can take this and put it into evidence." His mouth broke into a tiny, unmistakable grin, "Isn't that what you people say? *Put it into evidence.*"

Rowan squeezed the bulb pump and had a whiff. He nodded, finding the aroma most agreeable. "That won't be necessary. What about noises? Did you hear anything strange coming from the office this morning?"

Alan paused, pursing his lips together. Something he hadn't previously given much thought suddenly came to the fore of his mind. "I think I may have heard a hissing sound, like the faintest hint of a gas leak. Strange, but it was so faint that I didn't pay it close attention." He shook his head with frustration. "I could be mistaken."

"When did you hear this sound?"

"We have an occupant in office 3A, a Mr. Reynolds. He called me and asked me to come to his office. When I did so, he drew my attention to the crowd that had gathered outside. It was then that I spied the smoke coming from the window of Mr. Parnell's office. Naturally, I ran to the hall and tried to open Mr. Parnell's door. It was locked. At that point, I could hear the faint hiss and then a crackling sound."

"You tried the handle?"

"Certainly. I wanted to make sure Mr. Parnell was unharmed. I imagine I would have tried to smash the door open, but it was right then the heat detector sounded and the firemen appeared from the front stairwell. They ordered everyone on the floor to evacuate."

"As I understand it, Mr. Parnell owned that office space? Is that unusual?"

"Most of our clients rent, but Mr. Parnell was successful enough that buying made sense. He still paid the company service fees for security, cleaning service, and my services." He smiled that helpless smile of his. "I'm not cheap, you know?"

"How long had Mr. Parnell owned that office?"

"Six years if I'm not mistaken."

"And you've been here . . . ?"

"Nine months."

"Was there anything unusual about his activity in recent days? Anything at all?"

"Now that you mention it, there were a few things about this week that were quite out of the ordinary. On Monday, Mr. Parnell had a visitor, a young man I had never met." He pulled the register from a nook under his desk and opened it. "Farley Sage was his name. He arrived without an appointment, but Mr. Parnell agreed to see him." Alan shook his head. "Most irregular."

At the mention of *Farley Sage*, Walter looked up from his notes. Rowan and Walter had worked together long enough to communicate without words. Rowan registered Walter's concern at the mention of that name before resuming the interview. "How long was Farley Sage's visit?"

"Ten, fifteen minutes at the most. It wasn't long after Mr. Sage left when Mr. Parnell came out of his office. He looked…" Alan paused mid-sentence. His fingers momentarily adjusted the perfectly straight tie at his collar. When he finally spoke, his voice had changed. It was now hesitant and measured, almost as if he were afraid of implying something nefarious. "I didn't speak one word with him, you understand, but…the way he looked after meeting Farley Sage…it was unsettling." He hesitated again, his brows knitting slightly as he recalled the scene. "Mr. Parnell's face was drained after that meeting, almost ashen. His eyes had this wildness to them, as if he had seen something absolutely dreadful. I've never seen Mr. Parnell so rattled." He let out a nervous involuntary chuckle. "I almost didn't recognize the man."

Rowan took a moment to puff his cigarette. "Very interesting."

"The next day, Mr. Parnell received a telephone call that I found troubling. I asked the caller for his name. He wouldn't tell me." Alan leaned forward and whispered, "He said, *'That bastard knows who I am.'* I was certain Mr. Parnell wouldn't want to speak with someone so incredibly rude, but he didn't seem taken aback at all. He took the call without the slightest hesitation. Imagine my surprise. Mr. Parnell left for an early lunch after that phone call; he rarely, if ever, took an early lunch. And again, he had that frightened look on his face. He's had that look most of this week. I dare say, he had it when he arrived this morning."

This made perfect sense to Rowan. In his line of work, it was almost a pattern—murder victims often unraveled in the days leading up to their deaths. Irregular schedules, strange behavior, and erratic emotions were the telltale signs of someone caught in the snare of dangerous relationships or shady dealings. By the time they were killed, the strain of whatever threat loomed over them had already begun to show. Burt Parnell's worried demeanor was just another piece of a puzzle Rowan had seen too many times before, the final cracks in a man pushed to the edge.

"Is that everything you can think of, Mr. Figgins?"

"Just one more thing. On Wednesday, he received a telephone call from Anderson & Brookes while he was out."

"Who are they?"

"Real estate and development. The agent said to tell Mr. Parnell that they were interested in purchasing his office. In fact, Mr. Parnell was scheduled to meet with them this afternoon."

Rowan motioned to the busted door down the hall. "He was selling that office?"

He nodded. "Mr. Parnell had even filed paperwork with the city. He told me it was a done deal."

"Did he mention why he was selling the office?"

"I don't ask questions."

"Smart man. Thank you, Mr. Figgins. You've been most helpful. You can go home. We'll contact you if we need anything else."

When Alan had exited down the stairs, Rowan asked Walter, "Who is Farley Sage?"

"I've never met Farley, but I served with his father, Andrew. We haven't seen one another in years."

"Do you know where he lives?"

"Last time I checked it was in Back of the Yards."

"Can you pay him a visit? See if he knows anything about why his son would be visiting Burt Parnell?"

Walter hesitated.

"Are you not on good terms?"

"No, no. It's just…" He shook his head. "I'll go talk to him."

"Do that. Ask him for Farley's contact information and set up an interview. Make sure your friend understands that we do not have any suspects at this point. We only believe that his son might have information helpful to our case."

"Right."

Rowan stamped out his cigarette, carefully watching his assistant's reaction. From the shift in his partner's demeanor, Rowan could tell that something was gnawing at him beneath the surface.

"Something wrong?" Rowan asked, his tone as casual as possible.

"No," he replied, too quickly, clearing his throat. "I'll handle it."

Without another word, he pulled open the door and entered the stairwell. The pace of his echoing footsteps were steady, but Rowan could sense it—the hesitation that clung to the air after Walter was gone. He would inquire about it later. For now, he had to move on to the next witness.

Langston Foley didn't strike Rowan as having the intimidating nature necessary for a security guard. He was in his mid-sixties, had terrible eyesight, and his hearing wasn't worth a damn.

"What's that you say?" he yelled.

Rowan raised his voice. "Where are you usually stationed?"

"Ground floor, right near the stairwell. That's my desk."

The old man's jaw worked like a cow—up and down in a slow, deliberate chewing motion, though there wasn't a crumb of food in sight. It unsettled Rowan in a way he couldn't shake. The motion seemed reflexive, mechanical, as if Langston had lost control of some part of his brain and his body had taken over—thoughtless, like an automaton. It was the kind of habit that hinted at something deeper, something involuntary, and Rowan found it troubling. Would he be the same in twenty years? Perhaps, worse?

"You gonna ask me any more questions?"

"Yes, I'm sorry. I have a lot on my mind. How long have you worked for Cityscape?"

"A few years. Can't say when I began exactly. Cityscape would know. Why don't you call them steada' asking me?"

"I will. Mr. Foley, would you call this a *secure* building?"

He chewed the air a little slower. "How do you mean?"

"When I walked around the base of this building, I noticed several windows without locks. The locks on the offices are cut-rate. And you," he paused, forming a way to express his thought inoffensively. "You might be a bit past your prime. Security is not a top priority at Pinnacle Place, is it?"

Langston shrugged. "There ain't nothing to steal. No money, anyhow. And…and…no one came through the front door. At least no one who didn't have cause to be here like a leaseholder or member of the staff. I can guarantee you that much."

"I understand that Mr. Parnell had a visitor on Monday. Is that correct?"

"Yes, sir. He had a visitor. He also got himself a package delivered."

"Is it unusual for him to receive packages?"

"Not in and of itself, no. What was unusual was the man who dropped it off."

"What about him?"

"Tweren't the mailman."

"Who was it?"

"Didn't give his name, but he was awful distinctive—a cloak and gloves, all black. He had a beard too. Looked like a preacher, but not a good one, the sort of preacher you might see in a nightmare. He wore a big ol' piece of jewelry I've never seen before, a big metal circle round his neck."

"An amulet?"

"Could have been. I ain't never seen an amulet before, so I can't say. It was big. He had this way about him. He moved like he wasn't stepping. And his eyes—they were cold."

Rowan looked up from his notepad. "What color is cold?"

"Black. Ain't nobody have black eyes, I know, but his were so dark that the color wasn't apparent. He was a white fella. I'd guess early twenties. Hard to tell with the beard."

"Did he say anything?"

"Just that he had a package for Mr. Parnell. He gave it to me and left. Ten minutes later, that other fella came."

"Farley Sage?"

"That's the one. He had no appointment, so I took him upstairs personally. Mr. Figgins okayed it with Mr. Parnell and I delivered the guest and the package. After a while, Mr. Parnell came to see me. He asked me a lot of questions about the man who dropped off his package. I couldn't answer most of them. Everything I knew then is everything I know today…everything I told you."

"How big was the package?"

Langston held his hands apart by 14 inches. "That big. It was wrapped in brown parchment paper and there wasn't nothing written on it."

"Were there any other visitors or packages for Mr. Parnell this week?"

"No."

"I've been told that Mr. Parnell left early for lunch on Wednesday."

"That's right. I hailed the taxi for him."

"Do you know where he went for lunch?"

"He always goes to the Commodore. It's got good food. But you know something? That's the first time since I been working here that he left for lunch that early?"

The maître d' of the Commodore was most helpful over the telephone.

"I remember it well because Mr. Parnell didn't take his usual place near the window. He sat at the back with a strange-looking fellow wearing all black, a beard, and an amulet around his neck. He was straight out of Weird Tales."

"Did you overhear any of their conversation?"

"No, but it was heated, lots of finger pointing and such. After only a few minutes, the man with the amulet stood and began to walk out, but he stopped, turned around and said one more thing. One of our busboys passed by and heard it. It doesn't sound like an English word. I've certainly never heard it before."

"What was it?"

"Pazuzu. Whatever it means, Mr. Parnell turned white as a ghost at the sound of it."

Heavy industry sprawled across the outskirts of Back of the Yards, a relentless backdrop of metal scraping against metal in harsh, repetitive rhythms Cattle lowed in the distance, while conveyor belts groaned and saws whined through bone.

Walter's friend had come to live in this ratty little neighborhood.

Andrew Sage's yard was patchy and unkempt. A few hardy shrubs lined the walkway, but most of the plants had either died or begun the process in earnest. His wife, Betty, had always been a keen gardener, cultivating a lush and vibrant lawn and garden year after year. It seemed she had given up the practice.

Walter stepped onto the porch, taking in the weathered, chipped paint on the door. It had once been a deep green, but now the surface was cracked, flecked with white where time had worn it away. His knuckles met the wood, its rough texture biting at his skin, brittle beneath his hand. The knock echoed faintly, and for a moment, he expected it to splinter further under his touch.

Andrew answered the door wearing an apron. He was gaunter than when Walter had last seen him. Lines had developed over his face, sculpting it into deeply etched sections. His hair had faded into a washed-out gray, neither dark nor light—just nothing. He was only forty-three but could easily pass for elderly.

"Walter?"

"How are you, buddy?"

A spark resurrected in Andrew's glazed eyes. "You son of a bitch. You look fantastic."

"Why are you surprised? I always look fantastic."

"What brings you around these parts?"

"Is it a bad time?"

"God, no. It's perfect. Come in." Andrew stumbled backward, beckoning Walter to enter the kitchen. "I was just making breakfast for Betty. She woke up a few minutes ago."

"How's she doing?"

"Oh, you know. Good days and bad." He walked to the counter and dug a butter knife into a bottle of cod liver oil. "Are you…*uh*…still doing the gumshoe thing…with that detective."

"That's right." Walter looked around. The kitchen was cramped with cabinets that had seen better days. A single window with a lacy curtain let in weak sunlight, casting a pale glow over the mismatched dishes stacked next to the sink. Despite the wear, Andrew had kept the space clean.

"How about you? Still working for the city."

"Part time."

"Doing the same thing as before?"

"Yeah. It keeps me busy. That's all I need is to keep busy and I can get by." He spread the amber-colored oil over a plate of fried eggs.

Walter frowned at the dish. "That's an interesting breakfast you've got there."

Andrew laughed. "Betty has rickets and the doctor said she has to eat this every day. She'll be happy to see you, by gum." He called out to the living room. "Sweetie! Guess who's here!"

Sharp coughs filtered through the hall. A weak voice asked, "Who?"

"Do you remember Walter? He's come to pay us a visit." He picked up the plate of eggs and motioned for Walter to follow.

The living room windows were all wide open, flooding the

room with illumination. The sunlight pooled around Betty, making her seem even frailer, almost translucent. She was sitting on the couch, hands resting limply in her lap. Her skin was sickly pale and her hair was brittle and thin. When she spoke, her mouth barely moved.

"Won't you sit down?"

A pit deepened in Walter's stomach. The mantel was overcrowded with photos of the couple in better times, laughing or gazing longingly at one another. They had been vibrant and joyful before, but now looked to be dying slowly and quietly in private. He sank into the chair with a polite nod. "Betty."

Andrew put the eggs on the wooden table in front of his wife.

She covered her mouth and coughed. "Don't ever get sick, Walter. You'll have to eat such dreadful food."

Andrew chuckled. "I must say I feel better after eating it." He sliced off a triangle of fried egg white and forced it down his throat. "Doesn't taste half bad after you have that first bite."

"It's not nice to lie, dear." She took a nibble, wincing as she swallowed. "It's been so long since we've seen you, Walter. Have you been busy solving crimes?"

He nodded politely. "Murder never sleeps."

"We've read about your exploits in the newspaper. It must be exciting work."

Andrew said, "Whenever the boys and I get together, we talk about your cases. The last time we met was right after that Greenbriar murder. They always ask me about you—where you've been, what you've been up to, and such. I don't know quite what to tell them."

Walter preferred to remember the boys the way they had been during the war. He didn't want to see them in their present state. "How are they?"

Andrew's mouth made the motions of a smile, but his eyes didn't cooperate. "Good and bad days—the same as all of us. Freddie just got out of Cook County."

"For what?"

"Burglary. It was six months, but he's in good spirits now."

Freddie Lindstrom had survived a raid at Vittorio Veneto without a bullet coming near him. He was the squad's good luck charm. Throughout the tour of Italy, Freddie had given them the precious illusion of safety when they needed it the most. Walter considered him to be the bravest man he had ever known. It was hard to imagine a man like that turning criminal.

"How about Carlton?"

"Dead."

"Oh, no."

Andrew nodded. "Last Christmas. They think he must have passed out just before the blizzard struck. His body wasn't found for three days. At least he probably slept through the whole thing. Carlton never got used to being in country. Heck, most of us haven't."

Betty put a thin hand on her husband's knee. "You should ask Walter about next weekend."

Andrew's eyes lifted at the idea. "Yes. Freddie, Wilbur, Curt, and I are heading up to Fort Sheridan. You should come too."

Walter opened his mouth to respond, the excuse already forming. "Next weekend? I've got—"

Andrew cut him off with a raised hand. "They treat ex-doughboys like royalty at Sheridan. We can come and go as we please. There's free food and Lieutenant Horowitz always has the best rum. You can play some cards or just relax. It's always a good time. You don't have to work weekends, do you?"

"Sometimes." Walter forced a cough. "Actually, the reason I'm here has to do with my job. I need to speak with your son."

Betty stopped chewing.

"Farley?" asked Andrew. "He's at work. I can call him for you."

"Could you?"

"Not a problem."

Betty sat back, suddenly eyeing Walter suspiciously. "Why do you need to speak with Farley?"

"Just some minor questions. Nothing serious."

Andrew grabbed the telephone from the sill and dialed Farley's work. "I'd like to speak with Farley Sage." He grinned. " This is Andrew Sage. He's my son. What's that?" The smile disappeared. "Oh? That's odd… I suppose I'll try him at his apartment. Thank you kindly."

"What's wrong, Andrew?" asked Betty.

He didn't answer his wife. Instead, he tapped the switch hook several times and tried a different number. After about thirty seconds, he limply replaced the receiver, his hand trembling slightly as he let it go. His shoulders slumped, and he seemed to shrink, hunched over as if the weight of the moment had broken him. "No answer at his apartment," he muttered, his voice hollow.

"And he wasn't at work?" She coughed.

"It's the darndest thing. The receptionist at Sterling said that Andrew called in on Wednesday to say he was taking off the rest of the week because of a family emergency."

"Is there a family emergency?" asked Walter.

Andrew shook his head. "None that we know of."

Walter slipped the notepad out of his pocket. "Do either of you know a man named Burt Parnell?"

"We've never met him before, but we know *of* him."

"How do you know him?"

"Farley is engaged to Parnell's daughter, Lizbeth."

Walter paused his writing. "If that's the case, why haven't you met Mr. Parnell? I would think the parents of the bride and groom would at least have lunch together. A coffee. Something."

"Lizbeth and her father are not on speaking terms. We could hardly be expected to introduce ourselves if he doesn't even talk with his own daughter. Her mother has been dead for years."

Betty added, "She told us specifically not to contact him. It would be embarrassing for Farley if we went against his wishes. Besides, we don't mingle in the same social circles as Mr. Parnell."

Andrew snorted awkwardly. "We don't mingle *period.* Those days are well and gone."

Again, she tried to cut straight through the chatter "Is Farley in trouble?"

"Not at all," said Walter in a soothing voice. "I need to interview anyone who has had any contact with Mr. Parnell this week. There's a…long list of people. Farley is only one of them."

She scoffed. "Farley's never met Burt Parnell. I told you that Lizbeth doesn't want anyone contacting her father. We respect her wishes. So does Farley. He adores the girl. He wouldn't hurt her in any way."

Walter paused. He tapped the pencil softly against the page.

Betty stared at him. "What?"

A bead of cold sweat traveled down the left side of his ribs. "I have it on good authority that your son met with Burt Parnell on Monday morning." He waited for one of them to speak. When both remained silent, Walter blurted it out. "Burt Parnell was murdered today. That's why it's important I speak with Farley. I need to know what they discussed."

Betty mustered as much ferocity as her condition would allow as the vaguest hint of color returned to her face. "Farley is a *good* boy."

Andrew darted his eyes from his wife to Walter. "Gosh, that's a shock. Do you have any…any suspects, Walter?"

"It's too early in the case for that. I'm only gathering information. Farley isn't a suspect. I want to make that clear."

Betty said something under her breath that Walter couldn't hear.

"Pardon?" he asked.

"Get out."

Walter grimaced. "There's no reason to be upset. He'll be right as rain as far as alibis go, I'm sure."

Just as he said it, Walter understood how his words had acknowledged a terrible possibility. A moment ago, Farley wasn't a suspect. Now, the man needed to produce an alibi.

He stood. "Perhaps you're right Betty. I should go. When you speak with your son—"

"You turn your back on your friends for all these years and now this." She shook her head slowly, *damningly*.

"Betty," said Andrew gently.

But her anger had turned righteous. She couldn't hear her husband. "After all you and Andrew been through together, you can't find any time to see him. And when you do finally show, it is only to involve our son in this unspeakably nasty business." She coughed. "It's rotten behavior, utterly rotten."

Walter took a step backward. "It was good to see you, Betty." Without a proper goodbye, he marched down the hall and through the kitchen. He didn't stop until the street. Hunched over and panting, Walter tried to catch his breath.

"Jesus."

Andrew shuffled out quickly, tugging at his apron strings as he hastened to catch up, his voice already filled with apology. "Don't mind her, Walter. It's the sickness... the medicine makes her lash out. She doesn't mean it." The words tumbled out in a rush, his eyes full of a mixture of guilt and helplessness. "She becomes aggressive without even understanding why."

"I get why she's mad. Farley's your only child."

"It's more than that. He's the only good thing we have left. Betty's protective of him."

"Is there anything I should know, Andrew. If there is, you'd best tell me now."

Andrew nodded. "Farley gave me some troubling news earlier in the week. I would have told you in the house, but I didn't want to say anything in front of Betty. On Tuesday of this week, Lizbeth received a call. The man didn't say his name, but he knew about Lizbeth and her father."

Walter's immediately though of the telephone call from the morning. "Did she hear any bells?"

"Bells?"

"Yes, ringing in the background."

He shrugged helplessly. "I don't know. Farley didn't mention anything like that."

"I'm sorry for interrupting. What did the man say?"

"He claimed that Burt Parnell was being extorted for an exorbitant sum--$100,000. If he didn't pay, he would be murdered."

"Did the caller say how he would be murdered?"

Andrew paused, his lips trembling. "According to the caller, the extortionist was some sort of witch doctor, a man with the power to summon demons and the powers of hell. Burt Parnell was going to be slaughtered and set on fire." He hesitated. "Is that…is that what happened?"

Walter didn't answer. "Why didn't Lizbeth or Farley or you go to the police?"

"And tell them what exactly? That Burt Parnell was cursed and a demon was going to kill him?"

"Yeah, I see what you mean. Did you give Farley any advice?"

"The same advice I always give him; keep your nose clean and stay out of other people's affairs. This man who was calling was obviously a crank." He paused. "Wasn't he?"

"Do you think Farley listened to you?"

Andrew looked downward. "My wife was telling you the truth. Farley *is* a good boy. He wouldn't do anything against the law, but…"

"But what?"

"He would do anything to help that girl. He's snakebit. Bad. I honestly don't know where he is now. Farley tells me everything. He's straightforward with his old man; has been since he was little. If he was going somewhere, he would have said something to me or Betty. That's why I'm so worried."

Walter handed Andrew his business card. "When you hear from your son, tell him he has to talk to me. Otherwise, the cops are going to pick him up."

Andrew's fingers fidgeted with the edge of Walter's card as if it might offer some kind of reassurance. His jaw clenched, and a bead of sweat traced down from his temple. When he finally spoke, his voice was quiet, but the tremor beneath it betrayed his fear.

"You'll protect him, won't you? I mean from the police. They don't care about innocence of guilt. If pinning a murder on someone closes the books, Chicago cops will do it in a heartbeat. We both know that. I'd like your word that he'll be treated fairly."

"I'm handling the case, Andrew. Nothing bad is going to happen to your boy. But he needs to call me."

"I'll make sure he does." Andrew's mouth crumpled. His eyes turned wet. "You were always good people, Walter."

They hugged in the middle of the street.

The fire marshal scratched his head like a squirrel in search of a buried nut. "It's a strange scene in there, Manory. I've never come across anything like it."

"I should hope not."

"No, I don't mean the body. I mean the fire. It was mighty…*selective*. It didn't touch the books."

As soon as Manory entered the office, he understood. Most of the right side of the room hadn't been so much as touched by flame. The only real damage on that part of the office was from the pressure of the firehose; two rows of bookcases had been knocked back and now leaned like suspended dominos against the wall. Several ancient tomes lay scattered across the soaked floor. They were all leather-bound with embossed artwork. Rowan took note of the titles. *The Alchemist's Grimoire, Keys to the Abyss, Codex of Azoth*—not the typical office library.

Next to the bookcases was the bathroom door. One look

inside revealed it to be nearly pristine. Between the door and the bookshelves stood a three-foot mahogany cabinet with two small doors. On top of the cabinet lay a single book titled *Liber Daemonum.* Though not exactly proficient in Latin, Rowan understood the gist.

The left side of the room contained all the fire damage. The desk was a blackened ruin with bubbled varnish peeled back to reveal the scarred, raw timber underneath. Twisted handles dripped over the drawers and the ashes of partially burned documents littered the surrounding area. Mixed in were melted plastic and indistinct fabric remnants. The wall behind the desk had borne the brunt of the fire's fury. It was heavily charred with black soot marks that stretched upward over cracked plaster.

The marshal pointed toward what was left of the desk.

"It's such a huge concentration of damage that I imagine the ignition had to have started right here. The body was in the chair with a pile of entrails on the floor below. They were completely oxidized. You can still see the mark. The blood, it *uh*..." He grinned. "It *rusted.* I'd say an accelerant was used. Can't say which one just yet. The forensic laboratory will determine the specifics."

"Why didn't the fire spread throughout the rest of the room?"

He raised both eyebrows doubtfully. "A chemical reaction...maybe. Certain chemicals burn quickly and in confined areas, which could possibly explain why the fire just stopped on this side."

"But you don't believe it?"

He shook his head. "With the time frame I've been given, the fire should have spread to the books and the bathroom. Don't quote me, it's just my impression."

Rowan flared his nostrils. "Do any accelerants leave traces of sulfur in the air?"

"That's another strange thing." He drew Rowan's attention to the carpet near the center of the room. "Have a gander at those."

Rowan bent down to get a closer look. When he first entered the room, he thought the black stains over the carpet were simply soot marks. Now he saw them clearly. "Are those *crystals*?"

"It beats me. I've never seen anything like them before. All I know is they smell like sulfur."

The "crystals" were small and dark, each one only a few millimeters in length. Together they formed a cluster of tiny stiff points spread on one area of the carpet. The finish was dull, absorbing the sunlight from the window instead of reflecting it. They appeared to be lightly smeared with a dark brown residue. Rowan touched it with his handkerchief. It was some sort of sticky resin.

"Most interesting."

"Don't just poke at it. Get a good whiff—tell me if it matches what you noticed earlier. My guess is that those crystals are the source of the sulfur smell."

Rowan leaned in close. "You're right. This same odor was in the air when I arrived. It has mellowed, but I can still easily recognize it."

The book atop the cabinet was Rowan's next point of inspection. The pages were thick and sturdy with a toothy, fibrous texture. The edges had yellowed and the corners crumbled at the touch.

"This text is centuries old. It must be worth a fortune."

A careful flip of the fragile pages revealed sketches of demonic beasts with sharp horns and tails. Some of the pictures depicted burnt and eviscerated victims in nearly the same shape as Burt Parnell.

The fire marshal caught a glimpse over Rowan's shoulder. "Awfully coincidental. Guy gets butchered and inside that book is a drawing of a guy getting butchered. What do you think it means?"

"Burt Parnell may have been consulting it recently. That would explain why it wasn't on the bookshelves with the others. It may give us insight into why he died the way he did. I'll have to find someone who can translate it." He closed the book and moved on to the interior of the cabinet.

A twelve-inch dagger sat on the top shelf. It was clean of blood, but etched into the lusterless steel were several intricate symbols, a series of tapered triangles and interlocking spirals surrounding a crescent moon.

Rowan turned to the marshal. "We have a book about demons written in Latin and a knife engraved with ritualistic symbols." He ran a finger along the subtle depressions of the etchings. "It appears as if Mr. Parnell had involved himself in some nefarious activities. And look here." He reached inside and pulled out a glass jar containing chunks of yellow-brown resin. "It's a little lighter than the resin on the crystals."

"I bet that's what it looks like before it burns."

Rowan unsealed the jar, releasing a pungent odor much stronger than the crystals on the floor.

The fire marshal plugged his nose. "Good God, man. Cover that up."

Rowan sealed the jar and put it back on the shelf. The other items in the cabinet appeared to be ceremonial—candles, trays, and a red velvet cloth—and the rest of the room offered nothing of particular significance.

Rowan went downstairs to see Parker. "Is Clancy on the way."

"Ten minutes."

"Good. I want the jar and a sample of the black crystals on the floor sent to the lab straight away. The marshal will indicate them to Clancy. I'm particularly interested to know if the resin on the crystals is the same as the one inside the jar. I'll be taking two items with me, the dagger and one of the books. Catalogue the remainder of the library and put it into evidence."

Parker's broad face split into a grin that seemed too big for his features. "Am I a detective on this case?"

"You've always wanted to get out of escort duty, haven't you?"

"Yes, sir."

"Good. Don't muck things up and I'll put in a good word with Grady when he returns from vacation."

"Oh, boy! That'll be—"

"Have you gotten in touch with any family members?"

"There's only one. A daughter named Lizbeth Parnell. She isn't at her apartment and nobody from her building has seen her since Wednesday."

"Keep trying." Rowan put both hands on Parker's shoulders. "Now, I need you to speak with every one of your men. They are to keep the gory details to themselves. As far as the press is concerned, Burt Parnell died in a fire. Got it."

Parker saluted Rowan. "You can count on me."

The clock struck 10:00. With the investigation underway, Rowan had returned to his office to parse through his notes. Outside the window, car engines sputtered through the streets and the 'L' train clattered above the city. Faint strains of jazz floated from the clubs carried by a nighttime breeze.

In the gray confines of Rowan's office, it was a different world—one of convoluted clues and nonsensical facts. On his desk sat the evening edition of the Tribune.

BANKER FOUND DECAPITATED IN LOCKED OFFICE – SAVAGE RITUAL KILLING SHOCKS CITY!

Body Disemboweled and Set Ablaze – Hints of Dark Rituals Found at Grisly Scene

Rowan poured himself a glass of scotch. He wasn't angry. Most cops barely scraped by on their salaries, and the money they made slipping the lurid details to eager reporters was often the difference between making rent or not. His mind wasn't on the headlines. All he could think about was the cryptic phone call from the morning.

This murder will be a completely supernatural affair.

Someone had gone to great effort to make it seem that way. Why? And if Burt Parnell was being extorted, why was he killed before paying the money? That detail didn't make sense. Extortionists want money. Killing their victim before they have a chance to pay defeats the purpose. Besides, Parnell *was* attempting to pay. He had set up a sale of his office. Presumably, that was to raise the necessary cash. What was the detail Rowan was missing? Did Farley Sage and Lizbeth Parnell have anything to do with it? Was Parnell unhappy that his daughter was getting married?

He continued to ponder the mystery, drinking heavily into the night. By the time Walter walked through the door, the ashtray was full and the bottle was empty.

Rowan hiccupped. "Did you manage to find Farley Sage?"

Walter set down a suitcase. "I found both Farley and Lizbeth. They're in Cincinnati."

"Ohio?"

Walter cocked his head. "No, France."

Rowan squinted at him. "There's no Cincinnati in France, Williams."

"Are you zozzled?"

"Just a lil." He burped. "Why did you bring a suitcase?"

Walter exhaled sharply through his nose. He ran a hand over his neck, his fingers lingering there without apparent purpose. "Yeah," he muttered, shaking his head at the absurdity. "I'm going after them. Tonight."

Rowan sat in stunned silence.

"It's something I gotta do, Manory."

He struggled to pull out his pocket watch. "At this hour?"

"I have a seat on the overnight mail train. It won't be a comfortable ride, but I'll get there in less than six hours."

"How did you manage that?"

"My buddy, Tom is the head conductor at Union Station."

"I see. And how do you know Farley and Lizbeth are in Cincinnati?"

"They reserved a first-class train carriage on Wednesday. Farley's signature is on the register."

"Excellent work. I don't tell you that often enough. You do excellent work."

"They weren't trying to hide where they were going. I take that as a good sign."

"You don't have to go all that way. I can simply notify the Cincinnati police." Rowan slid the phone closer. "It wouldn't be a problem."

Walter looked downward and shuffled his feet. "No, I think it's a good idea for me to handle it personally."

"It seems as if you have an emotional investment in this case."

"Yeah, I suppose I do."

"Why hadn't you seen Andrew Sage in so long? Is there bad blood between you?"

"I lost touch with Andrew the same way I did with all the guys I met in Italy. It just…it happens."

Rowan took out another bottle from his desk and poured Walter a drink. "Do you have time for one?"

"Sure." He took hold of the glass, but he didn't drink. His thumb ran once along the rim. He furrowed his brow.

"Tell me what's on your mind, Walter. You look like a man in search of an ear."

"I found out today that Freddie Lindstrom got arrested for burglary."

"Who is Freddie Lindstrom?"

"He was my sergeant—a good man. I also found out Carlton Reynolds died. He took to drink when he came back from overseas, and I think it ended up killing him. Wilbur Goode was a machine gunner—used to play for the Cubs. Last time I saw him, he was barely holding a job bagging groceries at the A&P. Curt spent some time in an asylum. He lives with his parents now. And Andrew…" At the mention of his friend, Walter's voice wavered. "Andrew is an engineer. He should be designing the next Woolworth Building. Instead, he handles permit paperwork part-time for the city, and the Department of Buildings only gave him that job as a favor to the army."

"They've found it difficult to readjust to society?"

"All of them. But I haven't."

Rowan tilted his head back slightly, letting the pieces of Walter's strained relationships click into place like a solved puzzle. He let out a slow exhale. "And that makes you feel guilty?"

"That's it exactly. I saw and experienced the same things they did, and I'm perfectly fine. My heath is good and I don't have…" He snapped his fingers. "What do you call it?"

"War neurosis."

"I don't have any of that. And why not? Why did fate decide I'd get off lucky? Why was I spared? No reason makes sense. That's why I can't stand to see them." He frowned painfully. "Andrew knows that. He's just too nice to say anything to my face. His wife knew too." He knocked back the glass in one go and shivered. "And that's why I have to go to Cincinnati and bring back their boy. It's…" He nodded rapidly. "It's important to me, Manory. I know I should have asked you first. After all, you're the boss. Do you think it's a bad idea?"

Rowan sat in silence, his cigarette burning low between his finger and his eyes half-lidded from drink. His mouth twitched into something like a half-smile, more out of reflex than reaction. He tapped his ash, took a final drag, and exhaled a lazy stream of smoke. "Not at all," he said, voice calm and unhurried. "Of course, you should go."

Walter tilted his head into a side-eye glance. "Really?"

"Yes. We need to speak with Mr. Sage and Miss Parnell as soon as possible. I assume you have a contact in Cincinnati that can assist you in this matter?"

"Hawk."

"Pardon?"

"Frank Hawkins, used to be a patrol officer. He's been retired for eight years, but keeps his ear to the ground. I already called him. He's looking for them now."

Rowan grinned. "There you go again. The sheer number of people you call *friend* is a testament to your character—how you never burn bridges. I should take a page from your book. Go. Go to Cincinnati. Call me when you find out something useful."

"What are you going to do?"

"I'll be plenty busy tomorrow. First, I'm off to the Esoteric Library to speak with a man named Hollis Ashburn. He's a local demonologist, apparently one of the most respected in the field."

"I didn't realize demonologists were respected."

"Enough to teach at the University of Chicago. I'm sure he employs a scholarly-sounding euphemism for his class titles—*Ritualistic Obscurantism and Arcane Lore* or some other such nonsense. Hopefully, he can tell me something about the book, the knife, and Pazuzu." Rowan rolled a cigarette while the tiny remainder of the previous one burned in the ashtray. "After I speak with him, I'll see what the forensics department have made of the resin and the crystals. When I find out how the killer started the fire, his identity will be much more apparent. That's my hope, anyway."

"Do you think this guy with the amulet is our man?"

Rowan shrugged.

"Have you figured out how the killer cut up the body and escaped the room undetected?"

"I haven't a clue."

The belfry at St Michael's Church loomed large over Bradford Square, casting a long shadow over its mishmash collection of shops and cafes. Some Chicago staples resided here; Giovanni's Tailoring and The Corner Cup had been serving the public since the turn of the century, but an outgrowth of odd little businesses had sprouted throughout the neighborhood.

The Esoteric Bookshop fell firmly into this category. A tall, narrow building of dark brick with a moody, underlit interior, the shop seemed to exist beyond the demands of patronage or fashion. The opening of the door released the smell of old paper and aged leather. Inside, the walls were lined with uneven shelves overflowing with heavy tomes on demonology, alchemy, and various rites and rituals. Every inch of the wooden floors creaked from a single footstep.

The doorway behind the back counter was covered with a chime curtain. Most chime curtains jingled with bells or bright feathers. This one clinked with black chains, coins, and carved bone Something about that curtain made Rowan's stomach tighten, as if stepping through would drop him straight into hell. He hoisted his leather evidence case on the counter and tapped the service bell, waiting patiently as the sharp chime dimmed into a reverberating toll. Finally, the sound died into a dusty silence. Rowan cleared his throat.

"Hello?"

The chain was pulled aside with a gentle rustling of soft clicks and thunks. There appeared a tall, lanky man with large, bookish glasses perched over a bulbous nose. A trim thornbush of greying hair sat with dignity atop his head. His charcoal suit was tailored and the white shirt underneath was crisp.

"You must be Detective Manory." He grinned like a cheetah. "Hollis Ashburn."

"Thank you for seeing me, Mr. Ashburn."

"*Tut-tut.* It is my pleasure. We don't get much excitement here at the bookstore." He set an ashtray at the counter and pulled out a box of Kreteks Royale. "And we rarely entertain guests as renowned as you. What can I do for you, sir?"

Rowan began to roll a cigarette. "I have two items to show you. My instincts tell me they are very important to the case I'm currently working, but I lack the necessary knowledge of the occult to understand their meaning. I've been led to believe you're the only man in Chicago who can help me."

"Is this regarding the Parnell murder?"

Rowan froze, the loose tobacco in his hand suddenly forgotten. "Indeed. Did you know Burt Parnell?"

Hollis slyly shook his head as he lit his Kretek. "I knew *of* him. That's not really the same as knowing someone." His grin faded as his eyes took on an alert, almost predatory gaze. "Why don't you show me the items and I'll be more than happy to explain afterward."

"As you wish." Rowan removed the *Liber Daemonum* from the bag and set it gently on the counter.

Hollis exhaled a low, almost reverent moan at the sight of the book. "It is priceless," he whispered. "Do you know if it will be available at auction eventually?"

"I imagine it will be given to his daughter. What she chooses to do with it, I cannot say."

"I'll contact her with a tender offer." He cracked open the book. "What you've brought me is the *Book of Demons*, written in the 1340s, author unknown, but almost certainly Matthias of Trier, a renegade monk in Germany. It details the history and character of seventeen demons of the underworld. It includes the spells for summoning them and for abjuration."

"Abjuration—do you mean cancelling the summoning?"

"We are not discussing business meetings, so I wouldn't necessarily use that word, but…yes."

"I see. Mr. Parnell might have had a particular interest in a demon named Pazuzu. Is that one of the demons featured in this book?"

"Yes. Pazuzu is the single most destructive demon known to man. When summoned, it appears out of thin air, bringing the horrid stench of the underworld—a cross between burnt sulfur and rotting flesh. The creature uses its claws to render flesh from bone, and it has the ability to eject fire from its mouth and nose. Of course, I don't have to explain that to you; you've seen what happened to Burt Parnell." He exhaled a blue cloud of smoke. "Or so the papers tell me."

"Does it leave any residue at the scene?"

"Yes." He opened to the correct page immediately and translated directly from the text. "Witnesses of its attacks have reported the appearance of mineral deposits at the exact place it entered and exited the mortal realm. The dark energy necessary for dimensional travel creates these deposits from nothing." A sneering smile formed at the corner of his mouth. "This is the same exact energy which created our existence and, most likely, the one that will destroy it too."

"Mineral deposits?"

"Yes."

"Like crystals?"

"I've never had the pleasure of examining the aftermath of a Pazuzu attack, but the book goes on to describe them as geode-like." He stared into Rowan's eyes for a second as if he were about to say something important, but quickly shifted his attention to Rowan's evidence case. "You have something else in that bag, something far more important than the book. If my instincts are correct, there's a dagger with engraved symbols on the handle inside your case."

"Why do you say that?"

"Is there?"

Rowan took out the dagger and set it on the table.

Hollis froze, his breath catching as his eyes locked on the blade. Slowly, he stepped back, as though the dagger itself radiated a force that demanded distance. His hand trembled slightly, and a whisper of awe slipped from his lips.

"It's not often one encounters such a powerfully significant artifact." His gaze never wavered from the engravings, his words tinged with reverence and disbelief. "I'll show you exactly how I knew you had it. Wait here."

Without another word, Hollis vanished behind the clattering metal chains into the back room. When he returned, his steps were quicker, more focused. He laid two yellowed newspaper clippings on the counter, his hand hovering over them as if they held equal weight to the dagger.

"These articles are from the *Cincinnati Enquirer.* On March 14th of this year, a gentleman named Henry Thompson was found dead in his apartment. The details," Hollis glanced up, his voice lower now, "are eerily similar to those surrounding Burt Parnell."

One word caught Rowan's eye. Then another. Then another. *Decapitated. Mutilated. Blazing.*

Hollis underlined a passage with his finger and read aloud. "Found on the scene was a dagger with strange, symbolic etchings." He pointed to the other clipping. "The same thing happened on March 26th to Mr. Charles Wilson in Middletown. Same details. Same dagger."

"What is the connection between these two men and Burt Parnell."

"They used to attend the same church." He puffed at his Kretek. "You see, detective, during times of economic downturn, alternative sects, particularly those associated with the occult become more prevalent. The city of Cincinnati experienced such a period of hardship during the nineties. There were several religions that appeared, seemingly out of nowhere. One of the most notorious was called the Order of the Eternal Shadows."

Though Rowan had never heard of that particular group, he was certain of one thing—no religion with that name could be up to anything good.

Hollis showed Rowan a photograph of twenty men in suits posing in an auditorium. "These were the Order's members. Look at the third row—center."

Rowan's eyes locked on the image. "Burt Parnell?"

"And next to him are Henry Thompson and Charles Wilson. These three men were the High Wardens of the church. Rumor has it they committed the murder of a member of their flock." He pointed to one of the figures in the background. "This man, Matthew Blackwood."

"Why did they kill him?"

"Money. It was a ceremonial sacrifice which would ensure

the earthly riches of the three men who performed it."

"If they killed him, they would have…?"

"Fortune in work, life, bank account, you name it. They lured Matthew Blackwood to an abandoned warehouse on the riverfront where they bound him and stripped him of his clothing. After marking his flesh and performing the sacred chants, they killed him with three stab wounds to the chest. As per the ritual, they buried the body and the three daggers in the consecrated ground under an abandoned chapel."

"Why did they engrave the daggers?"

"They didn't. Someone obviously dug up the daggers and used them to cast a curse of vengeance." He flipped forward a few pages in the *Liber Daemonum*. "Here it is—The Rite of Retribution. Anyone seeking revenge could engrave the murder weapon with the correct symbols and then perform the necessary rites. The murderer—or in this case, the murderers—would be cursed, doomed to die by the hand… or rather, the talon of Pazuzu."

"How long does it take for the demon to appear."

"Five days after the curse is cast."

"Do you know who could have dug up the daggers?"

"Matthew Blackwood had a son named Elijah. He was just a small boy when his father was murdered. Now, he's a grown man. I just so happen to know that Elijah Blackwood was in Chicago this past week. It shouldn't be difficult to find him. He has a penchant for ceremonial garb and wears a pendant around his neck at all times."

"Do you think Elijah Blackwood is still in Chicago?"

"My guess is that he's gone back home to Cincinnati. The business he had here is finished."

"I only have one more question, Mr. Ashburn. You mentioned abjuration. Can the curse of Pazuzu be lifted after it has been cast?"

"Oh, yes. The person who originally cast it can lift it with a ritualistic cleansing done with black paraffin candles. When the sacred spell is spoken aloud, the candles are lit and continuously burned until all the wax has melted. At that point, Pazuzu no longer poses a threat." He lifted an eyebrow. "Obviously, Elijah Blackwood never lifted the curse. Or if he did, he did so far too late to save Burt Parnell."

"Yes," said Rowan. "Obviously." He placed the dagger and the book back into the case. "Thank you for your assistance, Mr. Ashburn."

"You will inform me how the case turns out, won't you? I'm sure it's obvious how interested I am in the subject."

"You'll read all about it in the newspaper. If I have any more questions, would you be willing to speak with me again?"

"After next week, yes."

"Are you going out of town?"

He nodded, "I'm on my way to Joliet to give an important speech to the Symposium of the Arcane. I'm the keynote speaker. They've opened a new spa down there. It's said to be the best in Illinois. I intend on examining that claim for myself. If you wish to attend, you might find me there."

Rowan left the shop and sat on a bench in the middle of Bradford Square. The soft warmth of spring hung in the air, carrying the scent of blooming flowers from nearby planters. A woman strolled by with a basket of fresh vegetables, while two children skipped around the fountain, their laughter mingling with the chirping of birds in the budding trees. Rowan barely noticed.

The puzzle pieces themselves were clear, but they didn't fit quite to Rowan's liking. Hollis Ashburn's involvement was undeniable. The problem was that he hadn't tried to hide it. He could have played dumb. Rowan would have probably seen through it, but that wasn't the point. Ashburn had laid out everything except a confession.

Rowan checked his pocket watch. Only six more minutes.

The Forensics Division was a blend of order and chaos. Low-hanging lamps cast a sharp glare over the room. The worn wooden desks were cluttered with glass beakers, fingerprint powder, and test tubes of mysterious liquids. A large chalkboard stood against the far wall, scribbled with chemical formulas and sketches of rooms. In the corner, a steel filing cabinet towered over everything, its drawers halfway open and packed with case notes. The place reeked of formaldehyde and acetone.

Rowan liked this room. It was a world apart from the bustling areas of the police station—a quiet, almost reverent space where science, rather than brute force, held the key to solving crimes. What's more, he completely trusted Clancy, the head of forensic investigations. Rowan didn't trust many cops.

He lit a cigarette. "Tell me something I don't know, Clancy."

"Whoever started the fire used a small, unassuming pile of thermite on the desk directly underneath the body. He surrounded the pile with magnesium strips, struck a match and—boom. He had ignition. Once the magnesium catches fire, it turns white hot. Then, the thermite erupts. A searing hiss fills the room and the desk and the body turn into a molten blaze. Both would have blackened within moments. That's why the wall directly behind it was scorched but none of the other walls had much damage. At that point, the fire has essentially burned through its super fuel. The flames lick at the walls but they don't spread as quickly as before. I'd say the fire was going for three minutes before the water put it out."

"What if the fire had been allowed to continue for 14 minutes?"

Clancy considered it for half a second. "The entire room would be gone. The fire would have spread to more of the building at that point."

"Are you certain?"

"Quite. Why?"

"This fire was burning for 14 minutes."

Clancy snorted. "Ridiculous."

"Yes, I thought so too. What about the crystals on the carpet?"

"I can't tell you what caused them, but their chemical makeup is simple—potassium chloride and black dye."

"Dye?"

"Traces of it, yeah."

"But…why?"

"Don't know yet. I've only been working on it for twenty-four hours. I'm not a miracle worker, Manory."

"And the resin on the crystals?"

"Sugar."

"Pardon?"

"Lactose to be specific. My guess is that the crystals formed as a byproduct of a chemical reaction, and the resin is another leftover residue. This is backed up by the fact that some of the soot and particulates are consistent with a fire while others, specifically the ones on or around the crystals, are most decidedly not. I just don't know what the reaction was."

"If you had to take a guess?"

"My first thought was fertilizer, but nothing else from that room confirms it. I'm in contact with an industrial chemistry teacher at the Armour Institute. He's coming to look at the evidence in a few hours. Hopefully, he can nail down the specifics."

"What about the resin in the jar?"

"Oh, that stuff's completely different. What you found in the jar is called Ferula Assa-Foetida."

"Pardon?"

"It's more commonly known as the devil's dung."

"Lovely."

"It's a dried latex made from several herbs. If you thought it smelled bad in the jar, you should get a whiff when it's set on fire."

"What is its purpose?"

"In the real world, it's primarily a digestive aid and it's been reported to relieve menstrual pain, but not enough to make it commonplace. There is, however, a much more unsavory use for it. As I understand it, the victim in this case was involved in occultism. Is that right?"

"Very much so."

"Devil's dung is used as an incense in certain rituals. It's supposed to muggle up the devil."

A fleeting memory flickered to life in Rowan's thoughts, something Alan Figgins had mentioned that didn't seem important at the time. It was in reference to the sulfur smell.

A knock came at the door. It was Parker, grinning like an idiot. "I found it, Manory. Just like you said."

"Well?"

"Curtain Call Outfitters on Dearborn. It's a popular place with all the theaters."

"And they sold that costume?"

Parker nodded.

"This week?"

"Thursday, the day before the murder."

Rowan smiled. "To whom?"

That night, Rowan's office felt colder than usual, the shadows longer, pressing in against the dim light of his desk lamp. He stared at the empty glass in front of him, his hand hovering over the bottle, but he hesitated, as if the act of pouring another drink would somehow set things in motion. The clock on the wall ticked steadily, but time felt like it had slowed to a crawl, each second stretching out, taunting him.

When the telephone rang, he grabbed it like a lifeline, his grip firm as if steadying himself against everything swirling in his mind. "Williams, is that you?"

It was.

"I've solved it, boss. I know it's hard to believe, but it's true. Farley Sage and Lizbeth Parnell are innocent. They had nothing to do with it."

"In that case, who is the killer?"

"I think you met him today."

"Hollis Ashburn?"

"That's right. I'll be on the 7:30 train in the morning. I want to be there when he's arrested."

"If you want to witness his arrest, you'll have to go to Joliet."

"Huh?"

"That's where Ashburn is now. He'll be there for a week. Some sort of conference involving the occult. I'm heading there tomorrow. I've already informed the Joliet Police Department. They're ready to assist me."

"You mean you already knew it was him?"

"I'm afraid so."

"Damn, and here I thought I'd beaten you to it. I should have known better. Do you want me to go to Joliet and meet you?"

"My dear Williams, I wouldn't have it any other way. I'll be waiting for you at the train station. We'll go somewhere and have a drink and discuss the case. Tomorrow evening, Hollis Ashburn is giving a speech. Once he's finished, we'll take him into custody. Does that sound satisfactory?"

"It does, it does. Say, Manory?"

"Yes?"

"I still don't know how Ashburn got out of the office."

"Well, when we meet tomorrow, you can tell me the motive and the evidence, and I'll tell you the method."

They said their goodbyes and Rowan hung up the phone. He poured another drink. He needed it.

The Lantern's answer to prohibition was odd but effective. The owner had filed a lawsuit arguing that the property was not actually on U.S. soil. It was beyond frivolous, but still required a court date. The County Judge was a frequent patron. He made sure the trial remained in limbo. It was an easy peace with local law enforcement because the Lantern, unlike establishments in Chicago, didn't attract criminal activity. The Lantern wasn't a speakeasy. It was a tavern. Pictures of the townspeople were framed and placed on the shelves.

Walter stretched his legs in the booth. "Cozy. I like it."

"It was recommended to me by the Joliet Sheriff."

The waitress was innocent-looking. She wore a fitted cardigan with low-heeled pumps and no makeup. Her voice was bright and friendly. "Gentleman?"

Rowan asked, "Do you have a local drink? Something we couldn't get anywhere else?"

"We're famous for our maple sour. It's Canadian whiskey, lemon juice, and syrup that we get from the sugar maples in our yard. I suppose that makes it unique."

Walter asked, "Is it sweet?"

"It's called a maple *sour*."

"We'll have two," said Rowan.

After the waitress walked to the bar, Rowan clapped his hands together and rubbed them. His smile was slightly awkward, but he was doing his best not to appear upset.

"I'm interested to hear your theory, Williams. It's rare that the two of us reach the same conclusion at similar times. I'm wondering how that could have happened."

"Maybe we'll have to start calling the business *Williams Investigations*."

Rowan squinted and shook his head.

"Just a thought." Walter set down his notepad on the bench. "Shall I begin?"

"Please."

Walter proceeded to tell Rowan everything he had learned about Burt Parnell, including his nefarious history within the Order of the Eternal Shadows. When he talked about the murder of Mathew Blackwood, all the details matched the ones given by Hollis Ashburn.

"I found out most of this from Farley and Lizbeth. They had hired their own investigator to research Burt Parnell."

Rowan lit a cigarette. "We are simpatico on the facts thus far."

"So, we know that Elijah Blackwood did not murder Burt Parnell."

"How do we know that?"

"Because Blackwood was extorting Parnell. Why kill

someone before they pay the extortion money?"

Rowan tapped ash into the tray. "That's a fantastic question. Indeed, it is the same one I posed."

"And we know that Burt Parnell was attempting to raise money very quickly. He'd set up the sale of his office that afternoon. He was going to use the money to pay off Blackwood."

"Again, we are in agreement on the facts."

"What's more, Elijah Blackwood had purchased a train ticket to Cincinnati for Friday at six o'clock in the evening. He was expecting to get paid that day, and he wanted to skip town as soon as possible."

"Really," asked Rowan, genuinely surprised. "How do you know he purchased a train ticket?"

"I'll get there, boss. Let me lay it out in time."

Rowan offered his hands, palms up, in a gesture of compliance. "My apologies, detective. I'm listening."

"Elijah Blackwood had grown up in Cincinnati. He'd heard all the stories about his father's murder. At some point, he learned of his father's burial site and exhumed both the body and the daggers. He next sought out old members of his father's church. That was how he knew about Pazuzu and a..."—he squinted at the notepad—"curse of retribution."

Rowan nodded along. "I see."

"One of the biggest clues is that Blackwood never tried to extort money from the other men who killed his father, Henry Thompson or Charles Wilson. He just killed them and butchered their corpses before setting them on fire. Why didn't he try to blackmail them? Because they were dirt poor. Thompson was a janitor at the local high school and Wilson shined shoes for a living."

"Funny that," said Rowan.

"What?"

"Just that the ceremonial murder didn't bring those two men the riches they were promised. Only Parnell seems to have benefitted from the murder of Mathew Blackwood. He was reasonably wealthy with a downtown office in Chicago. Thompson and Wilson ended up poor."

"That's because curses and rituals aren't real, old boy. Just like Pazuzu isn't real."

"An excellent point, my friend. Please, continue."

"Blackwood murdered Thompson and Wilson just the way Pazuzu would've. Why?" Walter pointed at Rowan.

"Do you want me to answer?"

Walter did his best impression of Rowan. "When I point to you, I want you to answer."

"Blackwood committed the murders in a Pazuzu-like manner because he wanted Parnell to be frightened and compliant. What better way than to give him two examples of the Pazuzu curse working exactly as described in the literature? The events were in the newspapers. The daggers were even described in the articles. It was a perfect set-up."

"That's very good, Manory. There's hope for you yet. Who knows? You might even become a great detective someday."

Rowan took a long, thoughtful drag. "So, we agree that Blackwood killed the two men in Cincinnati but wasn't responsible for Burt Parnell's death. He was after money, not revenge. That's all well and good. The important question is this: How can we link Hollis Ashburn to the murder of Burt Parnell?"

"I'm getting there. Don't rush me." He consulted his notes. "When Lizbeth got the phone call warning her about what would happen to her father, the mysterious caller knew everything about the extortion. He even told her the exact amount. $100,000. How would the caller know that?"

"My wild, unsubstantiated guess is that the caller had been at the Commodore restaurant when the details of the extortion were laid out."

"Close, but no cigar. I figure the caller had Blackwood tailed there. I later learned that the caller had Blackwood tailed the whole time he was in Chicago."

"Is that so?"

"Yes. Now, I know you get nervous when I start thinking too much."

"It's usually dangerous."

"But it occurred to me that this sort of job couldn't be done with a reputable firm like ours. We would ask far too many questions. It had to be some cheap dick who only took cash and didn't bother with ethics. Now, if there's anything I know about cheap dicks, they don't save their cash. No, they tend to blow their dough after they hit a good payday."

"A fine assumption, Williams."

He shrugged. "I took a chance and it paid off. I contacted a few brothels. There's one near Bourbon Street where a PI named Russell Harlow showed up last night and bought every girl they had. Russell clammed up when I called him, but a little cash loosened his tongue." He shook his head. "You can't trust private detectives."

The picture was clear now in Rowan's mind, but he wanted Walter to lay it out. "Step by step, Williams—let's hear it."

Walter flipped the page in his notepad. "Okay. This is what I learned from Russell Harlow." He took a deep breath. "On Saturday, Elijah Blackwood walked into Hollis Ashburn's shop and asked him all about Pazuzu. He probably wanted to know as much as possible before he threatened Burt Parnell. Hollis saw the amulet and the get-up. Naturally, he was intrigued. This occult mumbo jumbo is his whole life. He reads news from around the world to find anything he can use in his lectures or his books as evidence. He knew about the recent murders in Cincinnati."

Rowan nodded. "Hollis Ashburn had collected newspaper clippings about both murders."

"At this point, Ashburn knew something was up. He needed a professional to tail Blackwood and find out why he was in Chicago."

"So, he hired Russell Harlow?"

"Exactly. Harlow took the job and stuck to Blackwood

like glue. He was in the Commodore when Blackwood made the threat to Parnell. He heard the whole conversation. When Hollis got word about all the details, he telephoned Lizbeth and warned her." Walter bit his lip. "I'm not certain why he did that. Maybe, he wanted Parnell isolated, easier to kill."

Rowan already knew why Hollis had made the phone call to Lizbeth Parnell. He didn't say it straight away. He was interested in something else. "Tell me, Williams—during this week of surveillance, did Ashburn ask Harlow to break into Blackwood's motel room and look for anything."

"Yeah, but he didn't find what he was looking for."

"What was he looking for?"

"I can't remember. It didn't seem important." Walter had to search through his notes. "*Uh*...candles."

"Black paraffin?"

Walter leaned forward, the easy posture he'd maintained slipping away as he studied Rowan's face. He always knew something was amiss when Rowan asked questions about meaningless details.

"Yes. Why are the black paraffin candles important?"

"Everything is important, Williams. Please, continue."

"Okay." He sat back slowly, his head still askew. "On Thursday evening, Blackwood purchased a ticket for the 6:00 p.m. train for Cincinnati. His plan was to get the hundred grand from Parnell, tell him the curse was lifted, and go back home. Hollis Ashburn knew that nothing was going to happen to Burt Parnell. This didn't sit well with him."

"Why?"

"What do you mean *why*? For Hollis Ashburn, it would be worth a fortune for anther Pazuzu murder to take place. He's the foremost demonologist, yes?"

"Absolutely."

"He gets more speaking engagements and book deals and God knows what else if there are more Pazuzu murders. Hell, reputable people might start buying his bullshit, right?"

"Oh, yes, Hollis Ashburn will benefit greatly from the murder of Burt Parnell. I agree completely."

"You're damned right. Any day now, the Cincinnati police are going to find Elijah Blackwood and arrest him for the murders of Thompson and Wilson. There are eyewitnesses who can place him at both scenes. He's finished."

"How are Farley Sage and Lizbeth Parnell connected to the case."

"They are…what's that word you love to use all the time? Oh, yeah—*tangential* to the case. After they got engaged, Lizbeth made Farley promise never to speak with her father."

Rowan snickered. "It would appear that he broke that promise almost immediately."

"Farley thought he could fix the rift between them. He was upset that his fiancé and her father were estranged. He showed up on Monday morning to introduce himself and formally ask for Lizbeth's hand in marriage. According to Farley, Burt Parnell was thrilled. He wanted to reconcile with his daughter. He and Farley made plans to get together with Lizbeth and hash everything out. Those plans never happened because Lizbeth got the phone call from Hollis the next day."

"And that inspired the couple to travel to Cincinnati and find out if it was true?"

"Exactly. When Farley got home from work, she tearfully told him everything."

Rowan softly clapped his hands. "Terrific, my friend. Your investigative abilities have rarely been so thorough."

"Thank you." He closed his notepad. "I believe I've proven the case against Hollis Ashburn beyond a shadow of a doubt. I'd like to know *how* he did this murder. There are too many obstacles to—"

"I still have a few problems though." Rowan knocked back the rest of his drink aggressively and repositioned himself in his seat.

"Problems?"

"Yes. There are several insurmountable problems that make Hollis Ashburn a very unlikely killer."

Walter face paled. "Such as?"

"You'll recall the ringing sound I heard over the phone on Friday morning?"

Walter nodded freely. "You told me it sounded like a bell."

"There's a church right across from Ashburn's bookshop. He called us at 10:00. The bells, of course, ring on the hour. After I interviewed him, I sat in the square and waited for the hour to strike so I could make sure. I'm certain Hollis Ashburn was the one who called us on Friday."

"That's what I said."

"You fail to think things through, Williams. If he was at the bookshop when he made the call, he couldn't have committed the murder in the office on Pinnacle Place."

"Then…then…he must have had an accomplice. Sure. He planned it and someone else did the murder."

Rowan ignored the feeble suggestion. "Tell me; why do you think Ashburn told the PI to look for black paraffin candles?"

"I don't know."

"I do."

"Then, why did you ask me?"

"Those types of candles were necessary to lift the curse. Their absence would indicate that Blackwood had no intention of lifting it. That's why Hollis Ashburn called us on Friday. He knew Pazuzu was going to strike. He knew that Blackwood wasn't going to perform an…abjuration of the curse."

"But that's ridiculous. Hollis Ashburn doesn't believe in Pazuzu."

"Doesn't he? The man has built his entire career around the subject of demonology."

"Yes, but…"

"That's why he called Lizbeth—to warn her. He was genuinely concerned about the woman. If she were to be visiting her father while the demon attacked, she would most likely be killed as well. So, in a sense you were right. He did it to make sure Burt Parnell was isolated."

"But Hollis Ashburn is a monstrous murderer. He wouldn't care if she died."

"Nonsense. Hollis Ashburn is a nice, caring man. He's good friends with the priests at St. Michael. They enjoy robust discussions of theology over lunch. Why would you think he's evil?"

"Why didn't he admit to making the phone calls?"

"Obviously, he would be seen as the prime suspect. You've proven that just now."

"Because I…he…" Walter shook his head. "I'm in shock and I'm completely lost."

"Take a breath."

"So, who killed Burt Parnell?"

"Before telling you the *who*, I should give you the *how*. Breaking into the office was done the night before. As I have already established, it was not a difficult task to pick the lock on Parnell's door. The killer lay in wait for Burt Parnell to arrive. That happened at 9:00. The killer performed his task. The exact cause of death was impossible to discern due to the degradation of the corpse. Suffice it to say, it was fast and silent. Let's say strangulation. The killer then took a full hour to commit the butchery so that it would appear to be a crime of Pazuzu. Are you with me so far?"

"Yeah, sure."

"At that point, the killer was trapped in the room. Alan Figgins was at the desk outside and there were several people in the rooms surrounding Parnell's office. They were free to roam the building at their leisure. Escape would seem to be impossible."

"I'll say."

"It's at that moment when we received the telephone call from Hollis Ashburn. Mind you, he didn't say when the demon murder was going to happen. In his mind, it could have been that morning or the next day. It would depend entirely on the exact time when Elijah Blackwood had cast the curse. Pazuzu would come exactly five days from the moment it was cast."

"He called us and…and he had no idea there was a killer inside Parnell's office at that very moment? Is that what you're saying?"

"Correct. At 10:04, the killer called the fire department from inside the office and reported the fire. *Pinnacle Place, fire,* and *quick*. In order to corroborate that time with witness statements from outside the building, he created a literal smokescreen. People from the outside would say it started at 10:04 and the report was at 10:04."

"How did he create a smokescreen?"

"I'll *uh*…get to that. For now, we'll say the killer had a device that allowed him to produce unlimited smoke in order to create the appearance of a fire."

Rowan stared at the burning tip of his cigarette, as if the murder were taking place within its smoldering ash.

"One thing about this case that was always troublesome was the odd nature of the crime scene. There simply wasn't enough damage to the office, especially considering the length of time and the sheer amount of smoke that was pouring from that window. Alan Figgins testified that he was able to grab the door handle without suffering any burns. It is obvious that the fire hadn't been burning for fourteen minutes. The killer would have been terrified to set the room on fire considering he was locked inside. All these facts point to the fire being started later than 10:04."

"When was it started?"

"At about the same time we arrived on the scene. The killer started the fire when he heard the sirens coming toward Pinnacle Place. Figgins heard a hissing sound just before the heat detector went off. This was no doubt caused by the magnesium strips heating up. The use of thermite created an incredible amount of damage in seconds. Half the room was charred to a crisp when the water was shot through the window, putting out the flames. Of course, the killer had already changed into his costume by that time."

Walter did a double take. "Costume?"

"His fireman's costume. Curtain Call Outfitters has actual fireman uniforms, hand-me-downs that were sold by retired firemen. The shop even sold the sacks used by firemen. They came in quite handy for the killer. He was able to transport the instruments of decapitation and evisceration to and from the office. One thing the costume shop didn't have was a smoke mask. The killer must have already had access to one. They all look the same. Especially in a room full of smoke."

"Do you mean the killer pretended to be a fireman and…and just walked away?"

"Do you recall the statement by the fireman who discovered Parnell's head. He kicked something, but he couldn't tell what it was. He had to bring it close to his mask in order to see that it was a human head. That tells us a great deal about the lack of visibility. When the killer walked past the firemen, they saw a partially outlined figure wearing the proper uniform."

"That seems *too* easy. Like it couldn't possibly work."

"Nonsense, Williams. It must have been a chaotic scene, the firemen running around a room filled with smoke. You can't see someone's face in a smoke mask, even in broad daylight. They certainly wouldn't have spotted a ringer in those smoky conditions. The killer walked out of the office and down the back stairwell unmolested. Occupants from the other floors were still coming down the stairs in unorganized batches. They thought nothing of a fireman walking down the stairwell carrying his sack. The killer went into the abandoned second floor which had already been cleared by the real firemen. He quickly changed out of his fireman's uniform and stuffed it in his sack. Then, he filed out of the building and vanished into the crowd—just another occupant fleeing the fire. Who cared if he was carrying a burlap sack? No one was looking for a killer yet.

No one knew anyone had been murdered."

Walter sat back, wide eyed. "How very simple."

"Well, the exact process was simple, but the elements that allowed for it were complex."

"And the smoke?"

Rowan pursed his lips. He nodded. "Are you going to have a drink?"

Walter took a sip. "It's good. Now tell me how he caused the smoke?"

"We had a clue about the smoke. It left residue of lactose, potassium chloride, and black dye. There was a smell as well—the sulfurous odor we detected in the air. Alan Figgins explained it away as a common smell coming from Parnell's office. He also mentioned that the smell was usually much stronger. This is because Burt Parnell often performed rituals in his office. He had the candles and a red velvet cloth in his cabinet. He also had a jar of the devil's dung. It smells similar to potassium chloride, just much stronger. This similarity in odor was merely a coincidence. Coincidences in cases are frustrating, but they do happen."

"Yeah, yeah. Was Clancy able to figure out what caused the residue?"

"It took a bit of time, but he finally nailed down what would have caused that combination of elements with a slight sulfurous odor, yes."

"And?"

Rowan grew quiet.

"Are you going to tell me?"

"Smoke grenades. A lot of smoke grenades set off in the same place over a short period of time. More than twenty between the time the first visual sighting of the smoke and when it finally stopped. The succession in the same spot is why the crystals and lactose formed on the ground. The black dye is used in smoke grenades to maximize the decrease in visibility."

"Okay."

"I already knew where the fireman's uniform had been

purchased. Naturally, I turned to the question of where one could find smoke grenades in bulk…along with a smoke mask. The most logical place turned out to be a military base."

"Okay."

"Yes." Rowan picked at his nails, his head tilted slightly downward, the dim light catching on the fine creases of his forehead. His jaw flexed, then relaxed, as if he were testing the motion, wary of what might slip out if he spoke too soon.

Walter blinked, his eyes dimming for just a moment as the realization hit him. His hand tightened around the glass, but then he shook his head slightly, as if trying to dismiss the thought before it fully formed.

"No," he muttered under his breath. His gaze darted away from Rowan and settled somewhere over the dimly lit bar. He took a quick, shallow breath, leaning back in the booth as if distancing himself from the idea. "No. That makes no sense."

"But it does. You told me that Fort Sheridan gives veterans free reign to come and go as they please. It would not be difficult for Andrew Sage to steal a box of smoke grenades and a smoke mask, would it?"

"No, but…I mean…there's no reason."

"The financial well-being of his son was the reason, Williams. It's not terribly obvious, but once you see it, there's no other way to look at the case. On Tuesday, Farley called his father and told him about the extortion—one-hundred thousand dollars. What is Andrew Sage's job?"

"He…he files permit paperwork for the Department of Buildings."

"On Wednesday, Burt Parnell informed the city that he was going to sell his office. Andrew handled the paperwork. That's when he knew Burt Parnell would soon be destitute. His daughter-in-law had no job and his son made very little. Andrew couldn't leave his son anything substantial. You told me how broke they are. His wife was dying; his life was over—his son was all he had to live for. He knew all about Pazuzu and the manner of death. He was an engineer in the army—brilliant, as you said. Killing wasn't a problem. He had done it before. This way, his son would have a great start in life."

"I still don't believe it."

"He's already confessed. It's already happened. I'm sorry, Walter."

He gasped. "Then why…why'd you bring me down here? Why the charade? Why…why all of this?"

"I saw how broken up you were about your friends and their struggles. I didn't want you to be in town when Andrew was arrested. I wanted to spare you the pain. Joliet has a new spa. From what I've heard, it's the best in the state. I think you should stay here for…as long as you need. Relax and get your mind off things. Whenever you feel up to coming back, you start work again."

Rowan went to drink, but his glass was empty. He set it on the table and bowed his head.

"I'm so sorry, Walter."

Walter stared at the table. He sank deeper into the booth. The lively hum of the speakeasy faded into the background.

When he finally spoke, his voice was quiet.

"Thanks."

3.

INSTRUMENT OF DEATH

Violet Reynolds walked the wet, uneven streets in a frenzy, her breath ragged, her knees wobbly. She should have taken a cab. The street was too open, too exposed. Footsteps clattered behind her—just another pedestrian—but she couldn't shake the feeling that they were too steady, too deliberate.

She turned a corner, pressed herself against the wall, and listened. A long, empty pause. The air turned thick with unfallen drops, the pressure sitting heavy on her skin.

A look around the corner revealed an empty sideway. She must have imagined it.

A streetlamp flickered to life. The shops were closing up. Curtains drawn, lights dimmed, doors bolted. The city curled inward, shutting its doors against the night, leaving her alone with the oncoming dark. Nowhere to go but home.

And Bobby.

Bobby wouldn't be there.

The thought of his absence caused Violet naked grief—the kind that made you forget who you were. It was at that low point of confidence when Violet saw the sign—hand-painted in bold scarlet.

Madame Dunkel, Clairvoyant

Fortunes Told, Futures Revealed.

Violet had walked this street before. Many times. But she'd never noticed this storefront. Had she really passed it again and again without seeing it?

It was tucked somehow unobtrusively between a dry goods shop and a tailor. Her discovery of it felt like divine intervention.

"Of course," she whispered. "I have to go inside." Without giving the idea a second thought, she found herself knocking aggressively at the indigo-colored entrance.

The lock popped open with a heavy *ping.* A long creak of the door. "Good evening. I am Madame Dunkel."

The woman wore a shimmering robe of deep sapphire and garnet tones. The folds of the fabric gave her an almost regal appearance, though her face, all sharp lines and shadowed eyes, carried none of the genteelness of royalty.

Her sharp cheekbones jutted beneath pale, lined skin, and her hooded eyes sank into her head. The faint smell of clove smoke clung to her, mingling with the scent of sandalwood wafting from within.

"And you," she said with a hint of amusement underlining her gravelly voice. "You are lost."

Violet blinked. "I…I was just walking and saw your sign. I thought—"

"Nonsense." Dunkel's lips curled into a grim smile. "You are here because you have no choice. The voices in your head, the turmoil you feel—they have brought you to me. Yes?"

"Yes." Violet's own voice startled her. Why had she answered so easily? And how had Madame Dunkel known?"

"I can reveal your future for three dollars. But beware, once the money is paid, there are no refunds, no matter the fortune—good or bad. And all fortunes are bad… eventually."

"Of course."

The room was dimly lit, its atmosphere heavy with incense. Drapes of deep crimson and midnight blue lined the walls. A circular table sat in the center, carved with intricate patterns of stars and moons. Atop it rested a crystal ball, its surface eerily clear in the warm amber light of a table lamp.

As Violet lowered herself into the chair, her fingers brushed the carved wood of the armrests. They were smooth from years of use, and she wondered how many others had sat here. Were they all as desperate as she? Did they fear losing everything too?

"You are nervous," Dunkel said as she sat opposite her.

"A little," she admitted. "I'm always worried about the future."

"The future is already determined. There is no sense in fearing it." She placed her hands on either side of the crystal ball, her long fingers curling around it. "I can tell you the future or you can find out for yourself. The choice is yours."

"I want to know about my husband, Bobby. I think he's fallen out of love with me. I need to know if we have a future together or if he's going to leave me."

"Perhaps you will leave him."

"No. I would never do that."

"We all find ourselves shocked at times at what we will do in the right situation. Or the *wrong* one." She gazed into the crystal ball. "I shall find the path you will follow."

Dunkel closed her eyes and took a deep breath. She moaned. It was an awful sound, born of ruin, low and ragged, dragging itself from her throat like a creature clawing free from the depths. It rasped and cracked, each note unraveling with an uneven rhythm, dragging something primal and unspeakable into the air. Her face twisted in agony. When she opened her eyes, only the whites remained. Her pupils had rolled back in her head, staring at her brain.

After the moaning had ceased, Dunkel leaned back from the ball and shook her head in complete disbelief.

"Das Ende kommt schneller, als du glaubst!"

"That sounds awful. What does it mean?"

Dunkel regarded Violet with a heavy stillness, her expression unreadable at first—then shifting, just slightly, as if something inside her had gone cold. The color seemed to drain from her face. Her eyes held too long.

Violet's voice began to break in panic. "What did you see? Tell me!"

"I saw a man standing over your corpse. He was leaning over you and watching you take your last breath and he was smiling."

Violet felt her throat tighten. She placed a hand at its base, massaging the skin as if to soothe herself. "What…what does he look like?"

"He is large," Dunkel said, holding her arms wide. "And…and Ugly."

"That's not Bobby. Bobby is the most handsome man I've ever seen." She tried to think of every large, ugly man she knew. No one came to mind. "When will it happen?"

"Soon," Dunkel replied, her tone devoid of sympathy. "Perhaps tonight. Perhaps tomorrow. But there is no escape. The die is cast. Your fate is sealed."

"There has to be something I can do. Can't you—"

"You have no future, not even a small respite of hope. Death is coming for you.," Dunkel said firmly. "I'm sorry, my dear."

The journey home was a blur—vague memories of stepping out into the pouring rain, her T-straps splashing through puddles. She recalled hailing a taxi and shivering in the backseat, but the sights and sounds of the ride were not part of her consciousness. When she got home, she downed two amytals. Bobby wouldn't be home for hours. She couldn't endure the night with Dunkel's words echoing in her mind, not without Bobby's arms wrapped around her. The worry would kill her before any man did.

She donned her favorite nightgown and lay in bed, clutching the blankets to her chest. If the large, ugly man came that night, Violet would be asleep. She wouldn't have to see that awful smile as her life slipped away.

Dickie Daubert grinned, all teeth and no joy.

"Where the hell is it?"

His heavy boots scraped against the hardwood floors as he muttered obscenities under his breath. He yanked open a drawer in the sideboard. Its contents rattled as he rifled through them. The frustration grew with every fruitless search. His sharp movements made the house seem to flinch around him.

Dickie glanced at Julie's lifeless form sprawled on the floor, her stillness an eerie contrast to his restless fury.

"Hiding it from me, huh? Real clever, smartass."

Julie said nothing.

Even in death, her face carried a ghost of the softness he used to adore, now twisted, ruined until a mortician could fix it. Her lips were tinged a faint, ethereal blue, her half-open eyes dull and glassy. A sickly purplish-blue groove encircled her throat like a macabre necklace carved into her skin. Near her collarbone, a small cluster of puncture wounds stood out, surrounded by faint, thin rivulets of dried blood. Her mouth hung slightly open, as though one last word were stuck inside—something she didn't have time to say.

Dickie traced her ligature mark with his dirty fingers.

"At least, it don't hurt no more. Ain't that right? Nothing hurts you no more, not after this."

Again, she had nothing to say.

"Come on, baby." He hoisted her with one arm like a sack of grain and flopped her over his meaty shoulder. "I'd love to chat with you all night, but I gotta get going. That means your carcass has to vanish. It wouldn't do for the police to think I was back in town."

He strode into the kitchen, the floor shaking with each heavy step. Right over the table was a narrow scuttle hole.

"The attic will have to do for now. They'll find you in a week or so and put you in the ground proper. That's the best I can do for you, baby."

He fetched a rope from the bottom cabinet and tied her arms and legs close to her body.

"Look at me—talking to a dead woman." With a raspy laugh, he wrapped the opposite end of the rope to his waist. "You always said I was crazy, Jules. Maybe you was right."

He stood on a chair and leapt, catching the edge of the hole and hauling himself upward. His broad shoulders barely squeezed through the space.

He took a moment to rest in the attic. Sweat slicked his forehead. His breath came out in hard, angry huffs.

"All right. Let's finish."

He hauled the rope, dragging Julie's corpse upward. Her head banged against the ceiling a few times. "Come on, Jules. I ain't getting paid for overtime here." He licked the exposed bit of gum at the front of his mouth and, with a final yank, pulled her through. The force lifted the body into the air. It landed face first onto the attic floor with a comedic splat.

"Good girl!"

There wasn't a hiding spot anywhere in the attic, but Dickie didn't mind.

"As long as there ain't no sign of a struggle, they won't search too hard, 'specially up here. They'll probably figure you skipped town. You used to do that sometimes, didn't you? Not anymore."

He dragged the body into the corner and piled a few old sheets on top. He tucked and pulled at the edges until no form was visible. It looked like a pile of old laundry, nothing more.

"Good enough."

He straightened up the house, replacing the couch pillows and closing every desk and cabinet drawer. Satisfied, he closed the door behind him and replaced the spare key under the mat.

Dickie Daubert moved through the night with quick, purposeful strides, his head swiveling just enough to clock the alleys and doorways without looking nervous. He blended confidently into the night.

Why wasn't the violin there? Al swore she had it. Al's a smart fence. He wouldn't send me unless he knew for sure Julie had the thing. He better not be trying to get me caught. If this is a double cross, I'll break his skull.

Julie's corpse sat alone in the attic, slowly rotting under the sheets.

Violet woke up with a start. The room was dim, the gray light of morning filtering weakly through the curtains. She reached across the bed, fingers brushing against cold, empty sheets. Bobby was gone.

She sat up slowly, rubbing her eyes. Her head felt thick, as though she'd been drugged, but the bottle of amytal on the nightstand told her the truth. The pills had done their job. No dreams. No voices. Just sleep—heavy, merciful, and dreamless.

A folded note sat beside the bottle. Bobby's handwriting, sharp and precise.

Got in late. You were dead to the world. Didn't want to wake you. Had to be out early. See you tonight.

She ran her thumb over the words, tracing the ink like it might tell her something more. He hadn't signed it *Love, Bobby.* But maybe he never did. Maybe she was only noticing now.

For a moment, she sat still, listening. The apartment was silent. The voices—gone. The night had passed. She was still here. And life, for now, went on.

One hour later, Violet sat at the back of the Lynn Stratton Community Hall, letting the din of activity wash over her. All around the room, women flitted between chairs in animated clusters, their chatter rising and falling like fleeting breezes.

She unscrewed the clarinet's ligature, the familiar motions steadying her hands as she wiped down the reed. The routine helped calm her nerves and improved her outlook. And she needed to stay calm. There was nothing she could do about Dunkel's premonition. It would either happen or it wouldn't.

The sudden *thud-thud* of violin cases landing nearby jolted Violet from her thoughts. Her hands tensed as her gaze snapped toward the pudgy frame of Pearl Ennis.

"Hiya, Violet." Pearl's face flushed pink and sweaty. Her chest rose and fell as though she'd just run a mile. She pushed her glasses up the bridge of her nose with one finger and pressed awkwardly against her hips with her knuckles. "You haven't seen Julie by chance, have you?"

Violet gave an obligatory look around the room. She knew Julie wasn't there, but she looked anyway. "Gee, it looks like she hasn't arrived yet, doesn't it?"

"She's usually one of the first ones here."

"Not today."

Pearl pushed out her lips. "Yeah, I can see that."

"Then why are you asking me?" Violet returned her attention to the clarinet as if she didn't expect an answer, removing the barrel and bringing it to her lips. She blew a sharp, decisive breath, stronger than necessary. The short, hollow whistle carried her impatience with it. Dust puffed out from the open end, swirling in the light that streamed through the high windows.

Pearl had to have known Violet didn't want to talk with her. She didn't seem to care. "I tried to call Julie last night, but she wasn't home. I'm starting to get nervous."

Violet inserted the barrel back onto the upper joint. Her fingers tightened on the smooth wood. Without looking up, she asked, "Why is it so important for you to see Julie."

"I have her violin."

"What violin?"

Pearl patted the case. "I don't feel comfortable carrying it around. It costs a lot of money. Makes me nervous. This is one of those *vee-homes*?"

Violet looked up and laughed. "Surely you don't mean a Vuillaume?"

"That's what I said—a *vee-home*."

"Julie can't afford an instrument like that."

"She didn't buy it. Her mother gave it to her."

A faint curl of disdain tugged the corner of Violet's mouth. *"Mrs. McPhee?"* The memory of Julie's miserly, tight-fisted mother flashed through her mind. Ann McPhee had neither the funds nor the inclination to treat her daughter with such generosity.

"That doesn't make a lick of sense, Pearl."

"Julie said it. I have no reason to believe she's lying. That's just silly."

"Her mother doesn't even play the…" Violet shook her head with frustration. "Why do *you* have it?"

"Loose soundpost," Pearl said cheerily. "My uncle's a luthier. Julie asked me to get it fixed for her. I did, and now I don't want to carry the thing around. What if it gets stolen. If she doesn't come to practice today, can I just leave it with you? She's your friend."

"Give it to her mother. She lives at the Oakmont Residence."

"Which room?"

"I'm sure their front desk knows the answer. I don't have her room number memorized." Violet glared at her.

"Okay." Pearl lingered a moment longer, clutching at the straps of her coat as though they might anchor her. Finally, with a resigned sigh, she turned back toward the cases, her movements slow and heavy. "Thanks anyway."

Violet heard her whisper something. It might have been the word *jerk*, but she didn't exactly know because the sound was drowned out by the hall doors creaking open. A woman in a crisp white apron stepped inside—Millie Carpenter, the hall's steward. She weaved through the room directly toward Violet.

"Mrs. Reynolds."

"Yes?" Violet cringed at the slight quaver in her voice. For some reason, the words of Madame Dunkel had returned to the very fore of her thoughts right at that moment.

"There's someone here to see you. A woman named Alice Dahlen."

The air seemed to leave Violet's lungs. Her grip on the clarinet tightened before she forced herself to relax. "Alice?" she said, the word catching on her tongue.

Millie nodded. "She came here looking for Julie. When I told her that Julie hadn't yet arrived, she asked for you. She says the two of you are friends. Is that true? Do you know her?"

"Yeah." Violet set the clarinet down on her chair. She stood abruptly, nearly knocking over a music stand in her haste. "Excuse me," she mumbled, already moving toward the door.

Millie stared wide-eyed at Violet's response. "Are you all right, dear?"

She didn't look back. She didn't respond. Violet Reynolds was looking straight ahead to her future.

The alley behind the music hall was damp, ivy-scented, with the faint sourness of unseen garbage. The gloom seemed alive, curling around her ankles as she walked, and the faint cooing of pigeons overhead sounded like whispers. Violet's chest tightened as she stepped deeper into the passage. With every step, Madame Dunkel's voice echoed in her mind.

Death is coming for you.

Alice stood at the far end, looking as delicate as a paper doll, her long hair falling in untamed strands across her freckled face. Her hands were clasped tightly in front of her, fingers twisting and fidgeting, and her pale skin seemed even more ghostly in the eerie light. "It's good to see you, Vi."

Their embrace was delicate. A year ago, Alice and Violet would have squeezed each other until it hurt. Now their touch seemed perfunctory. Alice sniffled, but it was unclear whether it came from emotion or the chill in the air. "It's been a long time."

"You came here to see Julie?" It wasn't the warmest way for Violet to start the conversation, but it was all she could think to say.

"I want to see you too," Alice added quickly before looking downward and brushing the hair from her face. "I'm worried about Julie though. No one knows where she is."

"Pearl Ennis told me she tried calling Julie last night."

"About fixing the violin?"

"Yeah. Pearl has it inside right now."

"Last night, Julie was supposed to pick up her violin from Pearl and stop by my place for a drink, but she never made it. I figured she got tired and fell asleep early. I went to her house this morning to check on her. She wasn't home, so I used the spare key to have a look inside."

Violet held her breath. "And?"

"She wasn't home."

"Huh?"

"But her purse was still there. Julie wouldn't go anywhere

without her purse. It didn't make any sense. Do you think somebody kidnapped her?"

"Are you…are you sure she wasn't there? Did you look everywhere?"

"Yes. I called the police, but there's nothing they can do until 72 hours have passed. The only way they'd look for her now is if there was evidence of foul play. Nothing in the house was stolen. And it was obvious no one broke in." Alice's shoulders trembled as she folded inward, clutching her arms tightly across her chest. "I know Jules. She's in trouble."

"You can't be sure of that."

Alice's breath came in stuttering gasps, each one sharper than the last, until a sudden sob wrenched free, shaking her whole body. "There's nothing I can do about it. I can't help her and it's breaking my heart."

"Julie's impulsive. Remember that time she took the train to St. Louis and didn't tell anyone. She might have wanted to leave for a week and said to hell with everybody."

"That's impossible."

"Why? She picks up and leaves whenever she wants."

Alice shifted her weight from one foot to the other, her movements abrupt and jerky. Her fingers flexed at her sides, then stilled before curling into tight fists. Then she opened her mouth, closed it again, and swallowed hard.

"Are you having a stroke? What's wrong with your face?"

"Julie's pregnant." The words came tumbling out in a blurted confession.

That word *pregnant* had landed between them like a hammer. Violet lowered herself onto her haunches. "*Wow* ," she whispered. "Pregnant? How? Who?"

Alice threw up her hands. "I don't know. I only heard part of the story. It was one night, one drunken night. He was a soldier on leave. Julie doesn't even know his name. He could be halfway around the world by now." She looked away, suddenly deciding to play with a button. "But it changed her, Vi. It made her start thinking seriously about her life. There's no way she would leave town. And she wouldn't leave her violin."

Violet wasn't listening. There was only one thing on her mind. "Why didn't Jules tell me she was pregnant? I can help her. My uncle is a physician. I can—"

"You haven't been around lately, Vi. I think she and I…we wanted to leave you alone. You're married," said Alice, treading gingerly around the subject. "We aren't exactly part of your new life."

"Yeah," Violet whispered. "I know." She thought for a moment. "Who would want to hurt Jules?"

"Do you remember that boyfriend she had for a few months?"

"Dickie?" The name brought a chill. Violet had only met Dickie once when Julie brought him to an orchestra fundraiser. He was a nasty piece of work—unwashed, mean-eyed, and towering. Not one musician left the function with a positive opinion of Julie's grotesque fella. "Didn't Dickie skip town?"

Alice nodded. "He had to. The police were looking for him. They probably still are. He beat a jewelry-store clerk to death during a robbery."

"Oh, God."

Madame Dunkel said he would be large and ugly. That's Dickie in a nutshell.

Alice rubbed her nose. "But he might have come back. Maybe he thought Julie would wait for him. Can you imagine what he would do to her if he found out she was carrying another man's baby. He'd kill her."

Violet bowed her head. "I'm sorry I haven't been around, Ali." Her eyes glistened, just shy of tears. "The terrible thing is that I feel so alone without you two."

"You're not alone. You have Bobby."

"Yeah," she murmured, not entirely convinced.

Halfway across town, Dickie marched through a narrow hallway, his steps moving with urgency toward his goal. He passed by a few doors to empty rooms when he finally saw the man he was looking for. He leaned in and knocked on the open office door. "Hello, Tommy. You're looking good."

Tommy Benson looked up from his paperwork. His face scrunched up in confusion. "Can I help you, sir?"

Dickie rasped a gentle laugh. "You don't remember me? That's all right. I forgive you."

Tommy snapped his fingers. "Oh, gosh. Dickie Daubert. The orchestra fundraiser." He stood and offered his hand. "It's been a while." Dickie's handshake was stronger than Tommy had anticipated. He did his best to hide his wince. "Sorry about that. I'm terrible with faces and names."

"No need for an apology. It was seven months ago and we only met that one time." He gave the office a quick, disinterested once over. "Nice office. Nobody else is here, huh? You work in this building all by your lonesome?"

Tommy flexed his fingers, trying to loosen them. "We have a garage with the loaders. It's a few blocks down the street. All the drivers are gone. I have the afternoons to catch up on my work. It's nice. No one's around to bother me. What are you…*uh*…"

"I remembered you said you was a bookkeeper for Sangero Trucking. I was in the neighborhood going for a walk, see? I passed by the building and I said to myself *Hey, that's where Tommy works.* Figured I'd say hello."

"How did you…how did you get inside?"

"The side door was cracked open. I knocked for a good while, but you musta not heard me."

"Those morons are supposed to lock up before they leave."

"Good thing I'm not a burglar, huh?"

Silence.

Tommy shifted his weight awkwardly. "Well, uh…how…how have you been? Are you still with Julie?"

"No. Jules and I decided to go our separate ways."

"That's too bad."

"People come and go. You can't get too wrapped up in one of them." He clapped his hands together like thunder. "Say, now that I'm here, I was wondering if you could help me out."

"I…can try."

"At that party all those months back, there were two friends of Jules's there. They went to high school with her. Do you remember their names?"

Tommy looked away, trying to remember. "Sure, I do. Violet…" He stroked his chin. "She got married, so her name is different now. It's …uh…Reynolds. Yeah, Violet Reynolds."

"You told me you were no good with names. You must know her pretty well."

"I've donated services a few times for the Women's Orchestra. She's a clarinetist with the group, so I've spoken with her plenty of times."

"That's the group Julie was in?"

"Yes, Julie's the violinist. She—" He froze. "Wait—did Julie quit?"

Dickie vaguely shook his head.

"It's just you said *was*. I didn't know if—"

He didn't answer. "What's the other girl's name?"

"Alice Dahlen."

He grinned wider. "You lied to me, Tommy. You ain't awful with names; you're awful *good* with 'em."

Tommy chuckled. "She's not with the orchestra. I only remember her because…" He turned a little red. "Well, she's my type—real mousy with freckles. I like that sort of thing…I mean, that sort of woman."

"Ooh la, Tommy boy. That's great. I like the mousy ones too." He smirked. "They scream the loudest." He produced a tiny notepad from his jacket and scribbled the names. "Do you know where they live—these dames?"

"No, I'm afraid I don't."

"No matter. That's what phone directories are for, right?" He pulled out a cigarette, plucked it into his mouth, and reached back into his jacket. "Say, Tommy—what's that on your desk?"

Tommy looked behind him. He hadn't even registered the items on the desk when a white-hot burst of pain tore through his chest. He staggered, his breath hitching. His eyes dropped downward. An ivory handle jutted from his breastbone. He turned forward, but no air entered his lungs. Panic rose in his throat. He began to gurgle.

Dickie took a deep, serious breath. "I'm sorry to have to do this to you, Tommy, but I can't afford nothing tracing back to me. It just can't happen. You understand, doncha?"

Tommy's legs began to wobble. He blinked rapidly, his hand instinctively reaching toward the knife as if to pull it free. His knees buckled, and he slumped against the desk, smearing the papers with blood that had trickled from his mouth.

"Thanks for working alone today. If you hadn't been here alone, I woulda had to come back later. You saved me a lot of time." He placed a hand on Tommy's shoulder for leverage and yanked out the knife.

Tommy fell to the floor in a dead heap. Dickie wiped off the knife with the dead man's shirt.

"I better get that violin soon, or else this town's gonna get bloody real fast."

Violet was dying. That's how it felt.

Her body was pinned, frozen under a crushing weight. Her eyelids refused to open, and her chest ached with the effort to breathe. Panic clawed at her as she struggled to move, to cry out, to escape the void pulling her under.

She knew she had to be asleep, but the line between dream and reality blurred. Small shifts in her body weight gave her the illusion that fidgeting could break the paralysis. But the harder she tried, the stronger its hold became.

What if someone's here in the room with me now? Sitting on top of me? Crushing me? And I'm just asleep.

The very thought sent a jolt of terror through her. Her

arm twitched. Then again. The pressure eased, and she snapped awake.

Bobby's face hovered, his features shadowed by the dim light. For a terrifying moment, his expression seemed wrong—too sharp, too foreign.

She screamed.

"Violet, it's okay. It's me."

Her chest heaved as she clutched at her throat. "Bobby? I—I couldn't move. I couldn't breathe."

"You were dreaming," Bobby said, turning on the lamp. "It's all right now. I'm here."

Her worries melted away when she got a good look at him—the cut of his charcoal suit sharp and clean, his white shirt crisp against his tanned skin. His tie was knotted perfectly, as if he'd walked out of a magazine advert. His symmetrical features—strong jaw, faint cleft in his chin, straight nose—looked sculpted, deliberate. And those eyes—clear and calm—looked at her with an almost boyish sincerity.

That's all Violet needed, that warm swell of pride and comfort he brought to her life. He was a handsome man with a presence that made her small bedroom feel more like a safe haven than a trap. How lucky she was to have him.

"Bobby," she whispered, her voice trembling but steadier.

He crouched beside her. "You okay now? You know you're awake."

"I just needed to see you."

He laughed softly. "You're adorable."

"Don't laugh at me." She pulled the sheet higher, hiding her face. "It's not funny."

"You're beautiful when you're scared."

With that assurance, she sat up, rubbing her arms against the chill. "It's 11:30. You must have worked hard. Do you want me to make you something?"

"No." He loosened his tie. "I'm exhausted."

As he turned toward the closet, his foot caught the vanity. A cascade of jewelry clattered to the floor.

He bent down to retrieve the fallen pieces. "Oh, shit." He picked up one of her necklaces. "I think I broke it, honey. The quartz is chipped." He looked back at the floor. "Maybe I can get it fixed if I can find the piece. It might have gone under the vanity."

"Don't worry about it," Violet said, sliding off the bed and joining him on the floor.

"I'll fix it," he insisted. "I bought this for your birthday." He ran a thumb over the jagged quartz pendant. "It's your favorite. I can't just break it and not do anything about it."

She took the necklace gently from his hands and set it aside. "I don't care about jewelry." She wrapped both arms around his neck, and kissed him softly, deeply. She took great care to breathe on his skin. She knew he liked that.

"I miss you when you're at work."

He kissed her neck. "Of course you do. I'm a fantastic husband."

"I was talking with Alice today."

He continued kissing her. "And?"

"And I came to the realization that I don't have any friends."

He pulled back. "Come again?"

"Since we got married, I haven't spent any time with Alice or Julie. I don't even know what's going on in their lives."

"Nothing's stopping you. While I'm at work, you should get together for lunch."

"You aren't following me."

"Then, explain it to me like I'm a child."

She paused, biting her lip. "I've thrown myself into this marriage without abandon. I made the rock garden with that stupid birdbath. I've rearranged the living room at least four times this year. And I've done a hundred other stupid projects for the house, but I never see you. I gave up my old life for you, but you haven't done the same for me."

His jaw tensed. "Violet, honey, we've been over this. I'm responsible for the company. The hours I work now will pay off later—for both of us. I'm working my ass off for us."

"I know."

"Not for me. For *us*. You want nice things and so do I. What if—"

"What if someone killed me tomorrow?"

"Come on, honey!"

"I'm serious. I didn't marry you to secure our future. That's about the least romantic thing I can imagine. I don't worry about that. I worry about our lives now. About how much time we spend apart. I know you think it's silly, but I need you here to protect me."

"From what?"

She didn't even think about mentioning the psychic. Bobby wouldn't approve. "You keep telling me that we'll have more time together, but I don't feel it happening."

Bobby sighed, rubbing the back of his neck. "Violet—"

"Julie's pregnant."

His head jerked up. "What?"

"Alice told me this morning. It hurt to hear it Not because she's pregnant, but because she didn't have to wait. She didn't even have to get married. We've been married half a year, and you don't even want to talk about children. It hurts. To think about it like that."

"We have talked about it, and we agreed. You said—"

"I'm lonely, Bobby. All I want is for you to make more of an effort. Just a little. If you did that I'd be…happier." Her voice broke on the last word. She reached for his hand, placing it over her heart. "Do you still love me?"

He pulled her into a hug, letting her literally cry on his shoulder. After she had quieted, he whispered. "I feel the same way I did when I first met you."

She rested against him, her breath slowing. For a moment, it was enough. This embrace could last forever. She could die like this.

He broke it though. He stood up and walked into the kitchen. "When did you see Alice?" he called out.

"This morning, she came to rehearsal looking for Julie.

She thinks Julie's gone missing."

"Why does she think that?"

"Because no one's heard from her. She didn't show up for practice." Violet managed a small smile. "But I told Alice not to worry. Julie's always been flighty. She picks up and leaves at the drop of a hat. It is strange though. She wouldn't leave if she was pregnant. And she's left behind a very expensive violin."

"I'm sure she'll turn up." Bobby stood in the doorway. "I'm going to wash up. Do you want a glass of water?"

"Yes, dear."

Violet slid back into bed, relaxing into the cool of the satin sheets. She sighed, the tension in her chest easing. She shouldn't have gone to Madame Dunkel. No good could come from dwelling on such dark thoughts. No one was coming to kill her. And marrying Bobby was the best decision she had ever made.

Detective Rowan Manory sat upright in his bed with his eyes closed. He wiped the drool from his mouth and scratched his fat stomach. Something was ringing. Probably the telephone.

He lurched toward the noise, stopping at the nightstand to light a decent-sized butt from the ashtray. The frayed, black tip burned acrid for a moment before the sweet-but-stale taste of tobacco flooded his lungs.

Now, he could open his eyes. Now he was awake.

Look at the time.

He yanked the receiver off the table. "Whoever this is, it's three o'clock in the goddamn morning."

"Manory, are you up?"

"What do you think, Grady?"

"It sounds like you're up."

"Your powers of deduction truly have no equal."

"There's been a murder in Edgewater. The victim's parents have friends in high places. I promised to send the best detective in Chicago. That's you."

"Full fee?"

"All expenses."

"Full control?"

"You're the boss, kid."

Rowan fumbled for a pencil. "What's the address?"

"2242 Norwood."

"And the name of the victim?"

"Dahlen. Alice Dahlen."

Rain streaked the patrol car's windshield. Combined with the orange glow of the streetlights, it created a mood of oncoming danger and the sort of trauma that buttered Rowan Manory's bread. He sat in the back seat, smoke curling from the cigarette parked between his fingers.

The thrill of the hunt consumed him, as it always did. He loved it—the details, the questioning, the slow, steady unraveling of the truth. It was why he was put on this earth. Most men had no idea of their ultimate purpose. Rowan had figured it out early in life.

Near the intersection of Norwood and Broadway, a man with a flashlight waved down Rowan's ride. He stood under an umbrella, the light reflecting off the rivulets of rain coursing down his black slicker.

"That'll be Officer Kegan," Rowan's driver said.

Rowan stubbed out his cigarette in the ashtray and stepped into the rain. He pulled his coat tighter, though the damp air already clung to him.

"Detective Manory?" the man asked, offering a firm handshake. "Steve Kegan. Midnight shift. I found the body. Sargeant Grady says I am to be your liaison and extend you every courtesy."

Rowan gave a curt nod. "No time like the present, officer."

Kegan gestured toward the sidewalk. "Follow me."

To their left stretched a strip of grass and trees, partially obscured by the misty rain. Beyond that, a fence lined a row of houses, their dimly lit windows barely visible. Broadway Avenue hummed with the occasional car or truck, headlights splashing against the asphalt.

Kegan spoke as they walked. "It was 2:00 a.m. I was on my beat, same as always. Got to the last house before Norwood and saw the kitchen window smashed. It's visible right over the fence." He pointed at the last house before the intersection.

Indeed, Rowan clocked the smashed window. It was lit by a lawn lamp and easy to make out at night.

"I turned right onto Norwood, and checked the front door. It wasn't locked, so I let myself in."

Inside the house, the air was heavy and faintly damp. Several officers milled about. Some of them taking photos, other making notations. The forensics examiner, Davis, was curled against the wall with a coffee in his hand.

"Any mud, Davis?" asked Rowan.

Davis yawned. "Huh?"

"Are there any tracks through the house, any footprints?"

Davis shook his head. "None."

"And outside the house?"

"Nothing."

"Does anyone know when it started raining?"

"A little after 1:00 a.m.," said Kegan.

"So that would mean the killer probably entered the house before it began raining. Do we have a time of death?"

Davis and Kegan looked at each other.

"What?" asked Rowan.

Kegan spoke up. "When I found her, she was still alive. She died right in front of me. About seven minutes after two."

"I see." Rowan turned toward Davis. "In your expert opinion, would that suggest the killer was here just before Officer Kegan arrived on the scene?"

"I think not. Her injuries suggest cerebral hypoxia. The force of the attack was enough to render her unconscious, but not immediately fatal. After the assailant left, her body likely began compensating. Residual oxygen in her blood could have kept her alive for a while, albeit in a deeply unconscious state. As her body tried to recover, she may have regained enough partial brain function to briefly regain consciousness. It's not uncommon in cases of strangulation or hypoxia for victims to experience a final moment of lucidity, almost as if the body makes one last desperate attempt to communicate or survive. The damage to her airway and the prolonged lack of oxygen eventually became too much for her system to sustain, leading to cardiac arrest."

"You sound quite sure of that."

He yawned again. "That's just my guess. As soon as I cut her open, I can be more certain. But she could have been attacked several hours before Kegan arrived. That's not a problem."

Rowan rolled himself a cigarette and licked it shut. "Let's have a look at the corpse."

The living room was sparsely furnished: a sofa, a small armchair, and a coffee table with a lace runner. The wallpaper, faded and floral, spoke of practicality rather than style. Alice Dahlen lay on her back, her freckled face pale and stark against her red hair. The ligature mark around her neck was unmistakable, and the sash lying nearby left no doubt about what had been used to accomplish the dastardly deed.

"When I found her, I checked for a pulse. It was weak, but there. Just as I was heading for the phone, she woke up."

Rowan kept his gaze on Alice.

"Did she say anything?"

"Well, she couldn't talk at first. She was gasping like she'd just surfaced from the water. Her face—" Kegan's voice faltered. He took a moment to compose himself. "I'm sorry."

Rowan saw this more and more on the force—men for whom death was still an emotional affair.

"Not a problem, officer. Take your time."

Kegan continued. "It was all twisted like she was in agony.

She couldn't catch her breath. I think she was suffocating. I tried to calm her, but she kept squirming, gurgling, like she was choking on air. She grabbed me by the collar and pulled me close to her. That's when she spoke. She only whispered one word. I think it was all she could manage."

"Which was?"

"Violin."

"Do we know if she played the violin?"

Kegan shook his head. "No. According to her parents, she never played any instrument—tin eared. But she did have a couple of friends in a local women's orchestra." He checked his notes. "Julie McPhee and Violet Reynolds. Julie plays the violin."

Rowan nodded. "Let's have a look at that window."

The scene was all wrong. That much was obvious. No footprints marked the sill and the muddied garden just outside had not been trampled or disturbed except for the glass shards that had submerged themselves into the soil. Only a few pieces lay in the kitchen.

"*Hmm*," intoned Rowan. "Rather odd, isn't it?"

Kegan said, "I didn't want to step on any toes and suggest something."

"Suggest away. You and I are both working this case."

"Are you sure?"

"Speak your mind, Officer."

"Well…the entire reason I checked out the house was because of this window. I saw it smashed from the sidewalk."

"Yes, you told me."

"So, obviously I figured that someone had broken in. But that's impossible. Most of the glass is outside. If someone broke in, there would be more glass in the kitchen. And the garden shows no sign of entry or exit."

"That's terrific. I have had the same revelations as you. What does this evidence tell us?"

"It means somebody broke the window from the inside."

"Very good."

"But why? There are no signs of a struggle in the kitchen. Everything was done in the living room. There's no reason to break the window."

Rowan shrugged. "There may be or they may not be—accidents do happen—but I fear you are not concluding the more important fact derived from this evidence."

"Like what?"

"I'll give you time to mull it over."

Rowan continued his inspection of the kitchen. Hidden away in a corner was a small shelf of liquor consisting of mostly cheap bottles. The lone exception was a nearly full bottle of Martell Cordon Bleu with the seal partially intact.

Rowan unscrewed the cap and had a sniff. "That's a damn fine cognac. No one would drink it from the bottle."

He opened the cabinet doors until he found the section with glasses. The first two lowball glasses were still wet, as if recently used. "These glasses could be a clue."

"You mean fingerprints?"

"Doubtful. They've been washed. However, if the killer was in a hurry to wash them and failed to do it properly, the glasses might still have scant traces of alcohol." He tilted one of the glasses. "See how the drop of liquid clings to the glass. I think I may be right. Have Davis run a test on them, see if he can identify the substance. Tell him I'm looking for a good cognac."

"What would that tell us? I mean what would it mean if Alice Dahlen and her killer drank that cognac?"

"Well, it would obviously corroborate the information we got from the window."

Kegan looked doubtful. "I don't see it, Detective. Maybe, you should get somebody else to help you out. Somebody smarter than me."

"Nonsense. Look here. My assistant is on vacation in Joliet. I need someone to fill in. You seem to be roughly his speed. Grady, in his infinite wisdom, has bequeathed me your services. Are you interested in the job?"

"Oh, yes, Mr. Manory."

"Excellent. I'm going to take a quick look around the rest of the house and then pay a visit to Julie McPhee. I'd like you to follow up with Violet Reynolds. Find out if she knows anything about a violin or why it would be the last thing Alice Dahlen said in this world."

"Will do."

Rowan took a long, thoughtful drag off his cigarette. "I wonder what the importance of a violin is. Was that why she was murdered?"

"An instrument seems like a trivial reason for murder."

"All reasons for murder seem rather trivial after the fact, Officer."

Violet stirred helplessly in her bed again, but this wasn't quite like before. This time, she was fully awake and she could move, but the movements were all wrong. Her limbs were heavy and uncooperative, as though her body were encased in syrup. Thoughts surfaced only in fragments.

She opened her eyes a crack and blinked at the darkness. What she saw made no sense. A tall, looming shape like a silo towered against the blackness. Her heart thumped unevenly as confusion rippled through her. Why would there be a silo outside her bedroom? Slowly, the shape resolved itself—the sharp, gleaming edges, the glassy surface catching the faintest glimmer of light.

It was her perfume bottle. Its reflection in the window.

How silly of me.

She blinked hard, her vision clearing bit by bit. The room around her swam into focus—the familiar curves of the nightstand, the thick quilt twisted around her legs. This was her bedroom.

Of course it was.

She exhaled a breath of relief and rolled onto her side, reaching instinctively for Bobby. Her hand brushed the cool sheet where his body should have been.

He was gone.

She fumbled for the clock on the nightstand, zeroing in on

the faint tick-tick-tick. She squinted at the face, barely making out the hands in the dim light.

4:30 a.m.

What in the world was Bobby doing up at this hour? He never left for work this early.

Her sluggish mind grasped for an explanation, but before she could make sense of his absence, a sudden crack shattered the silence. It came from the direction of the kitchen—a violent, jarring sound that made her flinch.

Bobby must have dropped something. Maybe he'd gotten up early to make coffee? That had to be it.

She flung off the quilt and swung her feet to the floor, nearly toppling as she stood. Her knees buckled, and she caught herself against the bedpost. Something was wrong with her balance. She felt lightheaded. Was she ill?

"Bobby?" she called out, her voice thick and unsteady.

She didn't wait for an answer. The thought of seeing him—her Bobby, her safe place—was enough to make her stumble forward, out of the room, down the short hallway toward the kitchen. Her legs felt like they weren't quite attached to her body, and she half-lurched, half-staggered as she moved.

When she reached the doorway, she stopped cold.

A man who was not Bobby stood in the kitchen.

He was enormous, his broad shoulders filling the narrow space. His head was shaved, and his jaw jutted like a block of granite. He wore a battered overcoat, the kind that had seen too many winters. His hands hung at his sides, but they looked capable of terrible things.

Dickie.

Violet froze, her heart pounding so loudly she thought he might hear it.

Alice was right. He had come back. More importantly, Madame Dunkel was right. Dickie was here to kill her.

Dickie didn't seem to notice her panic—or maybe he did and he was quietly enjoying it.

"Howdy, Violet. You look a little sleepy."

Violet's thoughts spun, searching for an escape. Could she make it to the back door? No, he was between her and it. What about the window? No, it was too small, and her balance was still unsteady. Her eyes flicked to the knife in the sink. It was closer to him than to her. She'd never reach it in time.

Stop staring at the knife.

She forced herself to speak, to try to act normal. "Dickie. It's…it's good to see you."

"You remember me. That's so sweet. How ya doin?"

"Good. Real good."

"You called out for Bobby. Is that your husband's name—*Bobby*?"

"I…yeah. He stepped out for a moment, but he'll be back." She stumbled, but quickly caught her balance. "I'm sure of it. He'll be back any minute. Probably just walked to the newsstand. He reads the paper and—"

"Nah. Ain't no car in the garage. My guess? He ain't coming back for a while. It's just you and me, doll."

"Oh." She looked back to the knife. Maybe she could grab it if she distracted him, but what then? He was so big, so strong. Even if she stabbed him, he could probably kill her before he bled out. Maybe if she just played along, he'd leave. "What do you want, Dickie?"

"Straight to business—a dame after my own heart. I want the violin."

"The vio—" For a moment, her mind blanked. Then, she remembered. "Oh, the Villaume."

"Yeah, that's what it's called. I'm sure glad you said it. I can't pronounce it so well. I just call it the violin. Where is it?"

"P—p—Pearl."

"Who's Pearl?"

"She's in the orchestra. I swear it's the truth. You have to believe me."

He held up a calloused, swollen hand. "Simmer down, Violet. I believe you. Keep going. You're doing real good.

Tell me about Pearl."

"Yeah, the violin needed repairing, and her uncle is a luthier. He specializes in repairing old stringed instruments. She brought it to practice this morning. She has it because she couldn't get ahold of Julie."

"Where does Pearl live?"

Violet pointed to the fridge. "There's a paper up there that has the address and phone number of every woman in the orchestra. Take it. Her name is Pearl Ennis." Violet nodded aggressively. "Just take it. It's yours. I don't need it."

Dickie took the paper from the top of the fridge and gave it a quick once-over. "That's good, Violet. Now, I got one very important question for you. When I go over to Pearl's house—and I'll be there shortly—I'm gonna find the violin?"

She nodded. "I swear."

He folded the paper and pocketed it. "I'm glad, 'cause otherwise, I'd have to come back."

They smiled at each other. For a moment, Violet dared to believe he was leaving. Maybe he was satisfied. Maybe she was safe.

Then he walked forward. "Just one more thing."

"Anything, Dickie."

His hands rocketed forward and gripped her neck.

Her fingers clawed at his iron grip, her nails raking against his skin. She couldn't breathe. His massive hands clamped around her throat, the prickly points stabbing into her skin.

"Please…" she croaked, her voice barely a whisper.

He leaned in closer, his breath hot against her ear. "I want you to know this ain't personal, Violet. I like you just fine, but you have to disappear. I'll make it quick though. I'm good at making it quick. Ask around."

She tried to speak more, to beg, to reason with him, but the only sound she could make was a pathetic rasp. And then it hit her. She was going to die. Right here, in her own kitchen. No one would save her. Bobby was gone, and no one else was coming.

Her fists flailed against his arms, a feeble resistance. The blows landed with dull, useless thuds—like trying to punch through stone. Her strength was nothing against this monstrous force that had stormed into her safe little life and torn it apart.

She thought of Madame Dunkel. That strange, cryptic woman who had warned her, who had tried to tell her that something dark was coming. Violet had talked herself out of believing. But Madame Dunkel was right.

Pain exploded behind her eyes, a bulging, throbbing sensation as the lack of oxygen took its toll. Her vision began to pulse, the room flickering in and out of focus like a dying candle. Her feet kicked wildly, searching for the floor, for any kind of leverage. Then, with a sickening jolt, she realized—her feet were off the ground. He had lifted her, her legs dangling, useless.

A numbness began to creep over her, radiating out from her chest and into her arms and legs. It was a terrifying sort of calm, like her body was surrendering even as her mind screamed at it to keep fighting.

This isn't fair. The thought came, sharp and bitter. All her plans, her hopes, her dreams—they were gone.

Was life always like this? Had life always been this cruel, and she had just been blind to it? She had stupidly invested in it, trying to find happiness in the darkness.

Her head lolled back as the pressure around her neck grew unbearable. Her vision tunneled, colors smearing together into a gray haze. There was a noise somewhere—sharp and loud—but it sounded far away, like it was coming from the end of a long tunnel.

Suddenly, Dickie's grip loosened. She fell, hitting the floor hard and crumpling into a coughing, wheezing heap. Air rushed back into her lungs in painful, ragged gasps. Her throat burned, every breath a jagged knife slicing through her.

Her vision began to clear. She looked up, and there he was—Dickie, still standing, but something was wrong. He was swaying. He turned around, revealing the dark stain spreading across his back.

Another crack, louder this time. Dickie's face jerked violently to the side. His massive body lurched backward, the impact slamming him to the floor with a bone-rattling thud. His legs fell across her, pinning her down.

She stared, uncomprehending, as the room spun around her. She tried to move, to push his legs off her, but her body wouldn't cooperate. She was too weak, too broken.

Then she saw him—a man standing in the doorway. He was holding a gun, his face set in a grim mask of determination.

"Ma'am? Are you alright?" His voice cut through the haze, low and steady, but it sounded distorted, warped.

Her lips moved, but no sound came out.

"Ma'am?" He stepped closer, crouching down. "Stay with me, okay?"

The world tilted, the edges of her vision going dark again. She focused on the man's face, trying to commit it to memory, but it was already slipping away.

The last thing she saw before everything went black was the man's badge glinting in the dim light. *Officer Kegan.*

Rowan struck a match, puffing his cigarette to life. The smoke mingled with the sour, sterile tang of hospital air. The smell was an unsettling mixture of carbolic soap, boiled cabbage and something vaguely metallic—an odor that seeped into the back of your throat and lingered. The hallway stretched ahead, dim and unwelcoming, its greenish-gray walls illuminated by flickering electric sconces that cast long, jittery shadows. The floor tiles, a worn checkerboard of faded black and white, were scrubbed to an uneven dullness, their sheen broken by scuff marks and cracks.

"Well, Doctor Kelly?"

The doctor spoke without pause or correction. "She has significant trauma to her neck from manual strangulation. The pressure applied to her throat caused damage to the soft tissues and blood vessels, which explains the redness in her eyes—these are burst capillaries from the strain. Fortunately, her trachea is intact, meaning no permanent damage to her airway, but her voice is hoarse due to bruising of the vocal cords and the surrounding tissues. That will take time to heal."

"But she has no trouble speaking?"

"No."

"Superb. Is she critical at all?"

Of this, the doctor was far less certain. He wobbled his head side to side, his face pinching into a tight grimace.

"There's noticeable swelling along the neck, which could impair her breathing if it worsens. For now, we're keeping her head elevated and applying cold compresses to reduce inflammation. Internally, she's showing signs of hypoxia caused by the interruption of airflow during the attack. While she didn't lose consciousness for long, she was dangerously close. Honestly, I'd say exhaustion is the most serious problem. Her nerves are in shambles. I insist that any questions you ask her be of an unstimulating nature."

"Gentle as a lamb, I promise."

"There's a nurse stationed in the room. If she asks you to leave for any reason—"

Rowan finished the sentence. "I know better than to argue with a nurse."

The doctor nodded. "She's in room 12B."

The drawn curtains blocked the intruding daylight, allowing only faint rays to sneak through the edges. The lines they cast on the walls were fractured and pale, like faded scars of daylight. It was a room that stifled any emotion. In the corner, a nurse sat in a straight-backed chair, her head bowed over her knitting. The soft click of needles was the only sound, a rhythmic metronome to the stillness. She didn't say anything when Rowan entered, but her thin lips tightened at the sight of the cigarette dangling from his mouth.

Rowan recognized her disapproval and roundly ignored it.

He stood beside Violet's bed and rested one broad hand on the curve of his gut, the other flicking ash absently into a nearby tray.

Violet lay propped up slightly on the hospital bed, her head turned toward the drawn curtains. Her eyes were rimmed and bloodshot, glistening faintly in the dim light like polished stones. Her chest rose and fell in slow, shallow movements, and the jagged edges of her breathing remained barely audible in the oppressive quiet.

Rowan studied her, his expression unreadable behind a veil of curling smoke. Finally, he spoke, his voice gravelly yet softened, like sandpaper worn smooth. "Mrs. Reynolds?" He forced a little cough. "My name is Rowan Manory. I'm a private investigator."

Her eyes fluttered open, unfocused at first, before settling on him. "From the newspaper?" she whispered.

Rowan allowed himself a faint grin. No matter how often people mentioned it, the recognition never failed to stir a spark of pride. He nodded. "Yes, ma'am."

"I'm not dead." Her voice cracked as she said it, her disbelief raw. "I was... sure it was going to happen…sure I was dead."

"You very nearly were," Rowan said. "Had it not been for Officer Kegan's quick thinking, you might have perished. Luckily, he killed Mr. Daubert before that happened. It's over. You're safe now."

Her bloodshot eyes blinked slowly. "What about Julie? Did he…"

Rowan's expression hardened. "Miss McPhee is dead… as is Miss Dahlen. Both were strangled in their homes. We are still investigating, but it appears Mr. Daubert was the culprit."

Her head fell back against the pillow, and she seemed to shrink further into herself. "No," she finally whispered, the word frail and pleading.

"We don't know why he killed your friends," Rowan continued gently, "but I was hoping you could tell me why he wanted you dead. We are at a loss for a motive."

She licked her cracked lips, wincing. "He thought I had the violin."

Rowan's eyebrows lifted, betraying his excitement. "Violin?"

She nodded weakly and began to explain. Rowan took mental notes as she spoke. Her voice rasped and faltered, but she managed to provide details—the Villaume, Pearl, and everything else—spilling out in an unfocused mass.

When she finished, Rowan adjusted his tie and leaned slightly closer. "Did Alice know that Pearl had the violin?"

She mouthed the word, "Yes."

Rowan exhaled slowly. "Is Pearl your friend?"

Violet's frail body shook with a faint, silent laugh. "I don't like Pearl at all," she croaked. "When you meet her, you'll see."

"Why did Dickie think you had the violin?"

"I don't know," she whispered. "I met him once. Why would he remember me?"

Rowan let the question hang in the air, his brow furrowed in thought. "I'm certain the answer will become clear eventually," he said at last. "I'll leave you to rest now. It's vital for your recovery."

Her lips moved again, barely audible. "Bobby?"

"Pardon?" Rowan leaned closer.

"Is Bobby here to see me?"

"Yes," Rowan said. "I believe he's waiting in the lobby downstairs."

"I want to see him."

"Of course, Mrs. Reynolds. I'll send him up shortly."

He hesitated for just a moment longer, his eyes lingering on her frail form, before nodding to the nurse and leaving the room.

The hospital lobby was as dim as the patient rooms. The dark wood paneling absorbed whatever shafts of daylight spilled through the narrow windows. A fan spun lazily overhead, stirring the scent of wax and faint traces of coffee left on the desk nearby. Bobby Reynolds sat in a hard-backed chair, his posture rigid, hands resting on his knees. He wore a shirt that looked like it had seen better hours and slacks that had begun to crease at odd, haggard angles.

"Mr. Reynolds?" Rowan's voice was steady, businesslike.

Bobby stood immediately, offering a quick nod. "Yes."

Rowan extended his hand, and Bobby took it, his grip firm but brief.

"Rowan Manory," the detective said. "I've been working with the police on your wife's case."

"Is she awake?" Bobby's words came quickly, clipped at the edges. His eyes searched Rowan's face for reassurance.

Rowan nodded. "She's very lucky."

"I know." Bobby shifted his weight, looking down for a moment. "I… I don't even know how to thank the officer who saved her."

"No need." Rowan motioned toward the chair. "Do you mind if I ask you a few questions? It'll help with the final report."

Bobby hesitated, then nodded. "Of course. Anything."

Rowan took a seat across from him, leaning back slightly in his chair. He reached into his pocket and retrieved his small notebook, flipping it open. "How long have you and Violet been married?"

"Five months," Bobby said. "It was a small ceremony—just family."

"And how did you two meet?"

Bobby's lips parted as if he hadn't expected the question. He blinked before answering. "I was working for her father's real estate company. She came to visit the office one day, and that was that—love at first sight, as they say."

Rowan glanced up briefly, his pen pausing mid-stroke. "Do you work with her father now?"

"Yes," Bobby said. "Edward made me a partner after we got married. He's semi-retired now. Checks in once a week."

Rowan nodded. "Do you have a card I can take?"

He quickly produced a holder and flipped one of the cards

out for Rowan.

Wheat, Olen, and Reynolds Real Estate
"Estates, Homes, and Investments"
Robert "Bobby" Reynolds -- Partner
Telephone: ST-7685
Address: 455 State Street, Chicago, Il
Telegram: WHEATOLENREAL

Rowan studied the card. "Who's Wheat?

"I don't know. He's a silent partner. I've never met him," Bobby said with a shrug. "Just an investor, from what I gather. It's really just me handling the day-to-day operations. Sometimes I go days without speaking with Fred."

"Fred?"

Bobby breathed a chuckle. "Mr. Olen. He's my father-in-law, so it's not strange I should be on a first-name basis with him. Is it?"

"Certainly not, sir."

"Speaking of that," he said, adjusting his collar, "Fred's currently in Kentucky scouting out locations for a new office. Should I contact him? I didn't know if it was legally—"

"We've already handled that. He's taking a train north tomorrow afternoon."

"Good. Violet should have everyone by her side."

Rowan tucked the notebook back into his pocket, his cigarette hanging loosely between his fingers. "Did you know Dickie Daubert?"

"No," Bobby said, shaking his head.

"What about Julie McPhee or Alice Dahlen?"

Bobby hesitated. It was the smallest of pauses, but Rowan had been working too long as a detective not to notice. "I met them once or twice, but I didn't know them well. Violet has her friends, and I have mine." He looked toward the window, his jaw tightening slightly. "She did say she hadn't seen much of them lately. Maybe something happened between them, but she didn't mention it."

"Where were you early this morning?"

Bobby's fingers twitched faintly against the armrest of the chair. "I was… at work."

"At work?" Rowan asked, his tone even. "Hadn't you just come home from a long day?"

"Sometimes I remember things I forgot to do, so I go back to the office. Alone. You can ask anyone who works for me. I'm in the office most of the time."

Rowan nodded slowly, as if the answer was routine. "What time did you leave to return to the office?"

"Right after she went to bed," Bobby said. His voice was steady, but he rubbed his palms together absently.

Rowan pocketed his notebook, pushing to his feet. "Thank you, Mr. Reynolds. You can head upstairs now. She's in Room 12B and she's wanting to see you."

Bobby stood and thanked Rowan again. He glanced back as he moved toward the elevator, his footsteps echoing faintly in the quiet room. Just before he entered, he offered a faint, awkward wave goodbye, and Rowan responded with a slow nod.

The elevator doors slid shut with a metallic click, and Rowan remained where he was. He lit a cigarette and exhaled a thin stream of smoke. His gaze lingering on the empty hallway before turning toward the window. The waiting room was quiet again, save for the faint hum of the overhead fan.

Rowan stepped out into the midday glare, shielding his eyes from the sun. The heat radiated off the pavement, wrapping around him like a heavy coat. He paused at the top of the steps, inhaling the sharp sting of car exhaust and distant bakery steam, his cigarette burning low between his fingers.

He had seen this before—cases that seemed cut and dried, all the evidence aligning in a neat little row. But murder was never neat. It was messy, twisting in on itself when least expected. He'd lost count of how many times he thought he had a case nailed shut, only to have some overlooked clue pry the whole thing back open. And something about this case—this tangle of dead women, a strangled survivor, and a success-driven husband felt like it had a loose thread waiting to be tugged.

Kegan was waiting by his car. “How is she?”

“She’s going to pull through.” Rowan flicked his cigarette to the gutter and ground it out with his heel.

Kegan sighed. “That’s good. After Miss Dahlen died on me, I don’t know if I could take losing another one.” He squinted at the sky. “Sometimes, you do everything right, and they still don’t make it.”

Kegan had a weary understanding of the job, but he still cared. Rowan found it charming. “What have you got for me?”

“We’re canvassing near both Julie McPhee and Alice Dahlen’s places. Might get lucky, find someone who saw Daubert lurking around. But I have something better.”

Rowan raised an eyebrow.

“We found an interesting business card in Julie’s home. It’s for a pawn shop owned by Al Grimm.”

“Do we know this Mr. Grimm?”

“He was suspected of helping Daubert pull that holdup months back. We could never prove it.” Kegan’s grin turned sharp. “We picked him up hiding at a friend’s place, beat to hell. Two black eyes, busted nose. Someone worked him over good. We know Daubert had a mean streak a mile wide. Wouldn’t surprise me if this was his handiwork.”

“Where is Grimm now?”

“We got him waiting in a room for interrogation.”

“Let’s go.”

“We’re going to put a lid on this case by nightfall,” Kegan said, slapping the car door. “Feels good, huh?”

Rowan gave a noncommittal grunt.

Back in 12B, Bobby sat in the wooden chair beside Violet’s bed, his hands clasped between his knees. He had said little since he arrived. She was awake, her breath slow and shallow, her fingers idly plucking at the stiff hospital blanket.

Violet turned her face toward him, her bloodshot eyes dull with exhaustion. "I must look awful," she murmured, touching her cheek, feeling the bruises, the swollen skin.

Bobby hesitated. "You look fine. No one expects you to look like you usually do after what happened."

A weak, bitter laugh fluttered from her throat. "You don't mean that. You just don't want me to be sad."

Bobby said nothing.

She stared at him, searching his face with an expression that was almost painful in its sincerity. "You don't love me anymore," she said. "I can see that now." There was no accusation in it—just a tired acceptance.

He combed his fingers through his hair.

"Maybe you never did."

For the first time, a hint or irritation entered Bobby's voice. "Stop it, Violet."

Her face crumpled, and she lifted a trembling hand to cover it. A dry, gasping sob escaped her lips, her shoulders jerking as tears slid down her temples.

The nurse was on her feet in an instant. "That's enough," she said briskly, moving to the bed. "She needs rest."

Bobby remained seated, watching Violet shake, unsure what to do.

"Mr. Reynolds," the nurse pressed, her voice firm but not unkind. "I'm afraid you'll have to leave. Now, sir."

He stood stiffly, glancing at Violet once more—her hand still over her face, her fragile frame trembling beneath the blankets—then turned toward the door.

The nurse followed him into the hallway, shutting the door gently behind them.

"She's not making any sense," Bobby said. "It's like she's a different person."

"That's because she's in shock," the nurse replied. "It's all perfectly normal, I assure you. Give her time. After some rest, she'll be better."

Bobby glanced back at the door. "You'll stay with her?"

The nurse nodded. "I'll be here until six. Then another nurse will check on her every forty-five minutes. If she needs anything, a doctor will be called immediately. You have nothing to fear, Mr. Reynolds."

Bobby nodded, muttered a quiet thank you, and walked away down the darkened corridor.

The interrogation room was one of the worst in the station. A forgotten corner of the precinct, where the walls had yellowed from years of cigarette smoke and the single overhead bulb cast a sickly glow. The wooden table bore the deep scratches of restless hands, and the chair across from it was deliberately uncomfortable—a design meant to break a man down just that much faster. It was the kind of room reserved for a man like Al Grimm. Small with thin hair and no muscle, Al looked like his parents hated him.

Rowan stepped inside, closing the door behind him. The stench of sweat, blood, and stale breath filled the air. Al sat slumped in his chair, his left eye nearly swollen shut, his nose twisted at an unnatural angle. One hand lay curled uselessly in his lap, its fingers bruised and stiff. He was the picture of misery, and the second he saw Rowan, he latched onto it.

"I need a doctor," Al whined, shifting gingerly in his seat. His voice was nasal, his breath whistling through his broken nose. "I'm suffering."

Rowan let the door click shut behind him. "You look fine, Mr. Grimm. Besides, you didn't seek medical treatment earlier. It must not hurt that bad." He pulled out a chair and sat down, stretching his legs out. "What changed?"

Al let out a low groan. "C'mon, I got rights."

"Sure," Rowan said. "You want a lawyer? I can get you one. But that takes paperwork. Couple of hours, at least. In the meantime, I can get you a doctor." He leaned forward, lowering his voice. "Hell, I can even let you walk out of here if you say the right things."

Al shifted, uneasy. "I don't know nothin'."

Rowan shrugged, as if it didn't matter. He took his time, rolling a cigarette and lighting it with slow, deliberate movements. He let the silence stretch.

Al squirmed. "Look, I—"

"Dickie Daubert is dead."

"Thank God."

Al froze. His swollen lips parted just slightly. It was too fast. Too natural. And Al knew it the second the words were out. His eyes darted to Rowan's, realization dawning like a slow-rolling storm.

Rowan exhaled a cloud of smoke into the pool of light between them. "Why are you so happy about that?"

"No reason," Al muttered, shifting in his chair. "I just—"

Rowan cut him off. "Julie McPhee was murdered." He let the words settle like dust. "Now that Dickie's dead, someone has to take the rap."

"I don't know any Julie McPhee. In fact—"

Rowan slammed his palm on the table.

Al jumped in his chair. "What are you so angry about?"

"Why did you give her your business card, idiot? If you're planning a murder, you don't plant evidence on the victim. Jesus Christ, Al!"

Al's whole body tensed. He winced at the pain shooting through his broken ribs. His battered fingers twitched against the tabletop. He saw the trap now, and it was snapping shut around him. Panic set in.

"I didn't tell Dickie to kill her," he sputtered. "All I wanted was the violin! Dickie was the hothead! Look at me—" He gestured wildly to his bruised, battered face. "Does it look like we was good friends?"

It was exactly as Rowan had foreseen. He eased back in his chair, flicking ashes onto the floor and sucking on cigarette like a man who had just had a steak. Al was talking—that was all that mattered. He let him rant, let him spill, let the desperation boil over. Then, when the moment was right, he cut in.

"You can tell me exactly what happened, or you can take

the rap. Those are your two choices. I already know you were involved. That's finished, over, done. I need to know the A-to-B stuff."

Al swallowed hard. His good hand clenched into a fist. Then, slowly, he started talking.

"She came into my shop with a Villaume," he began.

"Use names when you talk, Al."

"Sorry. Julie…Julie McPhee and she had the violin, said it didn't play so good, wanted to know what it was worth. I gave her a number."

Rowan cocked his head. "An honest number?"

Al snorted. "Hell no. Lowballed her. Told her five hundred bucks. But I could get a lot more. Soundpost was busted—that part was true. The soundboxes don't last on those old instruments."

Rowan nodded, urging him on.

"She didn't wanna sell. Said it was a gift, wanted to play it." Al sucked in a sharp breath, wincing. "That's when she gave me her name, and I realized she was Dickie's old flame. Of all the luck." He licked his cracked lips. "Dickie was hidin' out in Springfield. I knew the number. And I knew he'd want in on that violin because he needed the money. I'd be able to sell it for ten grand, easy. I offered Dickie an even split. His job was stealing it and mine was the sale. That was it—a simple burglary." He looked down at his busted hand. "Murder wasn't part of the plan."

Rowan studied him, waiting. "Don't stop now, Al. You're doing so well."

"I was waiting for Dickie to deliver the violin at the shop yesterday morning. But come 8:00, Dickie storms into my shop, outta his mind and without the piece. He starts pounding on me." Al's voice turned frantic, his body twitching with remembered pain. "Said the violin wasn't there. Said he was gonna kill me. He broke my damn hand!"

"What did you tell him?" Rowan asked.

"I swore she had it," Al said, sobbing. "He didn't believe me. He smashed in one of the glass counters and picked up this jagged piece of glass. He said he was going to stab my eyes. That's when I remembered—when I mentioned the soundpost to Julie, she said she knew someone who could fix old instruments." His swollen face twisted. "I told Dickie that, and he got this… look. Then he left. Said if he didn't find the violin, he'd be back." Al shook his head. "I didn't wait to get outta there. So, yeah, I'm glad the son of a bitch is dead."

Rowan leaned back, considering it. The pieces fit. The story tracked. He studied Al a moment longer, then stood.

"Where you goin'?" Al asked, panic creeping into his voice. "I told you what you wanted!"

Rowan ignored him, stepping outside into the hallway. He rubbed his forehead, putting the puzzle pieces into place.

Kegan was waiting, his face set, a notepad in his hand.

"Well?" Rowan asked.

Kegan exhaled. "You were right about the cognac." He flipped a page. "Traces of it were found in the glasses at Alice Dahlen's."

Rowan nodded. "What else?"

"We found a body at Sangero Trucking," Kegan continued. "The side door was busted open. Upstairs, a man was stabbed clean through the chest. Strong killer—had to be to drive a blade in that deep and yank it back out. I'm going to take a leap and say it was Dickie."

Rowan's eyes narrowed. "Who is the victim?"

"Tommy Benson."

"Do we know the connec—"

"He was a bookkeeper for some orchestra events—fundraisers and such. He knew Violet Reynolds fairly well. We also found out from some of the other players that Dickie attended one of these events. They remembered *him* quite well. The oboist said he pawed her pretty hard at the entrance to the lady's room."

"It's good that certain people are dead, isn't it, Officer?"

"That it is, Detective."

"Anything else?"

"Yeah. But I saved it for last." He hesitated, glancing down at his notes.

"You have my attention."

"Julie McPhee was pregnant. About a month along."

Rowan stiffened. His jaw tightened. "I think it's time we speak with the mother."

It was 6:00 p.m. A faded couch, a ticking clock, and the long shadows cast by dim, depressing light. Ann McPhee sat hunched in her living room, a crumpled handkerchief in her hands. She was in her mid-fifties but looked older, her face drawn, her posture stiff. When Rowan and Kegan entered, she barely acknowledged them. Her eyes were red-rimmed, her hands trembling in her lap. She was a slobbery mess.

Rowan cleared his throat. "Mrs. McPhee, I just want to thank you for agreeing to speak with us."

Ann dabbed at her eyes. "What else am I supposed to do? My baby is gone." Her voice cracked, and fresh tears rolled down her cheeks. "I saw her body. I saw what that monster did to her."

Rowan and Kegan remained silent, letting her speak.

Ann shuddered. "I knew he was bad. I told her—told her a thousand times. But she thought she could change him. Thought that if she just loved him enough, he'd turn into a good man." Her laughter was bitter. "But men like that… the same large hands that hold a woman like Julie, protect her, make her feel safe… can kill her in an instant. And Dickie had nothing good in his heart. I was so happy when he left town. Thought he was gone for good. Thought she was free of him. Now Julie is dead. Alice too. Violet's in the hospital."

She broke down, shaking her head. "They were best friends, you know. Ever since high school. Always together—Ali, Vi, and Jules. That's what they called each other. Those girls were like sisters."

Rowan nodded, letting her grieve in her own way. After a moment, Ann wiped at her face and looked up. "How is

Violet?"

"She'll live," Rowan said.

Ann exhaled shakily. "Good. Something good happened She survived."

A pause. Then Rowan shifted, his tone soft but firm. "Mrs. McPhee, we need to ask about something important."

Ann bristled. "What?"

"Your daughter was pregnant."

Ann's face twisted with discomfort. "I know." She looked away, shame creeping into her expression. "She didn't tell me the father's name." She wrung the handkerchief in her hands. "She said she wouldn't tell me unless he married her. And if he wouldn't, she was going to call it off and never see him again."

Rowan exchanged a glance with Kegan, then gave him a slight nod. Kegan lifted a violin case and set it gently on the coffee table.

Ann blinked at it, confused. "What's this?"

Rowan leaned forward. "This is what Dickie was looking for when he came to Julie's home."

Ann's brow furrowed. "Why?"

"It's valuable," Rowan explained. "Very valuable."

Ann let out a short, disbelieving laugh. "That's silly. Julie didn't own anything valuable."

Rowan folded his hands. "She did. She gave this violin to a friend named Pearl Ennis for repair. Pearl told us that you bought it for her."

"That's a lie." She gestured wildly around the room. "Does it look like I have a lot of money?"

Rowan studied her, then nodded. "No, it doesn't."

"I never bought that violin," Ann insisted. "I didn't even know she had it."

Rowan watched her for a moment longer, then stood. "Thank you for your time, Mrs. McPhee. I'll make sure you get the final report when the investigation is complete."

Rowan and Kegan stepped out into the evening air. The sun had dipped below the horizon, and the city was awash in the last pale light of the day. As they walked toward the car, streetlights began flickering to life.

Kegan slid into the driver's seat and started the engine. He glanced at Rowan. "Case looks wrapped up."

"Nonsense."

"Why?"

"Because Dickie Daubert didn't kill Julie and he didn't kill Alice."

Kegan turned to him, stunned. "How do you figure that?"

"How were they killed?" Rowan asked.

Kegan frowned. "They were strangled."

"With what?"

Kegan thought. "A sash and… something we don't know yet, but something harder and sharper than a sash."

Rowan nodded. "Implements."

Kegan squinted at him. "Yeah?"

"No implement was used in the attempted murder of Violet Reynolds."

Kegan paused. "That's true." He frowned. "But an implement was used on Tommy Benson."

Rowan let out a dry chuckle. "Difficult to stab a man with your hand."

"Fair enough," Kegan admitted. "Okay the first two were strangled with implements and Violet was strangled by hand."

Rowan exhaled smoke from his cigarette, staring out the window. "Killers tend to follow patterns. It seems to me that a man who strangles once with his hands is a man who will always prefer to strangle with his hands."

Kegan nodded. "I'm with you so far."

"We must admit to ourselves that both Julie and Alice knew their killer. Why? There was no break-in at Julie's home. She let her killer in. And she sure as hell wasn't going to let Dickie Daubert into her home."

Kegan shrugged. "He could've used a key."

"Sure. But Alice *definitely* let her killer in. The window was broken *after* the fact. I've seen the same trick before—a killer breaking a window from the inside to look like a robbery. It's amateur hour. Our killer wanted to hide the fact that the victim knew him."

"And what about the cognac?"

"That was the real clue." Rowan flicked ashes onto the street. "Alice poured her *best* liquor and shared a glass with her guest. Would she do that for Dickie?"

"No," Kegan admitted. "Besides, Dickie would've chugged straight from the bottle."

"Exactly," Rowan said. "The drinks were for a special occasion. And then there's the most important part. The part that really settled it for me."

"Which is?"

"Neither Julie nor Alice told Dickie that Pearl had the violin."

Kegan frowned. "Why does that matter?"

"Think about it," Rowan said. "Dickie Daubert—one of the most frightening monsters you can imagine—is threatening to kill them if they don't tell him where the violin is. Do you really think they'd keep quiet? Protect Pearl Ennis? Hell, Violet gave up Pearl's name right away. No hesitation."

"...Yeah."

Rowan pressed on. "Let's say he lost his temper with Julie. Maybe she told him she was pregnant, maybe he flew into a rage and killed her before she could tell him where the violin was. Fine. But would he really make the same *exact* mistake with Alice the following night? No chance. Alice would've told him about Pearl. And we know for a fact that Alice knew Pearl had the violin. Does Dickie go to see Pearl and get the violin? No. He goes to Violet and asks where it is. He wouldn't have gone to Violet's home looking for it. It doesn't make sense."

Kegan stared at him, the realization dawning. "You're right."

Just then, another police car rumbled up the street, its headlights cutting through the dusk. Kegan recognized the driver. "That's Billy."

Rowan knew the solution was near and he had a funny feeling it was being delivered at exactly the right time.

Billy pulled up alongside them, jumping out with a piece of paper in his hand. He rushed to Kegan's window, excitement on his face.

"Someone saw a man entering Julie's home," Billy said.

Kegan asked, "On Sunday night?"

Billy shook his head. "No. Last night."

Kegan blinked. "Last night? But she was already dead."

Billy nodded. "I know. But the witness swears it—said he saw a man enter at about 2:00 a.m., then drive off. He didn't get a good look, but he got the license plate."

Billy handed Kegan the paper.

Kegan read it aloud, then looked up in shock.

Rowan exhaled slowly, letting the facts arrange themselves in his mind like puzzle pieces. His jaw tightened. "To the hospital."

Kegan hesitated. "Why?"

Rowan flicked his cigarette out the window. "Because Bobby Reynolds is going to kill his wife."

The tires screeched as Kegan jerked the wheel, sending the car skidding into the hospital lot. The moment they saw Bobby Reynolds' car parked haphazardly near the entrance, both men bolted for the door.

"Go!"

Kegan took off like a gazelle, sprinting across the lot in even, rhythmic strides. Rowan followed close behind, but his breath came hard and fast, his heavy frame struggling to keep pace. As they burst into the hospital lobby, Rowan caught the gleam of the stairwell sign and waved Kegan forward.

"Take the stairs!" he huffed, bending over with his hands on his knees.

As Kegan charged up the stairwell, Rowan took his time, shuffling toward the elevator. He jabbed the button with a shaking finger. He leaned against the wall, sucking in desperate breaths. "Take him alive," he wheezed.

But Kegan was too far away to hear him. He took the stairs three at a time, his gun already drawn. His boots pounded against the steps, echoing up the stairwell. When he reached Violet's floor, a nurse gasped and flattened herself against the wall to avoid his furious approach. Violet's door was feebly blocked—a chair, a trash can, anything that could be shoved against it in a hurry. It didn't slow Kegan down. Fueled by raw adrenaline, he slammed his shoulder into the door. The barricade skidded back and the trash receptacle toppled over with a metallic clang.

The sight before him froze his blood.

Violet was convulsing on the bed, her eyes rolled back, her tongue lolling from her mouth. A curtain sash was wrapped tight around her throat.

And Bobby Reynolds was above her, pulling the ends with a wicked glee. His usually handsome features were twisted into something monstrous—pure, seething hatred carved into every muscle of his face.

Kegan didn't hesitate. "Stop!" he roared, leveling his gun.

Bobby's head whipped around, wild eyes locking onto Kegan. He let go of the sash and headed straight for the window.

Violet slumped onto the bed, gasping for breath, her body shuddering.

"No!" Kegan surged forward. His fingers grazed Bobby's sleeve—just enough to feel the fabric slip away as Bobby threw himself onto the fire escape.

Bobby stumbled, the metal grating under his weight. His foot slipped. His hand shot out—grabbing the railing just in time. There he dangled, nothing beneath him but empty air and the hard pavement far below.

Kegan holstered his gun and lunged forward, leaning over the sill. "Take my hand!" he shouted.

Bobby's wild eyes met his.

For a split second, it seemed like he might grab the

officer's hand. His fingers twitched.

For a second, Kegan almost had him.

Bobby took a breath—one deep, final breath. He let go.

Kegan saw it happen in slow motion—Bobby's body twisting as he dropped, his limbs limp as if the fight had already left him. The sickening thud echoed through the alley below. And then the red pool flowing from under his skull.

Kegan exhaled sharply, staring down at the crumpled figure on the pavement.

Behind him, the elevator dinged. Rowan arrived, still breathless, wiping sweat from his brow as he stepped onto the fire escape. He followed Kegan's gaze downward.

Kegan didn't turn. "He let go. I gave him my hand. The son of a bitch let go."

Rowan stood beside him, looking down at the body. He nodded once. "He'd lost his reason to live."

A few hours later, Rowan pulled up a chair beside Violet's hospital bed. He exhaled, rubbed his tired eyes, and leaned forward.

"Violet? Can you hear me?"

She gave half a nod in response.

"The doctors told me you can go at any moment."

Violet's eyes fluttered. Her lips moved, but no sound came. Rowan shifted closer, tilting his ear near her mouth.

"My father?" she whispered.

Rowan sat back. "Barring a miracle, he won't make it here in time. I'm sorry."

She gave no reaction—not because she didn't care, but because she didn't have the strength to show it.

Rowan folded his hands together. "There are still a few unanswered questions about your case. I was hoping you could clear them up."

Violet barely moved, but Rowan could see the faintest flicker of acknowledgment in her eyes.

"You already know your husband is dead. After he

attacked you, he fell from the fire escape trying to run."

She whispered faintly, "I loved Bobby."

Rowan nodded. "I know."

"He didn't love me."

"Your husband and Julie were having an affair. He was the one who bought her the violin. We traced it back to an auction. It was a gift for her, one I'm sure she treasured. Bobby married you to get a partnership in your father's company. He only stayed with you to be in your father's good graces. You know that now, don't you?"

"Yes."

"It appears as if Julie gave Bobby an ultimatum. She told him to divorce you and marry her, or else she would expose the affair. Julie's mother has confirmed this. Julie didn't give her mother Bobby's name, but she did say she was seeing someone and that she was going to demand he marry her."

Rowan exhaled as if the conclusion was obvious. "Alice knew that Bobby was the father. He had to commit a second murder to keep her quiet. Strangling both women made it look like the same killer."

A single tear tracked down Violet's cheek. "I knew Alice was hiding something from me."

Rowan leaned back slightly. "Why do you think Bobby tried to kill you? He had no need."

She managed to speak in a ragged whisper. "I told him... I knew... didn't love me... maybe..."

She never finished.

Rowan nodded, as if to himself. "I see. It's possible he thought you knew of the affair as well and that you might tell your father. He would lose his position in the company. Is that it?"

She tried to shrug.

"Difficult to know the exact thoughts of a madman." He reached into his pocket and pulled out a jagged piece of quartz. He held it up in the dim light. "We found this in his pocket."

Violet's eyes widened at the sight of the shiny mineral.

Rowan lifted a brow. "Do you recognize it?"

A faint, almost imperceptible nod.

"It's from your necklace," he said. "We found it cracked in your apartment. Why was Bobby carrying it with him?"

"He wanted to... fix it."

Rowan studied her for a long moment, then said, "But that's not true."

He let the words settle before moving forward.

"I'll try to explain. When Dickie arrived at Julie's to find the violin, she was already dead. And the violin wasn't there." Rowan sighed. "Dickie murdered Tommy Benson."

"Tommy?"

"That's how Dickie found you. He showed up at Tommy's work to get your last name. Once he had it, Dickie found it necessary to kill Tommy Benson. He did it to keep the police off his trail."

Rowan pulled out a business card, flipping it casually between his fingers, a subtle, deliberate motion—like a judge toying with his gavel.

"All for your last name. Reynolds."

He tapped at the card. "You'll want to change that now, go back to Olen. I realize you may not make it very long, but you'll surely want your maiden name on your tombstone."

Panic shimmered in her eyes.

"Olen is what Alice and Julie would have called you, right? Your friendship with them seemed to end once you were married. They would call you Violet Olen instead of Violet Reynolds, wouldn't they? Out of habit? Of course, Julie's mother mentioned that you all had little pet names for one another. They called you Vi."

For a fleeting moment, Violet thought of following Bobby out the window and onto the pavement. But she couldn't even stand, let alone jump from the fire escape to her death. She had to lie there and listen to Rowan lay out her sins.

"You know, if I were a cop happening upon a dying

woman, and she gasped out *Vi Olen* with her last breath... I might mistake it for the name of an instrument, too." His voice softened, but the weight of his words remained heavy. "The cuts on Julie's collarbone match the edges of your broken quartz necklace."

Violet rasped a breath.

Rowan pressed on. "Julie invited you over that night, didn't she? She told you about the affair. It must have been quite the shock. You took off your necklace and strangled her with it. You didn't know Dickie would find the body and try to cover it up. When Alice came the next morning and told you that Julie wasn't home, you must have been surprised. You left her corpse there, after all."

Violet's breath rattled. She whispered something.

Rowan leaned in close.

"Alice made up a silly story…said a soldier was the father of the baby…"

"You knew she was lying. Of course, Julie had told her that Bobby was the father. That's why you went to see Alice that night. When you arrived, she welcomed you. Poured you the special cognac she'd been saving. You two shared a drink." Rowan exhaled, as if weighing the tragedy of it all. "Old friends reunited." His voice turned sharp. "And then you killed her too."

Violet's eyes fluttered.

"You strangled her with a sash," Rowan said. "If she told the police about the affair, they might figure out you killed her. You broke Alice's window from the inside. That way the police trying to stage a robbery. It was a sloppy job—because you're not a criminal. Not really." Rowan sighed. "When you got back home, you told Bobby that Julie was missing. He panicked. He loved her."

A flicker in her expression. A tiny one. But Rowan saw it.

"We checked the water by your bedside," Rowan said. "Bobby crushed up one of your Amytal pills. He needed you asleep while he left the house in search of Julie." He shook his head. "He didn't know the correct dose. That's why you woke up early and that's why you were so groggy. He hadn't given you enough. You'd probably been taking a lot of it lately and built up a tolerance."

She nodded.

"Because you'd been so worried about your marriage."

She nodded again.

"When Bobby went to Julie's house, he found your broken quartz piece. And later, after learning of Julie's murder, he put two and two together. He knew you had done it. The nurse told him her schedule. He waited until the evening to return to this room and exact his revenge."

Rowan saw her now, truly saw her. The whole story was told in her anguished expression—a woman who killed to keep what she never truly had, and lost everything anyway. A soul gutted by its own choices.

"Look at you now. No friends. No husband. Nothing," he said, his voice almost sorrowful. "All you've got is me, describing your murderous deeds in horrifying detail."

Violet's lips moved.

Rowan leaned over one more time.

"What did you say?"

"When Madame Dunkel told me you were large," she whispered weakly, "…she meant fat."

Politely, almost quizzically, he smiled.

4.

THE PREMINGER CURSE

Manory Investigations had seen no major cases during the summer of '28—not for lack of murders in Chicago. Quite the opposite. Bloodshed in the Second City was rampant. But those ingeniously plotted murders, the ones that required elaborate unraveling, were in short supply.

Walter had returned from Joliet that fall, rested and ready to work. He and Rowan soon slipped back into their familiar rhythm. The two detectives were reading their newspapers and chatting, half a pot of coffee between them, when the telephone rang.

"Rowan Manory speaking. How may I help you?"

"Hello, Mr. Manory, my name is Jasper Dunn. I'm the lawyer for Dolph and Sophie Preminger."

"Dolph and Sophie? How are they?"

"They've both passed on."

Rowan frowned. "Oh, I'm...I'm sorry to hear that."

"I'm not at liberty to discuss the finer details over the telephone, but you'll be able to get more information if you come to Cairo."

"Cairo?"

Walter looked up from his funny pages. "Camels and pyramids?"

Rowan glared at him.

Jasper clarified. "In order to receive your inheritance, you must come to the reading at the family mansion. It's located in Cairo, Illinois."

"Why would I receive an inheritance? I'm not an heir."

A pause crackled over the line.

"I beg to differ. You see, before their untimely demise, Mr. and Mrs. Preminger added you to their will."

"That's...odd."

"The reading will be held tomorrow evening. Because of the mansion's remoteness and certain eccentricities of the will, you will be required to stay the night. One of the guest bedrooms will be at your disposal. Will you be able to attend?"

"That's not much time...I..." His curiosity got the better of him. "I suppose I can take the morning train."

"Excellent, Mr. Manory. I'll give you directions."

After he hung up the telephone, Rowan explained the situation to his partner.

Walter stroked his chin. "Did you know them well?"

"Not at all. Dolph and Sophie Preminger hired me more than ten years ago, when I was just getting started in the business. They were having trouble with a Chicago brokerage firm—claims the company was underreporting their tobacco shipments and skimming profits on resale. They wanted someone quiet to look into it. A mutual contact recommended me. I dug around for two weeks, turned up the paper trail, and passed it along to their lawyer. Nothing glamorous, but it helped them recover a tidy sum. They sent me a thank-you letter and a box of cigars along with my payment."

"And now you're an heir?"

Rowan nodded slowly. "Without so much as a heads-up. It doesn't make sense." Rowan looked away. His eyes went still, narrowing like a lens. "Late changes to a will—that's never a good sign. I wonder how they died."

"Look at you—already forming plots in your head." Walter smirked. "I suppose we should have a look at train schedules and a map."

"You don't have to accompany me, Williams. It's not as if I've been hired for a case."

"I should tag along. When you get that look on your face, something bad is about to happen."

"What look?"

Walter pointed at him. "*That* look. Like you're trying to see around a corner that isn't there…and you're worried about what you'll find."

The landscapes of Illinois unraveled in slow gradients: steel grey giving way to golden fields, the sprawl of Chicago softening into the patchwork quiet of farmland. Rowan nursed cigarettes. Walter dozed with his suitcoat draped over his body, his polished shoes on the edge of the opposite bench.

By the time they passed through Springfield, the clouds had gathered in bruised knots across the sky. Rain streaked the windows, turning farmland to flooded marsh. The conductor mentioned something about the Mississippi being high this season—swollen like a corpse left too long in the sun.

They stepped off the train at the Mound City station and into the sharp breath of October. The platform was little more than a strip of cracked concrete beside a red-brick depot. Grain trucks rumbled down the main road. A dog barked somewhere behind the general store. Across the street, a pair of farmers loaded feed into the back of a dented pickup while a teenage boy smoked beside the pump, watching them with the torpid stare of someone who had never left and never would.

It wasn't a broken town, not exactly. But it had the look of a place where the paint peeled faster than it was reapplied.

A few men in overalls were gathered outside the barber shop, arguing good-naturedly about baseball.

"We could sell Faber to the Yankees," said one of them to the consternation of the others.

"Faber's forty years old. We couldn't get a wooden nickel for the bum!"

Never one to ignore talk about his favorite sport, Walter had to chime in. "Faber's biggest problem isn't his age. It's the uniform. He should trade it for some navy blue."

All three men stopped smiling. The biggest one spit tobacco close to Walter's shoe. "What are you saying, Mister?"

Walter grinned. "I'm not saying anything. Only that The Sox are a bunch of pansies who couldn't catch a cold in January."

Rowan forced a smile as he took hold of Walter's sleeve. "He doesn't know what he's talking about. It must be his medication. We're sorry for disturbing you, gentlemen."

Walter didn't budge. "I'm just saying the Sox couldn't win a coin toss if it was rigged." He covered his mouth with exaggerated innocence. "I didn't mean to say the "R" word in front of you boys. Seeing as how your striped monkeys took a dive for a few bucks back in '19, that must really sting."

Boots scraped on the pavement. One of them cracked his

knuckles.

Rowan yanked Walter's arm, leading him across the street. "He's tired from our long journey. My apologies."

Walter looked back over his shoulder. "I'm sorry too. I'm sorry Cicotte and Jackson turned out to be such spineless ninnies."

Rowan whispered. "What is wrong with you?"

"You don't understand baseball. Cub fans are supposed to tell Sox fans the time of day. That's just the nature of things. It would have been dishonorable *not* to insult their ballclub."

"You had better be on your best behavior at the mansion."

"Of course. I'm a professional. I won't say anything out of line." He shrugged. "Unless one of the Premingers is a fan of the pansy White Sox. Then, I'm *obligated* to set the guy straight."

They found the garage a few blocks from the station, its wooden sign faded and swinging in the wind: *Wendell's Repairs & Auto Hire*. Inside, a barrel-chested man with a red face and a head like a boiled potato handed over the keys with a grunt.

"She runs a little warm. Don't mind the smell—my helper usually drives her. Eats in there, never cleans up after hisself. Some kinda spicy mush. Foreign stuff."

Walter opened the door and retched from the smell—cumin and burnt onions.

The mechanic cackled. "He's from India."

"The Indians must have been happy to get rid of him."

"If you wants, I ken air it out a little."

"No, no, my boss smokes like a chimney. This hunk of metal will smell like stale tobacco in no time."

Rowan pulled out his map and showed the mechanic the road. "We're headed for the high ground just east of Cairo."

"What for? T'ain't nothing there but the ol' Preminger place."

"That's our destination."

He spit derisively. "Nobody there. Dolph and Sophie

Preminger, they done got murdered."

Rowan cocked his head. "Is that a fact?"

"Alexander County said 'twas a car accident, but my cousin went over the car. The brake line were chewed up. Coulda been a rat, animal or relative, take your pick. But tweren't no crash that done it. Somebody wanted 'em dead." He threw up his hands. "That's what my cousin says and he's smarter'n most."

Rowan tapped tobacco into a rolling paper. His brow creased deeper as the man spoke. He struck a match and took a long, thoughtful drag.

"How long to get to Cairo?"

"Hour. If the roads is washed out maybe longer. It'll be dark when you get there."

They pulled out of town, the noise of the station and stores fading behind them like the tail end of a dream.

The road narrowed, the fields stretched wider, and the signs of life dwindled. Fields lay sodden and half-submerged, the land still weeping from the summer's flood. Here and there, the road rose slightly where crews had built it up with gravel and wishful thinking. Elsewhere, it buckled under the weight of time and water, reduced to ruts and stubborn mud.

They passed a line of cypress trees, their roots slick with moss. A heron flapped upward as the Ford splashed past, vanishing into the curtain of mist.

Rowan rolled down his window and let the damp air curl in. The silence out here was different—thicker. Not absence, but hush. No dogs. No farmhands. Just the suck of tires against wet earth and the low groan of the car as it trudged forward.

When Walter finally broke the silence, the grey sky had lost its silver trim.

"What do you think is waiting for us, old boy? Are we about to find ourselves in some trouble?"

"It feels that way, doesn't it?"

"I'd say it feels familiar—you and me, travelling south, a

flood, suspicious deaths."

"You and *I*, Williams."

"Yeah, the both of us."

It wasn't long before the shape of the Preminger mansion emerged through the trees. Looming in the darkness, it appeared unearthed rather than built. Its peaked rooflines silhouetted against the slate sky, its windows glinting like glass eyes. Vines curled up its stone skin like veins. A shutter clattered loose in the wind. And from the chimney, a thin ribbon of smoke drifted upward, gray as bone.

Walter parked next to the other cars. "Not ominous at all. Perfectly normal."

On the wide, crumbling porch sat a man with silver hair combed back with surgical precision. The faint pinstripes on his shirt vanished into the shadows, but his gold signet ring caught the last vestige of gray light like a dying flare. His Homburg rested politely on one knee.

"You must be Mr. Rowan Manory."

Rowan nodded. "This is my assistant, Walter Williams."

The man stood and extended a cool, dry hand. "Timothy Preminger. Thank you for coming. I wish the circumstances were less... theatrical, but with my family, there's no other way."

Rowan cleared his throat. "Mr. Preminger, can you tell me why I'm here?"

"Didn't Jasper inform you?"

"He said that your parents had changed their will and I was listed as an heir, but he didn't say why. There's no reason I can imagine."

Timothy offered a strained smile. Though not much over fifty, he moved and spoke with the hesitant stiffness of a man decades older— blinking slowly, voice slightly reedy, as if his thoughts had to be coaxed into words.

"I hate to disappoint you, but neither my siblings nor I have the slightest idea. Father and mother changed the will after my brother Cornelius and his wife Brenda passed."

"When was this?"

"July."

"Your brother died in July, and now, just three months later, your parents. My deepest condolences."

Walter's gaze grew gentle. His smile faltered at the edges. "That's a rough year, Mr. Preminger."

"I certainly hope it isn't an omen." He scratched his head. "Changing the will made perfect sense. My brother had only one child, a son named Ernie. Naturally, he should receive his father's share. But Jasper has hinted there were other alterations. *Significant* alterations." He paused, as if the strangeness were only now catching up to him. "Your inclusion is certainly one of them."

"Are we the last ones to arrive?"

"No, my nephew Ernie and his wife aren't here yet. Fashionably late…I suppose. I'll introduce you to the rest of the family while we wait for them." He motioned toward the door. "My apologies about the state of the mansion. My parents were quite elderly and they never bothered much with upkeep in their later years. It seems like everything to do with the Preminger family is fading away. In a decade or so, there won't be much left."

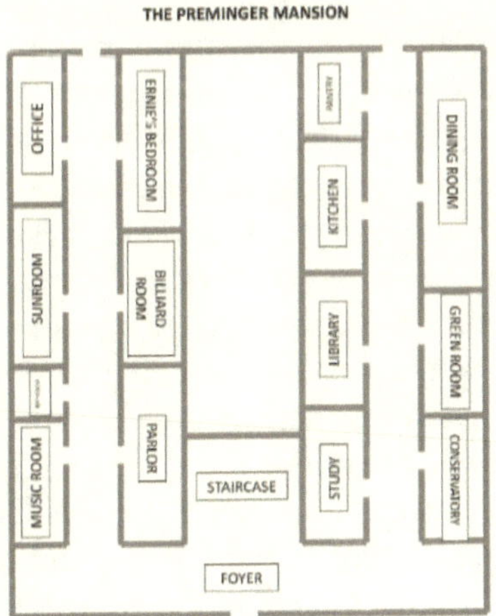

The scent of must and old paper thickened in the foyer as Rowan stepped inside. The wallpaper peeled in faint curls, like yellowed petals, and the old hardwood beneath his feet groaned with each step. A thin sheen of dust clung to the banister. The dulled brass fixtures caught the emerging moonlight filtering through high, grimy windows.

Timothy led them without comment, but as they passed a painting askew on the wall—two figures on horseback blurred with age—he offered another apology.

"It really is embarrassing—the state of this place."

"Not at all," said Walter. "It's got character. The sort that grows on you." When Timothy turned back around, Walter leaned toward Rowan and whispered, "Like a rash."

Rowan elbowed his ribs.

They turned down a sagging corridor. At the left, a set of double doors stood slightly ajar. The study beyond carried a faint odor of burnt coffee and wood polish, with a metallic tang beneath.

A voice came shrieking from inside. *"Don't give me any of that horseshit, Jasper."*

Timothy turned back with that same strained smile. "My brother, Robert. He has just as much *character* as the mansion." He opened the door.

The study was a dark, somber room illuminated only by the glow of a low-burning fire in the hearth. It didn't offer much warmth, but its flickering light threw slow-moving shadows that made the room feel faintly alive. A tall grandfather clock stood against one wall, ticking faintly like a weak pulse. There were a few books on a narrow shelf — mostly legal volumes and dusty ledgers — but the real weight of the room lay elsewhere. A filing cabinet hunched in the corner, its drawers dented and dull, and a small side table held a leather-bound binder stuffed with correspondence, its spine cracked from use. Everything was brown or brass, the color of old tobacco and tarnish.

Jasper Dunn rose from behind the desk. Neatly dressed in a dark vest and spectacles, he had a square jaw and a pencil mustache. His eyes darted toward the doorway, a trace of tension still in his shoulders. "Good evening, gentlemen," he said, a shade too brightly, as if trying to iron out the creases left by what they'd overheard. "We're nearly ready to begin."

Standing beside him, red-faced and glassy-eyed, was Robert. His tie was crooked, and so was his jaw. The wrath he had been directing toward Jasper turned instantly against Rowan.

"Here he is—the big-shot detective himself." He tugged at his trousers and rolled up his sleeves. "Listen here—if one red cent of the inheritance ends up in your pocket, I'll have my lawyer so far up your ass, you'll need a bottle of castor oil to get him out."

"Pardon?" asked Rowan.

Jasper shook his head. "Robert, *I* am your one and only lawyer, and I will do no such thing."

"You aren't my lawyer. Your father Langston was. You're just the result of nepotism." He pointed an accusatory finger at Rowan. "Listen up, fat boy." He walked forward with a slow, menacing gait. "I'll get myself a real lawyer who'll put the fear of God in you, believe that. I don't know what scam you were running with my parents, but…"

When Robert got three feet from Rowan, Walter stepped between them. His good-natured smile never left his face and his tone remained mild, but his eyes held a glint that didn't belong there — something hard, like flint beneath velvet.

"Let's slow things down, Robert. We don't want to do anything we'll regret."

Momentarily rocked back on his heels, Robert sputtered, "Like…like what?"

"Like getting laid out."

"Laid out?" He blinked, confused.

"Laid out. As in, busted nose, flat on your back. That wouldn't be good for anyone, least of all you."

Air seemed to leak out of Robert all at once — shoulders

drooping, face slackening, voice gone. "I…I…"

"Or we could just be friendly with one another. I think that's best, don't you?"

There was a tense silence. Both men stood still, watching each other.

Robert flinched first. He retreated to the fireplace, leaning against the wall like a jilted lover who'd thrown the first glass.

"The will had better be in order. That's all I know."

Walter nodded. "Good choice."

Jasper stepped from behind the desk. "Let's all remember," he said—his voice calm, but with an edge that suggested a practiced tolerance for outbursts like these, "that Dolph and Sophie were well within their right minds when they altered their will. No one unduly influenced them, certainly not Mr. Manory nor Mr.?"

"Williams," said Walter.

"Nor Mr. Williams." Jasper looked directly at Robert, who was now pretending the fireplace mantle required his immediate study. "What's done is done. We're here to learn the results, not argue with one another about your parents' wishes."

Timothy added, "Mr. Manory has as much knowledge of his purpose here as we do, Robert. Quite frankly, we should be thanking him. He came here on short notice and at his own expense."

Robert muttered something inaudible and kicked at the hearthstone with the side of his shoe.

Then came the sleek whisper of silk against wood. "God, I do love a good bit of masculine energy," said a woman's voice—cool, amused, and unmistakably entertained.

All five men turned.

Framed in the doorway, one hand resting lightly on the panel, stood a shapely woman with an amber colored drink in her free hand and a thin cigarette holder in the corner of her mouth. She snaked across the threshold, her perfume wafting in a floral cloud around her. The dress was velvet, deep blue, with a cut just daring enough to raise a brow without being indecent.

Her eyes flicked from Walter to Rowan with feline precision—then lingered, just slightly, on Walter. "I'm Beverly Preminger. Pleased to meet you." She flashed her teeth. "I know Mr. Manory from the newspaper. Are you a detective too, Mr. Williams?"

"I've been known to make a deduction or two."

Timothy rushed forward and snatched the drink from his sister's hand. "Can't you at least wait until after the formalities?" He took a whiff of the drink. His face twitched with a faint, involuntary wince. "Good God, Bev. That smells strong."

She threw her head back and laughed with all the subtlety of an actress playing to the last row.

"Why would I not enjoy myself? Mother and father always made sure to stock the parlor with spirits. They would have wanted us to be happy." She waltzed to the desk and hopped her backside onto the edge. "You're all too invested in the inheritance to have any fun."

Robert couldn't keep quiet any longer. "I'm invested in receiving my proper birthright. Some of us can't afford the luxury of multiple alimony payments."

"What good is your birthright if you don't survive the curse." She giggled.

He stared at her, the anger draining into something colder—tight-lipped, wide-eyed, as if she'd just spit on a grave.

The reaction of her brother seemed to sober her up a bit. "Come now. It was only a joke."

"It isn't funny, Bev," said Timothy solemnly.

"The curse?" Rowan asked, raising an eyebrow.

All three looked at Rowan helplessly.

Timothy stuttered his way to a general explanation.

"Well...It's an old family legend. Goes back generations. There's madness in the Preminger blood. Or so they say."

"It's nonsense," said a flat voice from the hallway.

A male figure stood in the doorway now—tall and still as a portrait. His dark hair was brushed back, and his clothes, though modest, were crisp and pressed. His face was pale, almost colorless, except for the eyes, which were sharp and steady, like wet glass catching the dark. His youth was in stark contrast to the rest of the Preminger children. While they were all around fifty, he looked to be barely in his twenties, not a wrinkle on his skin.

Jasper cleared his throat. "May I introduce Simon Preminger, the last of the Preminger children."

Robert scoffed. "He isn't one of the Preminger children. He has none of our blood. God knows he'll get a full share of our money though."

"That's enough!" A crack spidered across Jasper's composure—like glass under pressure. The room went still. The lawyer's voice had lost its usual polish—it was colder now, louder, and more human than anyone in the family had ever heard it. He continued, the words ringing against the study walls like a gavel strike.

"If you want to spew vitriol over your parents' bones, do it after the reading. But don't you dare stand there and insult Simon for the circumstances of his birth—something none of us get to choose."

Robert blinked in surprise. Again, someone had stood up to the bully and again, he had been robbed of any bravado.

Jasper turned slightly, readjusted his glasses, and smoothed his vest as though the outburst had creased the fabric. When he spoke again, his tone was far more composed. "The Premingers adopted Simon when my father was still their lawyer. After he retired, I took over. In all the time I worked for them, Dolph and Sophie expressed nothing but the deepest love for Simon. They considered him their child. No less than any of you."

"More," said Simon, addressing his siblings directly. "They considered me their only child—when all the rest of you had already vanished from their lives. I suppose that's why they adopted me. They wanted someone to fill the silence, after you had left the nest."

"They were in their fifties," Beverly said, her tone oddly neutral. "Everyone thought *they* were mad for wanting to raise another child when they'd finally finished with us."

"Maybe they were mad," Simon said. "But they were also kind. Generous. And entirely alone. You'd all scattered like seeds in the wind. Not one of you wrote. Not one of you visited. Only Cornelius, God rest his soul."

"That's not fair—" Timothy began.

"Isn't it?" Simon didn't raise his voice, but the chill in it was unmistakable. "You abandoned them. Now you come crawling back like carrion, hoping to scavenge what's left." His nostrils flared. "I hope they left you nothing."

"Easy," Beverly said. She'd retrieved her drink and was smiling faintly behind it. "You'll give yourself a nosebleed with all that righteousness."

The fire popped softly in the hearth, a single ember leaping and fading. Rowan felt the heat at his back, but it didn't reach the rest of the room. As he watched the family, unease crawled in beside him — not from the bickering or the grief, but from something else entirely. There was a silence beneath the conversation, something that moved under the words like a second current. The curse had only been mentioned once, but it lingered, shaping the air and the edges of every glance. He couldn't get it out of his mind.

"I'd like to hear more about this curse."

"We shouldn't even speak of it," Simon said. "There's been enough madness in this house without stirring up more. When Ernie arrives, we'll read the will and…and get on with our lives. I'll certainly never see any of you people again."

A low rumble of thunder rolled somewhere in the distance. It wasn't close, but it managed to draw a brief glance from everyone in the room.

Then came three quick knocks at the front door. The echo was just loud enough to carry.

"And there he is," said Timothy. "Our nephew."

Ernie sat in the high-backed chair with the posture and composure of a man awaiting coronation—spine rigid, shoulders squared. His hair was neatly parted, but sweat clung to his forehead in fine threads. One thumb slowly orbited the knuckle of the other, again and again. It was the only movement he'd permitted himself. His face had that ageless, bloodless quality you see in wax figures—or drowning victims.

To Rowan, the calm looked deliberate, as if Ernie were playing a part.

Irene stood behind Ernie, one hand resting lightly on his shoulder. The touch was protective, but also possessive—like a leash disguised as comfort. She had introduced herself as his wife, but Rowan had the impression that their bond was deeper—and far more unsettling—than matrimonial.

She is his handler.

Both of them stared with fixed anticipation as Jasper broke the wax seal on the envelope.

The others watched too, but their eyes kept sliding back to Ernie. Robert, Beverly, Simon, even Timothy— each of them cast quick, furtive glances at their nephew and his wife. They were gauging. Bracing. But for what reason?

Are they frightened of him? It certainly seems that way. The air in the room changed when he entered—heavier, somehow deadly.

A low growl of thunder stamped over the house as Jasper lifted his eyes.

"As executor of the estate of Dolph Randall Preminger and Sophie Marie Preminger, it is my solemn duty to read aloud their last will and testament, dated August 11, 1928. Please, reserve any questions or objections until the reading has concluded. This document was reviewed and sealed by the Premingers themselves."

Robert shifted by the fire, the glass rattling against the hearthstone. " Get on with it," he muttered, his voice raw and fraying.

Jasper unfolded the first page.

"To our daughter, Beverly Preminger, and our son, Timothy Preminger, we bequeath the same amount—one hundred thousand dollars. Though your lives have strayed from the values we instilled, you have not brought disgrace to the family name. More importantly, neither of you have borne children, Beverly through recklessness and Timothy through inactivity. Thus, you have introduced no new dangers…to the world." He adjusted his spectacles. "We wish you the very best."

Recklessness and inactivity—code for sins too delicate for parchment, no doubt.

Beverly blinked hard. All the carefree poise she had previously displayed about the inheritance seemed to vanish. "That's... significantly less than it used to be."

Timothy said nothing, but he turned red-faced and his jaw twitched.

"To Simon Preminger," Jasper continued, "our adopted child, who gave us such joy in our later years, we leave two hundred and fifty thousand dollars. No shadow of the curse falls on you. We pray you marry and build a future untainted by the burden of our name. We only hope you think well of us. We did the best we could for you."

Simon lowered his head slightly. His mouth opened and he sighed.

"And to our eldest son," Jasper said, voice sharpening, "Robert Preminger: we leave twenty-five thousand dollars. The reasons for this lowly sum are known to you and need no further explanation. We already gave you everything and you tossed it aside. Ungrateful. Contemptible."

Robert closed his eyes as if bracing for a blow. The fire snapped behind him. His shoulders sagged. The empty glass slipped from his hand and struck the floor with a hollow clink.

Jasper turned the page. "To Ernest Preminger, our sole grandchild: Though we fear what you may become, we recognize our duty to honor the offspring of our late son

Cornelius. He was not a good man—unfaithful and dishonest, but he was ours. We therefore leave you the Preminger mansion, all surrounding lands, and all remaining investments and properties, amounting to two million, one hundred thousand dollars."

Ernie showed no reaction. Irene's hand tightened minutely on his shoulder. She smiled.

"There are other bequests," Jasper said, without looking up. "Fifteen thousand dollars to each of the following: the Southern Baptist Orphanage Society, the Illinois Home for the Incurables, the Colored Freedmen's Mission Fund, the National Anti-Tuberculosis Association, the American Red Cross, the First Presbyterian Church of Cairo, the Salvation Army, and the SPCA of Southern Illinois."

Robert made a strangled sound—half gasp, half snarl. "I got more than the goddamned stray dogs," he whispered. "More than the fucking Baptists."

A laugh blurted out from Simon.

Robert snapped. "What's so funny, bastard?"

"I'm not finished reading." Jasper's voice had the clipped chill of a man reading aloud a diagnosis.

All eyes returned to him.

He continued. "However, should Ernest Preminger commit the crime of murder against any blood relative named herein on the night these provisions are made known, his inheritance shall be forfeit. The estate will be liquidated and divided equally among the surviving heirs. To ensure the proper observance of this clause, all heirs must remain on the premises for twenty-four hours following the conclusion of this reading. You are to sleep in your designated childhood rooms—no exceptions. This will settle once and for all the question of whether or not Ernest has been afflicted with the Preminger curse, for no one afflicted has ever failed to commit murder in this house."

The clock on the mantel gave a dry, mechanical tick. *Tick. Tick.*

"That leaves the last order of business. In the event that a murder occurs during this twenty-four-hour period, Rowan Manory, private detective, shall be entrusted with the investigation and determination of guilt. For these services, he shall be paid the sum of fifteen thousand dollars—equivalent to a full week's salary—even if no crime occurs. Mr. Manory, we have read of your career accomplishments. Your standing as the finest sleuth in the Midwestern United States makes you an obvious choice for the task. We have no doubt you will be up for the challenge."

Jasper folded the will closed. "These provisions are final."

The fire cracked and withered in the grate.

Rowan asked, "Could someone clarify what, precisely, this curse entails?"

The question hung in the air until Ernie finally answered.

"Isn't it obvious, Detective? I'm supposed to kill them all."

Simon excused himself, declaring that he had no interest in discussing the curse or spending time with the Preminger family before retiring early. Jasper remained in the study to prepare the releases for signature. Everyone else headed for the parlor.

Robert was the first to arrive. He went straight to the sideboard where the liquor was kept, hissing insults no one could quite make out as they followed him into the room. He sloshed brandy into a glass and took a hard, painful swallow.

"They lost their minds. That's the story. No court in the world would call that sane. I'll get it reversed. I'll have it reversed in a month."

"Calm down, Robert. You'll give yourself a stroke," Beverly said, striding in behind him.

Robert sneered at her over the rim of his glass. "It's a hell of a thing, isn't it? A woman with three marriages under her belt gets more than me. I've been with the same woman twenty years."

"Yes. Your wife." Beverly's smile turned razor-sharp.

"Funny, how Vera ran inside the moment she arrived. Didn't so much as say hello. Why is that, Robert? Is she afraid to show herself? I couldn't help but notice the bandage she was wearing. It was as big as her head. Did you do something to her face?"

The glass in Robert's hand trembled—then the rim cracked inward. "Damn it!" He covered it with a handkerchief that quickly soaked up the blood.

Rowan caught the look in his eyes—the kind of look a man has right before he forgets there are witnesses.

Across the room, Ernie and Irene had settled themselves on the worn velvet couch. Irene clasped Ernie's hand tightly in both of hers, not casually, but almost protectively—as though shielding him from the room's growing malice.

Timothy sank into an armchair with the heavy resignation of a man used to cleaning up after disasters.

Rowan rolled a fast cigarette, struck a match, and took a drag. The flame flared, then died, leaving a curl of smoke that drifted between him and the others like a veil. He exhaled slowly and leaned back, grateful for the brief illusion of calm.

"Timothy?" he asked. "Could you explain the curse for me?"

His voice came out in a clean, dry, whisper. "I know it started in 1784, but the exact details are not entirely agreed upon. As far as I can figure it, Konrad Preminger, the man who built this mansion, had several extra-marital affairs. This is standard with Preminger men."

"And women," added Robert, casting a long, lucid gaze at his sister.

Beverly disagreed. "I was faithful to all my husbands. In our family, Cornelius was the one with the wondering eye."

Timothy continued. "In the case of this particular ancestor, the affair was with a member of a group called the millenarians, a religious cult from Missouri."

"I've never heard of them," said Rowan.

"That's because they didn't last very long. Very little is

known about this woman, but it was said that she dreamed in tongues. There was one report of her weeping blood on the solstice."

Walter, who had been trying to stay professional for Rowan's sake, couldn't help himself. "Sounds like the kind you bring home to mother—if you *hate* your mother."

"Yes," said Timothy. "Konrad ended the affair soon after it began. In turn, the woman put a curse on our family. I'm sure it had a different name in the past. I've only known it as the Preminger curse."

"And what, exactly is the curse?"

"It's rather simple really. Every other generation, one of the Preminger offspring will go mad and attempt to kill the rest of the family. We would eventually be destroyed from within."

Walter gave a low whistle. "That's one way to keep the stork from coming."

"That's it exactly, Mr. Williams. Either the family would stop having children or risk annihilation."

"I take it," said Rowan, "the curse has been proven effective in the past."

"Oh, yes—with stunning regularity. Konrad Preminger himself was the first victim. The family history claims he laughed at the idea of the curse. But then...Christmas Day, 1834." Timothy got up with a curious litheness, all in one piece, without removing his fingers from the tongue of his tie. He nodded toward the fireplace. "Konrad's grandson, Federick, sank an axe into his grandfather's skull. Right there, in front of the fire. He also killed his sister and two cousins. The carnage only stopped when an uncle—I believe it was Detlef—shot Frederick dead with a Pennsylvania rifle."

Rowan's gaze traveled slowly around the room, taking in the faded wallpaper, the dust-choked drapes, the cracked crown molding. It was easy to imagine blood soaking into the worn carpet and the screams that followed.

Timothy's mouth thinned into a grim line. "And then it

happened again just like the curse said it would. The following generation—our grandparents'—was prosperous, fruitful. They built the house larger, expanded the holdings. The curse became a ghost story. I don't think anyone truly believed it." He paused to swirl the ice in his glass. "In 1885, Johan Preminger almost succeeded where Frederick had failed. Johan killed nearly everyone. The only survivors were our parents, Robert, and me."

"I survived too," Beverly said, lifting her chin, almost proud of it…"in Mom's belly. And I don't have any bad memories of it."

Timothy nodded. "I was an infant. Robert was seven. Cornelius hadn't even been born."

Robert downed half his drink in a single swallow. Then leaned against the fireplace, as though the memory had knocked something out of him.

"I'll never forget that day. We'd gone for a walk. Me and our parents, Timothy in the carriage. When we came back home and entered the foyer, good ole Uncle Johan was there... stabbing a body."

"A body?" asked Rowan.

"Yeah. It was a body. As I stared at it, I realized—even at that young age—that the body was already dead. Later, I found out it was his own son. He was stabbing his dead son…everywhere. You couldn't recognize the face—it was *gone.* Too many knife wounds for his face to hold its structure."

The room seemed to shrink around his words and the images they inspired.

Robert wiped a hand across his mouth. "We ran. Got in the car and drove to the next county to inform the police. When they came here, they found Johan wandering along the road. He charged at them and they shot him dead."

Timothy picked up the story. "Our family are the last to have the Preminger name. The four of us were warned never to have children. But Cornelius defied that warning." He turned to Ernie. "Our nephew here is the only member of his generation, the generation that is supposed to produce a psychotic murderer. That's why he is…*suspected.* I truly believe that is why our parents adopted Simon. He's not blood, meaning he cannot be inflicted with the curse. In theory, he could carry on the Preminger name sans madness."

"Monsters!" Irene rose defiantly from her place beside Ernie. "You talk about curses and bloodlines and madness like they're fairy tales passed down in storybooks." Her voice wavered, sharp at the edges, like something splintering beneath strain. "But you're the curse. All of you. You've treated Ernie like an outcast for his whole life. You locked him away. Made him fear his own shadow. You convinced him he was rotten. You made him believe he was destined to go mad."

Rowan asked, "Ernie? Have you had any issues concerning your mental state?

Irene answered. "He has a medical condition, Mr. Manory. With therapy and medicine, he's gotten better."

"What medical condition, exactly?" Rowan asked.

Ernie glanced up at him, his expression tight with shame, but it was Irene who continued speaking for him, squeezing his hand the entire time.

"Dissociative fugue," she said. "A rare condition—stress-induced. The patient temporarily loses awareness of their identity and surroundings. It's often accompanied by wandering behavior. In Ernie's case, the episodes are sporadic and brief. He enters fugue states, loses his sense of time and place. Often, he wakes up in places without remembering how he got there."

Rowan kept his voice calm, addressing Ernie directly. "I've known a few people with similar conditions. Tell me, have you ever attacked anyone during one of these fugue states?"

Irene spoke faster now, far more fiercely than before. "Lots of things happen when you're in a fugue. You can walk, talk, perform simple tasks. Once, Ernie walked nearly two miles through town in his sleep. He doesn't remember a second of it. If you truly know others who have suffered, then why—"

"Mrs. Preminger?"

She gasped, out of breath. "Yes."

"You are Ernie's wife?"

"Yes."

"Are you also his nurse?"

She stammered before answering. "I was. That's how we met."

"But now you are married. Do you still perform nursing duties?"

"I do. I take care of all Ernie's needs."

"What medication do you administer to him?"

"Chloral hydrate, administered in small doses when needed. And hypnotherapy, which I perform," Irene answered smoothly.

"Can I ask you one more question?"

"Of course."

Rowan gestured toward Ernie. "Is he allowed to speak for himself?"

She pursed her lips. No matter how much she tried to hide it, the underlying terror seeped through her expression.

She doesn't want him to say a goddamned word.

Irene's fingers, still wrapped around Ernie's, had gone white at the knuckles. She let go and stepped back from him.

Rowan eyed Ernie gravely. "Mr. Preminger, I'm curious—if your grandparents feared you, why do have a bedroom here?"

Ernie shifted forward on the couch, his voice flat and quiet. "It's the only bedroom on the first floor. That room used to be an office, but they remodeled it so that whenever my parents came to visit, I would have a place to stay. My own little prison."

"How do you mean, sir?"

"They had iron bars installed right outside the window

and a padlock on the door."

"I see."

"That wasn't the worst part. They wouldn't even let me near Simon. We were the same age, but I wasn't allowed to play with him. Can you imagine? I was practically a leper. I hated coming here. I hated seeing these people." He looked downward. "I hate being here now."

"And what do you think of this *curse*? Have you ever given it any credence?"

"Well, it's just like my wife said. I was led to believe it was true. For the longest time, I thought that way. But not now. Now, I'm free of the burden."

"And you've never found yourself holding a knife and not remembering why?"

"God, no."

"One more question, Mr. Preminger. As I understand it, your mother and father died earlier this year."

"That's right."

"How did it happen?"

Rather than answer straight away, he took the time to meet the gaze of his aunt and uncles.

"Mr. Preminger?" inquired Rowan.

Timothy answered. "It was a...a freak accident. A gas leak inside the home."

At that moment, Jasper entered, a clipboard tucked under one arm. "If I could trouble everyone—" he began, clearing his throat. He explained briefly: signatures were needed to acknowledge the reading of the will, acceptance of terms, and temporary lodging at the mansion overnight. A mere formality, but legally necessary.

Robert snatched the pen first. He scrawled his name with a savage flourish. "You could have stopped them, Jasper. My parents—you could have made them see reason. *Bastard.*" He stormed out without a backward glance.

Jasper did his best to maintain dignity. "Hopefully, there will be no further demonstrations."

The others signed in turn. When Ernie handed the paper

back, Jasper offered a stiff, professional smile. "Congratulations, Mr. Preminger."

Rowan signed last, his pen strokes slow and deliberate.

"Very good. I'll be in the study if you need me. There are documents to prepare for distribution to the estate's executors and I must update the sealed inventory list. I'll *uh*...get Simon's signature later." He offered a terse nod and retreated back toward the foyer.

Ernie and Irene rose. "We'll fetch our luggage from the car," Irene said quietly.

Timothy and Beverly excused themselves, heading up the staircase to their old bedrooms.

Rowan and Walter lingered in the foyer, near the massive staircase, speaking in low tones.

"Well, boss," Walter murmured, "we sure walked into it, didn't we? These people are goddamned crazy."

Rowan stared out one of the front windows, frowning at the rain tapping the glass like fingertips. "The will's structure makes the angle difficult."

Walter furrowed his brow. "Structure? Angle? What are you saying, old boy? I don't follow."

"Normally," Rowan said, "if someone wants the inheritance, they kill the person with the largest share."

Walter nodded. "Simple math."

"But this?" Rowan shook his head. "This will is twisted. No one gains unless Ernie kills someone first."

Walter stroked his chin. "So, if one of the others wants the money... they need Ernie to commit murder?"

"Exactly." Rowan exhaled smoke toward the rain-slick window. "The killer doesn't want to kill. He wants Ernie to do it for him." He took a drag off his cigarette, watching Irene and Ernie through the window. "That woman would be an obvious victim."

Irene and Ernie reentered the home, each carrying a small suitcase.

Rowan stepped forward. "Mrs. Preminger, before you and your husband retire, I'd like a word alone with you. Would you mind?"

She looked at him with an expression as plain as dough. "Fine."

Ernie gave her hand a squeeze before continuing down the hall toward the bedroom at the rear of the house.

She asked, "What is it, detective?"

"Earlier," Rowan said, "when I asked you if Ernie had ever hurt anyone during one of his episodes, you didn't answer my question."

She lifted her chin. "No, he hasn't."

Rowan studied her face for a long moment. Then he said, almost gently, "I think you wear too much makeup."

A scandalized pout played across her face—just theatrical enough. "What business is it of yours how much makeup I put on my face? I—"

"But if the light hits you just right, it almost looks like your cheek's been bruised."

She blinked.

"I can swear something has smacked against your face recently. Walter and I will be staying in the office directly across from Ernie's bedroom."

"It's entirely unnecessary."

He gave a small, humorless smile. "We're being paid a full week's wages for one night of work." He glanced down the hallway. "I intend to earn it. If something does happen in that room—"

"It won't."

"If it *does*, don't hesitate to call out."

"Curses don't exist, Mr. Manory."

"No, but murderers do."

She turned away defiantly, walking down the hall, stiff and straight.

"Williams, I have a terrible feeling we may never lay eyes on that woman again—at least not while she's alive.

Irene closed the door behind her and turned the latch with a soft click. The room was dim. The bedside lamp cast a faint golden spill that barely touched the gloom. Outside, the rain whispered against the windowpanes, soft but consistent.

The bedroom hadn't changed much since Ernie was a boy. But it had never been a child's room — no toys, no murals, no bright furniture. The heavy four-poster bed loomed like a judge's bench. A wardrobe with swollen doors crouched in the corner, and a scratched writing desk slouched beside it like a punishment. Damp had claimed a wall, and iron bars still gripped the windows, black and rain-slicked.

Ernie stood by those windows, his hands clasped behind his back, posture rigid.

Irene waited a few moments before plaintively asking for his attention. "What are you thinking, Ernie?"

"When my family came to visit my grandparents, and they locked me in here, I used to stand in this very spot." His voice was calm, but it trembled with an old, barely contained pain. "I used to stare out these bars and imagine myself somewhere else. I thought… maybe if I could fit between them, I'd run off into the fields, far away from this prison."

When he turned from the window and saw his wife, Ernie's composure buckled, collapsing like a paper mask left out in the storm. His body shook, and for a terrible moment, he looked much younger than he was — a boy trapped in a man's body, too frightened to breathe.

"I can feel it, Irene," he whispered. "Something inside me—waiting. It's always been there. It's been waiting for this very night."

She crossed the room swiftly and took his hands in hers. He flinched at first, but she held firm, steadying him. "You are not cursed. You are not broken."

"They're right about me." His gaze darted wildly across her face, searching for proof.

"Ernie!"

He stopped and stared into her eyes.

"Blood isn't destiny."

As if her words had cut through his anxiety, Ernie nodded once. "Right." His shoulders eased. A long breath escaped him, like air from a cracked bellows. "I…I know." He let her guide him to the bed, where he sat down heavily. "I thought I was going to lose it in the parlor. I could barely contain myself. That detective—he could *sense* it. He was looking right through me."

"Let's do our exercise," she said, smoothing his hair back from his damp forehead. "It always helps. You always feel better. Don't you?"

He nodded weakly. "O—okay. Yeah."

From the small leather bag she carried, Irene removed a compact travel clock in a worn green case. Its brass face glinted faintly in the lamplight as she flicked it open, revealing two small dials and a sharp little bell perched like a sentinel on top. She wound it with delicate precision, the ratchet ticking softly under her fingers.

"I'm setting the alarm for half an hour," she said, her voice low and sure. She turned the clock so Ernie could see the slender hands move into place. "When it rings, you'll wake calm and rested."

She placed it gently on the nightstand, the case angled toward him. Then she reached for the thin gold chain at her neck — a simple charm dangling at its end — and let it hang between them. "Watch the charm," she murmured, her words smoothing into a rhythm. "Let everything else fall away."

She knelt before him, and the charm began to swing, slow and deliberate, catching the lamplight in sleepy arcs.

"You are safe."

His panting ceased almost immediately, the breathing still unsteady, but far more measured. He spoke in a languid voice. "I am safe."

"Safe in this room. Safe with me. Your body grows heavy — not with fear, but with peace. Heavier… and heavier. The bars behind you don't matter anymore. The old fears don't matter anymore. You are strong enough to survive anything. You are stronger than they ever believed."

Ernie's eyes fluttered shut, his breath smoothing into

rhythm. "Yes," he purred.

"You will rest now," she continued, her voice a near-whisper. "Your mind will drift like a leaf on a river. But you will still hear me and do as I say. Do you hear me?"

"Yes." The word hissed softly from his lips.

"When you hear the ring, you will wake, free of fear. You will wake knowing you are your own master—not your family's, not your blood's, not the past's."

She remained kneeling in front of him, watching the tension leave his face by slow degrees. When she was sure he had sunk fully into trance, she set the charm aside and stood. "This place holds no power over you. Say it."

"This...place...holds...no...power...over...me."

"Good." Irene sat in the armchair near the door, her hands folded in her lap, watching the rain blur the world outside. "Now, my love," she said gently, "tell me about the future. Where will we go? What will we become?"

"We won't ever come back. The monsters... they can't find us. Not now. Not ever."

Irene closed her eyes. Outside, the rain whispered on.

Robert could pace no more. The path of his footsteps was well worn into the floor of the upstairs hall, but his thoughts were no less tangled than when he'd begun. He opened the bedroom door with all the hope of a man walking to the gallows.

A single candle burned low on the dresser, its wavering flame throwing shadows that danced restlessly along the walls.

"Well?" asked Vera. She sat at the vanity with her back to him — posture stiff, hands clenched in her lap. If she hadn't spoken, he might have mistaken her for a corpse.

He hovered near the door, unsure how to begin. His large hands flexed uselessly at his sides. "We'll think of another way," he said finally. "I—"

"How much?" she asked, her tone flat, exhausted.

He hesitated, knowing that to say it aloud would make it

real. "Nothing. Almost nothing… Twenty-five thousand."

Vera let out a small sound — something between a laugh and a sob — and pressed a hand over her mouth. Her shoulders quivered.

Robert crossed the room quickly and knelt beside her chair. "Don't cry, honey. Please don't. I couldn't take it now."

For all his swagger and bluster downstairs, here he was just a desperate man, clinging to the last good thing he had. He could only see her right profile — the unscarred side, pale and drawn in the candlelight.

"It's enough," he lied. "It'll buy us time. We'll figure it out. Just don't give up because I couldn't stand it."

Vera gave a broken chuckle. "It'll pay for a nice funeral. What shall I wear?"

Robert gritted his teeth. "Where's your ointment?"

"What's the point?" she whispered.

He stood up sharply, as if trying to rouse himself through motion. "We've been through worse. I'm not licked."

Vera finally turned toward him. A thick white bandage covered most of her left cheek, the gauze yellowing at the edges.

Robert flinched, a sick twist in his gut. He knew precisely what had been done to her face. Three men had held him and forced him to watch. The sight of the result mortified him, and though he tried to keep his expression steady, the revulsion showed—misread, perhaps, as disgust, when it was really grief. He wanted to offer comfort, to be brave for her, but his face had already betrayed him.

She caught the flicker of pain in his eyes and smiled bitterly. "Go ahead," she said. "Look at your beautiful wife."

"Healing takes time. I'll apply your ointment. Three times a day, that's what Doctor Healy said."

He lit the oil lamp and peeled away the bandage carefully, almost reverently. The gauze clung stubbornly to the wound, tugging at her skin. She sucked in a breath, eyes shut tight.

"Sorry," he murmured.

"Just get it over with," she whispered.

Inch by inch, the dressing came away. The cloth was darkened with dried blood at the edges. The wound was brutal — a jagged scar carved like a canyon through her cheek, raw and purple at the edges, pulling her features into something cruel and unrecognizable.

Tears slipped silently down her good cheek.

Robert set the soiled bandage aside, dipped his fingers into the small tin of ointment, and timidly dabbed the healing salve onto the scar. The candle wavered on the edge of extinguishing, its light barely keeping the dark at bay.

He smoothed the last bit of ointment over the twisted skin, then wiped his fingers on a cloth.

Neither of them spoke. The only sound was the rain crying across the window.

"Listen to me. The terms of the inheritance... they're not set in stone."

"What do you mean?"

"There's still a way for us to get the money," he said. His voice was low, but something hard had crept into it — the old gambler's edge, the way he sounded before every bad decision.

Beverly's bedroom smelled faintly of lavender — the same scent she remembered from childhood, clinging stubbornly to the drapes and heavy coverlet folded at the foot of the mattress.

She traced a finger through the dust on the vanity. The spotted mirror warped her reflection. In just the right light, she might glimpse the girl she once was — but not tonight. In this light, she looked as worn and weathered as the mansion itself.

"Oh, God," she sighed helplessly, hugging her arms around herself.

These days, she did her best to appear carefree. The opposite was true. Her flirtations were less effective now than in her youth. The looks she once inspired had curdled into double takes — half-pity, half-surprise. Beverly was becoming a joke.

The money—disappointing as it turned out to be—would help, but she understood deep down that she would be spending it alone. A cruel fate.

She gave herself one of her own mocking laughs. "At least you aren't crippled or mad." The smile half-faded. "Yet."

The sound of rain splattering against the window pulled her out of her thoughts. She crossed the room and drew the curtain aside with two fingers. A sharp gust rattled the pane. The storm seemed to shiver against the walls, more alive than it had been a moment ago.

"Gosh, it's really starting to come down now."

And then it happened. A flash of lightning revealed a figure outside.

Beverly flinched. "What the hell?" She leaned forward and pressed her face against the glass.

A shimmer of white moved at the edge of the trees. She leaned in closer, squinting through the rain. Now the figure came into focus.

It was a woman, barefoot and wild-haired, twirling in the rain just beyond the edge of the light.

"It can't be."

The figure spun once, twice, the hem of her dress plastered against her legs, then stumbled into a run — not purposeful, but manic, almost joyful, arms outstretched as though she were chasing something invisible.

Beverly's immediate, ridiculous thought was that this was a ghost from the past. One of the victims of Frederick or Johann. She had risen from the grave to witness the next incantation of the curse, to enjoy the screams.

Her mouth went dry. She took a step back, then another. Her breath snagged, sharp as a caught thread. All at once, the isolation jolted her into panic.

She was alone, in the room. Was everyone else dead already? Was she next? The idea struck her with sudden, absolute conviction. Her knees weakened. Had they all gone and left her behind — forgotten, like everything else in this house?

Without a rational thought left in her head, Beverly ran into the hall and pounded on Timothy's door with the side of her fist.

"Tim? Open up! Tim?"

There was a shuffling sound inside before the door cracked open. Timothy peered out, his hair tousled, his expression tight with irritation. "What's wrong?"

"I saw something," she whispered. "A woman — outside — she was *dancing* in the rain."

He stared at her, blinking. "Is this a joke?"

"No!" She grabbed his arm, dragging him down the hall. "Come on, you'll see." Back in her room, she flung open the curtain, pointing. "There—there, by the trees—"

But there was nothing. Just the rain, falling in silver threads, and the blurred shapes of the garden hedges beyond.

Timothy looked from side to side and frowned, letting out a breath, long and exasperated. "Bev, there's no one out there."

"I swear to you, I saw her. Right there." Beverly's voice broke slightly. "She was dancing. Like a madwoman. A…a…ghost."

"A ghost?"

"*Like* a ghost. I'm not saying she was a ghost. But she could have been."

"Bev, it's late." Timothy shook his head. "You're letting what happened downstairs get into your head. This house makes everyone feel like they're seeing things. Even I keep thinking I hear footsteps when no one's there." He nodded, as if reassuring himself. "But we aren't children anymore." He pulled the curtains. "Don't look outside. You'll feel better."

As he turned away, she grabbed his sleeve. "Wait—" She asked in a smaller voice, "Do you really believe in the curse?"

His mouth flattened into a hard line. "For God's sake—"

"You're a smart man, Tim. I…I trust your opinion." She leaned her head toward him in earnest. The expression was foreign to her, so little did she show it. "Do you believe it? Yes or no?"

He looked at her for a long moment, weighing whether or not this was an act. At last, he replied.

"I don't believe in magic, if that's what you mean. But madness… that's different. It runs in blood like poison in a well — slow at first, then everything turns. I'd be a fool to think we're immune. Just look at our family." He gave a short, humorless laugh. "The Premingers have always been a little mad. But that doesn't mean we're cursed. It doesn't mean you're doomed. This house—it gets into your head. That's all this is."

He touched her shoulder — awkward, but not unkind. "Try to sleep." Then he left, shutting the door gently behind him.

Beverly turned back to the window and brushed aside the curtain. The garden was still empty. The woman — if she'd ever existed — had vanished into the rain.

"Maybe I am going mad."

She turned from the window and caught herself in the mirror — pale, startled, unsteady. She no longer trusted what she saw.

Walter stood by the single window in the cramped office, peering out into the darkness beyond. The storm howled louder now, moaning against the eaves like a restless spirit. Rain battered the glass in spattering bursts, and the trees across the field writhed and bent under the rising wind.

He gave a low whistle. "It's getting ugly out there. I hope we'll be able to drive tomorrow."

Rowan didn't respond. He sat in a stiff-backed chair facing Ernie's door, hands steepled under his chin, eyes sharp and still. Watching. Waiting.

Walter crossed the room and dropped into the chair opposite him. "You don't think he's actually gonna kill her, do you? With us twenty feet away?"

Rowan's gaze flicked toward him, then back to the door. "It's the will. Sophie and Dolph wouldn't have hired me if they weren't certain something was going to happen. And the way this whole thing's been set up—I can't get over it. Normally, I'd be here to protect Ernie. That would make sense. But this setup doesn't."

"Manory, you've beaten a horse to death over this will business."

Rowan finally tore his attention away from the door. He gave Walter a look—head cocked, lips pressed tight, one eye narrowing as if trying to translate something deeply stupid into English.

"Why are you looking at me like that?" Walter asked.

"Don't you mean *beating a dead horse*?"

"Huh?"

"The expression is *beating a dead horse,* not *beat a horse to death.*"

Walter returned the look in kind. "Why on earth would anyone beat a *dead* horse? That's pointless."

"Exactly. That's what the expression means. That is why people say it."

"I don't want to argue semantics with you."

"Please don't."

"But if I were to beat a horse—and I'm not that kind of guy—but if I were to do it, I would beat a *living* one. Beating a dead horse will get you nowhere."

"You see—no—that's—" Rowan leaned back in his chair, rubbing his temples.

"You *do* this on purpose, Williams."

"I do what on purpose?"

"You pretend to be an idiot because you know it makes me angry. You think it's funny."

"Maybe I'm not pretending. Maybe I'm just that stupid."

Rowan narrowed his eyes. "It's not going to work."

"Good. The last thing I want to do is make you angry."

Rowan jabbed a finger toward Ernie's door. "The only reason that man is here tonight is because four people died under suspicious circumstances. Two of them believed he was capable of murder. No one in this house likes each other. And there's two and a half million dollars on the line. *That's* what I'm worried about. There has to be a plot. I can't see it." His eyes settled on the door. "What's the plot?"

Walter shrugged. "Plot or no plot, the windows are barred and the door is locked. Unless the curse is real after all, I don't see what could go wrong."

The old house groaned, its timbers creaking like bones unsettled by the storm.

Thunder did not break so much as *brood*. It rolled across the fields in a slow, ponderous swell, like the voice of some vast, sullen beast disturbed in its lair — a sound that belonged to no storm but to something older, something buried. The noise climbed up through the earth itself, creeping like a tide beneath the floorboards, into the soles of Jasper's shoes, and coiling in his chest. His eyes watered, not from fear but from pressure — as though the very air had thickened, or the house had drawn a sudden, shuddering breath and then held it. The floor gave a minute tremor. Somewhere in the walls, unseen timbers flexed with the faintest groan. And then — nothing. Silence. But not peace.

Jasper exhaled, adjusted his glasses with trembling fingers, and bent again over the open diary on the desk. The paper smelled faintly of iron. His eyes scanned the slanted, impatient handwriting of Dolph Preminger — a passage dated nearly twenty years earlier, scrawled in a hurried hand. Jasper had read the passage before, but now, reading it in a crumbling house during a storm, he felt the fear behind the words.

You can make excuses for a child. You can say he's tired, or hungry, or doesn't understand what he's done. But I saw what I saw, and no explanation will do. Cornelius and Ernie were playing with wooden swords. Cornelius was letting the child strike him harmlessly. Then, without warning or cause, Ernie struck his father hard across the face. When I ran forward and pulled him to the side, his eyes had gone flat — dead — like a doll's eyes. There was no shame in him, no fear. Just a cold amusement. He looked at me the way Johann used to look at birds before pulling off their wings.

Cornelius laughed it off, but he must have seen it too. I told him years ago — I begged him not to have children. He knew the blood wasn't clean. Sophie and I knew. But he had to be the clever one. The youngest, the loudest, the most impossible to reason with. His pride has cursed us all. When I look in his child's eyes, I see Johan. I see the evil reincarnated.

The storm groaned again above him. The sky let out a low bellow, like stone grinding against stone. For a brief moment, he imagined the whole house collapsing in on itself — a tomb sealing shut.

Buried alive.

A knock startled him. The ledger slipped from his hands, thudding softly onto the desk. He rose and crossed the room, smoothing his vest out of habit. He opened the door.

Simon Preminger stood in the hall — a tall silhouette swallowed in shadow. His dark hair was no longer brushed back but tousled, damp at the temples. The collar of his shirt was slightly undone, as if he'd dressed in haste or shed formality without realizing. His eyes, sharp as ever, seemed brighter now — reflective, fixed, unsettling — like frost on glass. He looked older than he had just hours ago.

"Can I come in?"

"Of course," Jasper said. "It's your house."

Simon stepped inside, then muttered, "Ernie's house… not mine."

"Well," Jasper offered, trying to sound casual, "not officially until tomorrow. And I'm sure he'll…he'll have you over any time you want."

Simon closed the door behind him. "What are you doing

in here?"

Jasper took a step backward, nearly tripping himself. "Paperwork. Diaries. Getting everything ready for the morning when I'll present these items to Ernie. I've catalogued everything for the record."

"I see." Simon's gaze dropped. He hesitated, as though weighing whether to continue, then reached into his pocket. He pulled out a small object and placed it on the desk.

It was a ring — a heavy gold signet ring, dulled by time. The face was rectangular, engraved with an ornate shield and tiny crossed swords. The craftsmanship was unmistakably expensive.

"It's lovely," said Jasper. "Why have you brought it to me?"

"I found it in my room," Simon said. "Someone must have left it there."

Jasper leaned closer, peering at it without touching. "I'm afraid I cannot help you. I don't know who would have done such a thing."

Simon picked it up again, turning it slowly between his fingers. "You stood up for me earlier. Against Robert. I appreciate that."

Jasper gave a tight smile. "It was long overdue. Perhaps it wasn't my place, but I have little tolerance for bullies. They treat you quite disrespectfully. Not just Robert. Beverly… even Timothy."

He nodded. "That's why I came to see you, Jasper. I have questions and I don't think my siblings are willing to help me." He looked downward. "I was hoping you might be able to."

"I'll certainly try."

"When I was a child, Dolph and Sophie wouldn't tell me the identity of my real parents. They put it off for years, hinting that the day might come. It never did. The last time I asked, they outright refused."

"Perhaps they thought it was for your own protection."

"I was hoping that your father might have known

something. He worked for them until the day he died. He would have almost certainly handled my adoption."

Jasper shook his head. "If my father did know anything, he never said a word to me. Everything I know about the Premingers is what I've read in these journals and the historical documents." He gestured toward the cabinet. "Of course, you're free to look for yourself, but there's a problem."

Simon frowned. "Yes?"

"I'll show you." Jasper opened the bottom drawer and pulled out a battered folder marked *Family Matters*, thumbing quickly through the contents. He lifted a brittle sheet, showing the yellowed index list.

"See here," Jasper said, tapping a faded line. *Adoption — Simon Preminger.* "According to this, the folder with your information is marked 17A."

"May I see it?"

"That's just it. The folder is gone. It's the only item missing. Curious. It's as if someone created the folder and then decided no one should read it."

Simon's gaze drifted past Jasper, unfocused. Then, without warning, he turned sharply, walking a short pace away before stopping again. His hand curled into a fist around the ring. "You're sure?" he asked, though the edge in his voice made it clear he believed him. "It couldn't be elsewhere?"

Jasper hesitated. "It's possible but all the other files are in their rightful place."

Simon exhaled, a clipped breath through the nose. He pressed his knuckles against the desk, eyes lowered, jaw flexing once.

A slow creak from the desk answered the tension in his body.

"Of course they are." The words weren't angry, but they were flint-struck — as if some quiet hope had just been dropped and shattered. He straightened again. "Do you have a glass?"

"Pardon?"

"A magnifying glass. There's an inscription on the bottom of the ring I found in my room. Too small to read."

"Yes, of course," Jasper said. He pulled open the desk drawer. His fingers brushed the handle of the magnifying glass — he fumbled slightly, the glass clinking against a fountain pen — then drew it out with deliberate care.

Simon handed him the ring. "Could you read it for me?"

Jasper peered through the glass. The words were engraved inside the band, worn but decipherable.

He paused.

"Well?" asked Simon.

"It says…it says *Cornelius Preminger.*"

Both men went still. The study seemed to contract around them, as if the very walls were listening. Rain scurried faster off the roof; the wind combed its long fingers through the eaves.

Simon took the ring back and closed his hand around it. "I wonder why it was put in my room. What could it mean?"

Silence settled, deep and unnatural — not a pause, but a breath held.

Then — from somewhere in the mansion's bowels — came the scream.

It was Ernie's voice, unmistakably. But stretched, broken, as though something had torn it out of him with a hook.

Rowan was up and across the hall in a flash. He seized the door handle. It barely rattled in the heavy oak doorframe. "Locked!"

Walter rushed to his side, pressing his shoulder against the door. "Solid as a vault. I can't break it open."

The whole mansion was in a state of crumbling disrepair, but this door—this door meant to keep Ernie at bay—had been constructed to last.

Rowan pounded with the flat of his palm. "Mr. Preminger! Open up!"

There was no answer.

Simon and Jasper barreled down the hallway. Behind them, Timothy, Beverly, and Robert spilled from the foyer, half-dressed.

"What's happening?" asked Beverly.

"We heard the ringing of a clock," Rowan said sharply. "And then a scream."

Before anyone could respond, a voice came from inside the room—thin and desperate. *"I didn't do this!"* Ernie cried. *"I swear to God—I didn't do it!"*

The sound of him—so raw, so broken—suggested the most terrible things awaited them inside that room.

Rowan took a step back. "Ernie, whatever happened, we can help you. But you have to let us in."

"Open the goddamned door!" said Robert.

There was a fumbling noise from inside—the scrape of a bolt, the turning of a key—and then the door swung open.

Ernie stood in the doorway—barefoot and trembling, his blood-spotted nightshirt clinging to his skin. The knife dangled from his hand, as if he barely realized he was holding it.

Behind him, Irene lay lifeless on the bed, her throat cut ear to ear.

The world shrank to a single frozen frame: the knife, the corpse, the man swaying like a ghost caught between guilt and madness.

Before Rowan could speak, Walter had already lunged forward, grabbing Ernie's wrist and wrenching the weapon from his fingers. He twisted the other arm behind his back and forced him to his knees.

Ernie gave the weakest resistance, crumpling to the floor like a marionette whose strings had been cut. Tears welled in his wide, terrified eyes.

"No… no—no—I didn't—I swear—" He gasped, shaking. "I didn't—I wouldn't!"

Beverly gave a small, strangled cry and buried her face against Jasper's chest. Jasper's face turned ashen as he awkwardly patted her head. Robert backed away with his hands raised as if warding off a blow. Simon stood stiffly by the doorway, unmoving. His face revealed nothing—neither horror nor pity. Timothy stepped forward to check on Irene, but Rowan caught his arm with a look that said, *Wait.*

Rowan stepped into the room and knelt, picking up the knife with a handkerchief, careful not to smear the blood along the blade. He rose slowly, eyes moving from the knife to the blood-slick bed, to the barred windows and thick door behind him.

The closet was empty. The bed, undisturbed. No signs of struggle.

The windows were barred—thick iron slats set into the stone like prison bars. The door had been locked from the inside.

Irene Preminger was dead. And Ernie had been the only one in the room.

Ernie was taken next door to the billiard room—a faded chamber of male leisure that now served as a kind of drawing-room gallows.

The air reeked of old varnish and older sweat, with hints of fur and smoke clinging to the wood-paneled walls. The paneling had dulled to a greasy amber, and a crack snaked down the ceiling like the start of a structural confession. The pool table sagged in the center, the green baize puckering like bad skin.

Over the hearth, a moose's head hung crookedly, one glass eye drooping with age. The beast's twisted antlers and mournful gaze gave it a grotesque tenderness, as if it pitied the man below—or judged him.

On the far wall, a massive oil painting loomed: a hunting scene gone wrong. Hounds with too many teeth lunged at a stag with a half-human face, its wide eyes filled with terror or some awful knowing. Smoke and time had blurred sky and blood into the same dull rust.

In the corner, an octagonal table crouched between two

chairs, its claw-foot legs frozen mid-pounce. One edge was worn smooth—darkened by decades of anxious fingertips.

Ernie sat hunched on a cracked-leather settee, hands trembling around a glass of water. Blood crusted on his nightshirt caught the light from the lamp and flickered black-red. He looked like a wax figure gone soft from the heat, his features sliding toward collapse.

Across the room, Rowan approached slowly, footsteps muffled by the rug, his eyes on Ernie—who hadn't looked up since they brought him in.

Walter leaned against the wall, arms folded, half-shadowed beneath a pair of crossed billiard cues mounted above the door. "It's going to be all right, kid."

"No," Ernie moaned. "It's never going to be all right again."

"How many times had she hypnotized you before tonight?" asked Rowan calmly.

"Nearly every day. It…helped me. At least, it did before."

"And you've never attacked her?"

"No." Ernie stared into his glass, as though some explanation of the violence lay at the bottom. "I don't know."

"You don't *know*? That's not the kind of thing a man forgets."

He shook his head helplessly.

Rowan took a slow step forward. "You're aware she tried to hide a bruise on her cheek with makeup. Any idea how she got it?"

At that, Ernie lifted his head, pain flashing across his face. "It wasn't what you think. I—I moved my arm in my sleep. Hit her by accident. I felt awful about it. She said it was nothing."

"Do you think perhaps she was lying to you? To protect you?"

"Maybe." His eyes teared up and he began to sob. "I wish I were the one who was dead."

"Earlier this evening you were adamant that you didn't

"Earlier this evening you were adamant that you didn't believe in the curse, and yet I sensed your feelings and words didn't entirely align. Do you believe in it now?"

"There's no other explanation, is there? I had no reason to murder Irene. I…I loved her. She was the only one I've ever loved," he choked, his voice dragging behind his tears.

Silence gathered between them, dense and smoldering.

Then the door creaked open. Timothy entered with his black Gladstone slung low in one hand. His expression was taut, his mouth a grim line.

"I fetched my bag," Timothy said quietly. "I can give him an injection of paraldehyde to help him sleep."

Rowan nodded. There was nothing more to pull from him now—not until Rowan investigated the room thoroughly.

Timothy produced a small vial and syringe. Rowan recognized the careful hands of a seasoned physician. Within moments of the injection, Ernie's body slackened, his breathing slowed to an even rhythm.

"He's out," Walter murmured. "Do you believe him?"

Rowan watched the firelight crawl across the floor. "I can't say."

They bound his wrists and ankles with rope—gently, though he didn't stir—then locked the billiard room behind them.

Back in the parlor, Robert was already holding court. He stood triumphantly by the bar, swirling a half-full glass of bourbon
with an expression that could only be described as *smug*.

"Well," he said, raising his glass to no one in particular. "Justice served. Inheritance back where it belongs. All's right with the world, eh?"

His voice rang hollow, but his grin didn't falter.

The shock of the murder prevented any disgust at Robert's celebration. The lone, mild objection came from Jasper.

"Not quite," he said, adjusting his glasses. "The outcome

of the will depends entirely on Mr. Manory's findings."

Rowan kept his expression neutral. "You can all rest assured in the knowledge that Williams and I will investigate this matter thoroughly and without prejudice."

Robert barked a bitter laugh. "There's nothing to investigate. The door was locked and the windows were barred. You were right across the hall. We all heard the scream. It's obvious." He stuck out a hand, open-palmed, toward the billiard room. "He's got blood on his goddamned nightshirt and he was holding the murder weapon!"

"Then you have nothing to worry about," Rowan said mildly. "The evidence will speak for itself."

Before Robert could fire back, Beverly stepped forward. "There's something you all should know."

All eyes focused on her.

"I saw someone outside my window. A woman." Beverly recounted her sighting—the pale figure darting through the rain—and Timothy's inability to find any sign of her afterward.

"Poppycock! You've been drinking too much and now you're hallucinating," Robert scoffed. "We've got a real corpse to deal with, not dancing ghosts."

Simon, standing near the fireplace, spoke up sharply. "Something strange happened to me too." He reached into his jacket pocket and produced the signet ring. "I found it on my nightstand. It hadn't been there earlier."

Timothy stepped forward. "Let me see that." He examined it before taking it over to Beverly and Robert. "Look."

They all gathered around it.

"That's Cornelius's," said Timothy. "I'd swear to it. We both purchased one." He made a fist to show off his own matching ring. "His went missing over twenty years ago."

"I smell a rat." Robert rolled up his sleeves as he moved toward Simon. "Where did you get this?"

"I just told you."

"Someone slipped into your room after you unpacked your suitcase. Is that it?"

"I was in the parlor with Beverly... for nearly half an hour. Anyone could've done it during that time. Maybe, it was you."

Robert shook his head. "I was in the study with Jasper."

Timothy said "I was on the porch."

Beverly grinned. "Don't you see—the woman could have done it."

"Shut up, Bev!"

"Enough!" Rowan's voice cracked like a whip, silencing the room. "Regardless of the circumstances, a murder has occurred. While I'm investigating the room, Walter will drive to Mound City to fetch the sheriff."

Walter frowned. "Not a good idea—you and me splitting up?"

"We can't delay with either of them." He gave a curt nod to his partner. "I'll be fine. You go and be quick about it."

Timothy cleared his throat. "Uh…Mr. Manory?"

"What is it, Timothy?"

"Before you say anything else, there's something I should have mentioned. I mean, I tried to find the right time to say it, but…" His face reddened.

"For God's sake, spit it out."

"When I went to fetch my bag from the car, I noticed... all the tires. Slashed. Every one of them."

The room froze. No one breathed. Even the rain shut up for a second.

"It'll take hours to reach town on foot," Timothy added grimly. "I don't think any of us are leaving tonight. We'll have to wait until the storm passes."

The rain came back with a vengeance, hammering the vast roof in mad percussion—deep thuds where slate lay thick, sharp tinny rattles over the attic eaves, a chaotic symphony of dread beating into every heart.

Beverly gasped. "Where's Vera? Is she all right?"

"Of course she is," said Robert. "Why wouldn't she be?"

"She's upstairs all alone. If there is a madwoman running around…"

Robert's face crumpled with panic. "Vera," he whispered. He tore from the room toward the stairs.

"Robert, wait!" Rowan called, but Robert ignored him, thundering up the stairs.

Everyone scrambled after him.

Rowan was only halfway up when he heard it—a scream that snapped through the house like a whipcrack. The second one that night.

When he reached the doorway to Robert's room, he saw Robert on his knees, reaching blindly to catch the hanging figure should she fall.

It was Vera. She hung from the chandelier by a twisted bedsheet, her body swaying gently in the cold draft. Behind her, the curtain fluttered like a dusty shroud.

They brought Robert to an unused bedroom. He swayed whether sitting or standing, his face slack with grief and dazed confusion. The words trickled out, mumbled, broken, and useless.

"Everything's fine, my darling. We have the money. We're saved. We'll start over." He kept repeating it—a mantra of regret, cried for no one.

Timothy prepped another injection from his doctor's bag. The syringe glinted in the weak lamplight. "I'm glad I brought this along."

Rowan knelt in front of Robert, guiding his wild, glassy eyes to meet his own. "What happened to your wife's face? Robert?"

For a long moment, Rowan thought he wouldn't answer. Then Robert's head dropped, and he gave a low, shuddering sigh.

"I owed money... a lot of money. To Meyer Danziger... in St. Louis." He rubbed his knuckles against his forehead. "Two hundred thousand. I thought I could win it back at the tables—Klondike poker. Always thought I'd turn it around. Just needed one good hand. One break. Vera didn't know... not at first. But then…"

"Yes?" Rowan prompted softly.

"They came to the house one night... three of 'em. Took a razor to her face. Said it was a message. Said next time... they'd do a lot more." Robert sagged forward. "This was our last chance. We would've paid them off—been free." He laughed madly. "All she had to do was wait." He started crying with a smile on his face. "Home free." He tried to stand, but his knees buckled. Tears dripped off his chin. "Why didn't she wait?"

"It's going to be okay, Robert," Rowan said as he and Timothy gently guided him onto the bed.

Timothy slid the needle into Robert's arm. "You'll feel better in the morning," he murmured. "Sleep now."

Robert slumped sideways onto the mattress. He shook for a moment and finally went limp. They eased him onto the bed and drew the covers over him.

Everyone who was left formed a circle in the narrow hall. They stared at one another beneath the uneven sconce light. Their faces had changed— creased, worn—not just tired, but clenched against whatever emotion or thought threatened to surface. The air had grown tense, heavy in the throat.

Beverly broke the silence. "Robert was foolish with the company he kept. It's his fault. Poor woman. I can't imagine the terror she must have felt…right up until the end."

"Some people inherit gold and still manage to turn it to rot," said Simon. "Robert could have done anything he Wanted with his life. Look at the path he chose."

"It's not the time for blame," said Timothy meekly.

Simon's voice cracked, brittle and loud. "It's far too late for civility. If someone had told the truth before, she might still be alive."

"We should be worried about that woman," insisted Beverly. "What does she want from us?"

Jasper's arms were folded tightly across his chest. "If

someone *is* in this house, they want us stuck here and they want us fearful. Unfortunately, it's working."

As they argued back and forth, Rowan tilted his head slightly. There—beneath their voices, beneath even the hush of the storm—something else.

A sound.

For a moment, he thought he was imagining it, but Walter's expression let him know it was real. It was music, soft and far off, drifting through the house like something from a dream. No—not a dream. A memory, half-forgotten and warped by time. The distant warble of a record spinning somewhere below them.

Walter raised a hand. "*Shh.* Listen."

Everyone fell quiet.

"The sweetest girl in all the world is my sweetheart of Sigma Chi…"

Beverly let out a sharp breath, stumbling back a step. "Cornelius."

"What?" asked Rowan.

"That was Cornelius's favorite song. He played it every time he
came back from the university—said it reminded him of escaping from here. It made him forget about being a Preminger."

Rowan headed for the stairs, his short legs stumbling into a desperate gallop. The others followed. They were pulled downstairs by the sound, by the impossible presence of that music.

They reached the parlor—and stopped.

The phonograph stood open. The turntable spun, slow and steady. The stylus drifted in lazy circles over the record, the melody blooming from the horn like a ghost rising in smoke. The sound filled the room—soft, nostalgic, droning an eerily cheerful melody.

Each sweet co-ed like a rainbow trail fades in the afterglow…

Rowan stepped forward. The crank lay flat, freshly turned. He snapped the needle arm away, killing the music with a sharp crack of static.

Beverly said, "Do you believe me now? Am I crazy now?"

"Williams, check on Ernie. Make sure he's still bound and asleep."

Walter grabbed the key to the billiard room and disappeared back down the hall.

Rowan looked toward the others. They were gathered at the back of the room, eyes wild and faces ashen. "We have an intruder in the house," he said bluntly. "We need to search every inch."

"How?" Beverly asked. "It's enormous. There are countless hiding spots. Besides, she should be on this floor if she just got this phonograph playing."

"She might have gone upstairs in the short time we've been standing here." Rowan turned to Timothy. "What's the layout of the mansion?"

"The house has four main areas. The ground floor. The second floor where the bedrooms are. The attic—though there's no proper lighting up there. And the basement."

"How do you get to the basement?" Rowan asked.

"There's a separate entrance," Timothy said. "Outside. Stairwell leads down. No interior door."

"Good, we can rule that out for now."

Walter returned, breathing a little hard. "He's still tied up. Same as we left him." He put the key back on the bar.

"All right," Rowan said. "Here's what we'll do. Simon and Jasper—you'll stay here and search the ground floor. Every room, every closet, every hall. Beverly and Timothy—you take the second floor. Check the bedrooms, the closets, everywhere. Everyone, lock the doors after you finish searching each room. Walter and I will take the attic."

"Of course we'll take the room with no light," Walter muttered.

"Move carefully. If you find the woman—or anyone else—you shout. No confrontations and no heroics. Understand?" Something in Rowan's voice—blunt, calm, immovable—quieted the rising nerves. They looked at him like someone holding a map in a burning maze.

The six of them gathered at the bottom of the stairs—each looking toward a different corner of the house, as if expecting something to emerge.

Then, silently, they split.

Jasper and Simon remained below, shadows swallowing them as the candlelight retreated. Beverly clutched Timothy's arm and led him up the staircase, veering left at the landing. Their footsteps faded, cautious and close, into the west wing.

Rowan and Walter followed, but at the top of the stairs, instead of turning down either hallway, Rowan pressed forward into a narrow nook tucked between two oil-dark cabinets. At the end of it, a lone pull cord hung from the ceiling like a noose. Rowan reached up and gave it a tug.

With a reluctant groan, the attic hatch dropped open, and the staircase unfolded downward, clattering as it struck the floor. A thick gust of stale air spilled out—carrying the scent of old wood, mildew, and something wetter, like a drowned parasol dredged up from a ruined pond.

Walter waved his hand back and forth in front of his nose. "I change my mind."

"About what?"

"About tagging along to fucking Cairo. I should've known when we got off the train and ran into Sox fans. What was I thinking?"

"It's too late to complain about it now."

"It's too late to go back. It's never too late to complain. I can complain right up until I'm murdered in this goddamn attic."

They went up the creaking steps. At the top, Rowan pushed aside a thin floorboard, and the smell intensified. He raised his candle. The weak flame barely lit more than a few feet ahead, swallowed quickly by the dark.

The attic yawned open before them—an endless sea of shadow, broken only by the angles of low-sloping beams and hulking forms beneath draped sheets. Their candle flames shivered with every faint breath of wind that the roof inhaled.

They advanced shoulder to shoulder. The floor groaned beneath each timid step. Their light only caught fragments—an overturned baby carriage, the rusted skeleton of a phonograph, a mountain of sagging boxes bound with brittle twine. Dust hung close to the flames, threatening to burst in mid-air.

Walter took an uneasy step and tripped on a fallen hat rack. The clatter cracked the silence like a gunshot.

"Shit."

"Be more careful."

The house murmured back: a tap-tap-tap of loose shingles, the furtive scurry of something small, a distant settling creak.

Rowan cleared his throat and called out, "If anyone is in here, make yourself known. We can help you with whatever it is you want." His voice fell strangely flat, absorbed by the dark.

They waited. Then—from somewhere ahead and to the left—a faint creak. Not the house. A footstep.

Walter glanced at Rowan. "I'll take the right side."

"Sounds good."

As Walter veered into the shadows, Rowan pressed left, deeper into the attic's long body. The air grew colder here. His candle caught a row of shelves full of disused craft supplies—faded bolts of cloth, wax flowers, cracked jars of feathers and buttons. The space felt haunted by a hundred abandoned hobbies.

As he moved forward, the nagging thoughts of the case threatened his concentration.

Why would Ernie kill Irene? Was it madness, rage, or something colder and more calculated? And the woman—who is she? Why here, why now? Why Cornelius's music? Why his ring? Did she place it in Simon's room on purpose? Or had someone else been there first? Why Simon? Did someone think it belonged to Simon?

Then he saw it—a figure posed near a tattered privacy

screen. It was completely still. Human-sized. A woman, he thought. She stood half in shadow, her posture unnatural—too stiff. Her dress clung as though soaked; her shadowy hair hung down, hiding her face.

Rowan's pulse thundered in his ears. "We don't want to hurt you," he said softly, stepping closer. "Who are you?"

From the far side of the room, Walter called out. "What do you see, old boy?"

"I think I've found her, Williams."

But no response came from the figure. No movement. Just that eerie stillness.

He crept forward, lifting the candle. The flame danced, illuminating pale hands, a curve of shoulder, the slack drape of a bodice. He thought he saw her face. He reached out—closer, closer—and touched it.

What the hell?

It was canvas, hardened with age. Cold and unyielding beneath the dust. Rowan exhaled, a shaky breath half-laugh. "Christ." He laughed harder now. "Never mind, Williams. It's just a mannequin. A dressmaker's mannequin."

"You scared me, old boy."

"Not as much as I scared myself." He backed toward the old privacy screen, the torn fabric fluttering faintly as if breathing.

He turned—

A face. A human face. Inches from his own. Twisted. Wild. The mouth wide, mid-scream. The woman's eyes caught the candlelight and gleamed.

She exhaled a puff of breath, vanishing the flame. Then — a damp hand against his cheek. Her breath, sour and sweet like spoiled lilacs.

Before Rowan could scream, he was shoved onto the floor.

"Manory!" Walter's voice echoed from somewhere in the dark. "Where are you?"

Coughing, Rowan scrambled backward across the boards, heart hammering, trying to make sense of the shapes around him. But the dark was solid now—thick and unmoving—and behind it, somewhere, the woman was breathing hard.

"Williams, she's here!" Rowan gasped, feeling the cold where the woman had stood, the wetness clinging to the floorboards.

A second later—*thud*—something slammed into his shin. A boot. Then a body. Walter tripping over him.

"Argh!"

"Jesus!" Walter yelped, pitching forward with a curse. He landed hard beside Rowan as his candle skittered away, casting mad shadows up the beams before dying out. "Is that you?"

"Of course it's me," Rowan groaned, still sprawled.

Then the attic door slammed.

"She's gone," said Walter.

They scrambled to their feet, taking off toward the front of the attic—though it wasn't clear which way that was anymore. They bumped into cloth-covered furniture, ducked low beams, and shouted over one another in the dark as they fumbled their way toward where they thought the entrance had been.

"Did she attack you?" asked Walter.

"She blew out my candle."

"How clever!"

Rowan lit a match. "There it is!" A sliver of pale light leaked around the hatch door.

They reached it—hands fumbling for the edge of the frame. Rowan felt for the latch and caught the inner handle. The attic yawned again, and a fresh gust of air rushed up from below—cool, living air that felt like a rebuke.

Beverly and Timothy appeared at the bottom of the stairs. "We heard yelling," she said. "Are you all right?"

"You didn't see her?" asked Rowan.

And then, the lights of the house went out all at once.

Darkness rushed in—not just absence, but something with weight and texture, as if the attic's shadows had spilled downward and soaked into the walls. For a moment, it was like falling into a dream where nothing had edges: the staircase, the hallway, even the people beside them blurred into suggestion.

Timothy whispered, "The generator in the basement—it must've been shut off."

Rowan didn't waste time. "Timothy—take Walter outside and try to get it running again. Beverly and I will find the others."

They all sprinted down the staircase toward the foyer. The moonlight from the front windows cast weak but welcome illumination. Walter and Timothy threw open the heavy front door and dashed into the storm, vanishing into the night's deluge.

Before Rowan and Beverly could move, a figure stumbled from the left hallway toward them. It was Simon.

"Where's Jasper?" asked Rowan.

"I don't know. We split up to search. When the lights went out, I heard him scream from somewhere down the left hall. I—I ran toward it, but someone—big, heavy—ran into me. I panicked and came back this way."

"Let's find him together." Rowan lit another match and crept toward the left wing. Simon followed with Beverly gripping his sleeve. They called out for Jasper.

A sound came back. Not a voice, but a thick moan of pain.

They turned the corner. On the floor of the hall, just past the study, lay a body. As Rowan got closer, the flame revealed Jasper lying sprawled, blood pooling beneath him and a butcher knife jutting from his side. His face was gray with pain, lips flecked with red. When he tried to speak, a bubble of blood popped from his mouth.

"He…st…st…stabbed me."

Beverly screamed just as the lights snapped back on, blinding after so much darkness.

Rowan dropped to his knees next to the lawyer's twisted, bloody body. "Who was it?"

All Jasper could manage was a rasping whisper. "Don't…

don't know. I struggled with him... in the dark... tried to grab the knife..." He raised a trembling hand, revealing a long, bloody gash across his palm. "He cut my hand and then…" Jasper looked down at the knife handle sticking out from his body. "Oh, God. I'm going to die."

Rowan leaned closer. "Which way did he go?"

Jasper gurgled more blood. He lifted one shaking finger down the hall.

"Did he run to the end of the hall?"

"N…no." His finger twisted to the side. "In…in there."

Rowan stared at the door to the library. It was slightly ajar.

Walter and Timothy stumbled back inside. They were both soaked and panting.

At the sight of Jasper, Timothy screamed. "My God! What happened?"

Rowan said, "Timothy, Simon—carry him to the parlor. Dress his wounds as best you can."

They obeyed, picking up Jasper up carefully as possible. He let out a weak protest before passing out. They carried him around the corner with Beverly following.

Rowan pointed to the library door. "Jasper said someone stabbed him in the dark and headed in that room."

"Right. I'll head in first, old boy."

"I wouldn't have it any other way."

They moved to either side of the door. With a nod, Walter nudged the door wide with his foot and stepped inside with a smooth, low motion.

The library wasn't laid out in rows but ringed with bookshelves that climbed the walls to the high ceiling. Each shelf was heavy with spines in faded leather and dark cloth, the dust thick and undisturbed. A pair of chairs huddled before the cold fireplace, and a bronze globe stood in the corner like an idle sentry.

It didn't take long for Walter to rule out every possible hiding spot. "No one's here," he said. "Jasper must've been wrong. Maybe he's concussed. It was pitch black. He probably just thought he heard someone come in. Let's check down the hall."

"Just a moment." Rowan stood in the middle of the library, unnaturally still. Something wasn't right. A faint change in pressure—like a thread pulling gently against his skin. He stepped to the right wall. His fingers grazed the seam of the shelves, then paused.

"What's wrong?"

A smile flickered at the corners of Rowan's mouth.

"There's a draft." He reached toward the shelf. "Right here. Come see for yourself."

Walter stepped beside him, placed his palm near the shelf, and felt it too: the soft whisper of moving air, thin and cool. His eyes sharpened. "There must be a passage," he said. "Behind the wall…in the middle of the mansion."

"I should have guessed. Most of these old mansions were built with passages."

Rowan's fingers drifted over the books, pulling and pushing random spines. "There's always one that hides the mechanism." He pulled on a slim green copy of *The Murders in the Rue Morgue*—a soft *thunk*.

"Poe is always an excellent choice."

The entire side section of the shelf groaned and shuddered open, revealing the narrow, dimly lit passage beyond. The only light came from a single electric bulb wired crudely to the ceiling—a low hum accompanied its pale glow.

They stepped inside and slowly made their way. Halfway through, there was a small switch embedded in the wall—antique brass, shaped like a toggle, with a cracked porcelain base and wiring that ran into the masonry. "This must cut the generator," Rowan said. "The person who stabbed Jasper must have triggered the blackout here."

They continued along the passage, footsteps echoing dully on the stone floor. At the far end, a large rectangle of wall faced them.

"Where do you think we are?" Walter's eyes widened. "Ernie's room?"

Rowan shook his head. "We aren't far enough. Remember

that strange painting in the billiard room?"

"Oh, yeah. I wondered why it was so big. But that means...no. Ernie was tied up. He couldn't have done it."

"Only one way to find out." Rowan stepped closer, crouched, and ran his hand along the base of the wall. Just above the floor was a recessed iron lever. He pulled it. With a low *clack*, the panel swung outward, revealing the billiard room beyond.

Ernie was still there, sleeping calmly on the settee—but the ropes had been cut and now hung in limp curls at his sides. His hands were smeared with blood glistening fresh in the dim light.

Walter moved toward him warily. "He's breathing. And he's not cut anywhere. The blood isn't his."

On the octagonal table, the mechanism that opened the hidden painting panel was still exposed—its cover wide open.

Rowan stared at Ernie's limp form—at the bloody hands, at the painting swinging quietly on its hinges.

"He's out cold, Manory. Unless Timothy lied about injecting him, there's no way he woke up. Do you think he can go into one of those fugue states while he's sedated?"

Rowan didn't answer. He couldn't.

After tying Ernie up again, they returned through the passage and locked the library door. Now he was sealed in from both sides—a prisoner for everyone's safety.

"What the hell do we do now?" asked Walter.

"I want you to go upstairs and make sure Robert's okay. When you come back, we'll investigate Ernie's bedroom, see if anything is amiss."

"Who do you think that woman is?"

"I don't know."

Walter smiled. "Some detective you are. What are you going to do in the meantime?"

"I'll check on Jasper's condition."

Inside the parlor, Timothy mopped blood from his hands

with a rag. He shook his head.

"Jasper's losing blood faster than I can stop it," he said, his voice low but steady. "I cleaned the wound as best I could, packed it with gauze, and wrapped him tight. Gave him something for the pain." He hesitated. "There's nothing more I can do. If he makes it through the night, it'll be a miracle."

Rowan nodded grimly. The corpses were piling up.

Jasper lay stretched out on the couch. His ashen face glistened under the weak glow of the floor lamp. Beverly knelt beside him, wringing a wet cloth into a makeshift basin and dabbing it lightly against his forehead. Simon sat stiffly in an armchair with his hands clasped tightly between his knees.

"The woman was in the attic," Rowan said. "She's loose in the house now…somewhere."

Beverly asked, "Was she the one who stabbed Jasper?"

"I...don't know."

Simon lifted his head. "What do you mean you don't know? Did you find anyone in the library?"

"No, but we did find a secret passage leading from the library directly to the billiard room. Did any of you know about it?"

They all seemed surprised.

"I find that hard to believe. You all grew up in this house and none of you were aware it contained a secret passage?"

Simon stood, suddenly edified. "It must have been Ernie then. He killed Irene and he stabbed Jasper."

"That's impossible," said Timothy quietly. "There's no way he could have woken up. I gave him 10 ml of paraldehyde. He'll be out five hours minimum. More likely, he'll sleep until morning."

Simon slammed a fist onto the bar. "Then how do you explain it?"

"I'm not the detective."

All eyes turned to Rowan.

"I sent Walter to check on your brother. As soon as he

returns, we'll investigate Ernie's bedroom."

A cough came from behind them. Walter stood in the doorway. "Manory?"

"Yes, Williams?"

"Can I have a word in the hallway?"

The look on Walter's face told the story. Beverly began to sob. Simon sat back down helplessly. Timothy buried his head in his hands.

Out in the hall, Walter told Rowan what he found. "Robert's dead. His throat's cut. There were no signs of struggle. I'm sure he slept through it."

With slightly trembling hands, Rowan rolled a cigarette, lit it, and took a drag. "Thank God for small favors. We'd better solve this case soon, Williams—before there's no one left to claim the inheritance."

The rain had thickened into a hissing sheet against the windows, whispering against cracked glass like a voice through broken teeth.

Rowan stood in the center of Ernie's bedroom, cigarette in hand, the ember casting a dull red eye in the gloom. He stared at Irene's corpse.

The pool of blood had already begun to vanish into the floorboards, as if the house itself had drunk it. The thought came to Rowan unbidden

The mansion feeds on its own.

Her throat had been opened with a single, precise stroke — deep, clean, *surgical.*

There were no bruises. No torn fabric. No desperate scratches on her arms.

Rowan exhaled a slow stream of smoke through his nose. He gestured with two fingers toward the body. "Look at the angle of the cut. Right-handed. From behind. Very controlled. Not a wild lunge, not a drunken swipe. Clean as a butcher's hook."

Walter frowned. "But he said she hypnotized him. Sat him right in front of her."

"Which makes it unlikely that he was the killer," Rowan said. "You can't creep up behind someone who's already staring into your face. And if she'd seen him coming—"

"There'd be some sign on Ernie," Walter finished. "A scratch, a bruise, anything."

Rowan moved to the walls and began tapping with his knuckles. The hollow thump of aging plaster answered him, but nothing more. "No hidden doors," he said. "No secret passages except for the one connecting the library and the billiard room."

"That doesn't do us much good." Walter's eyes swept the dim corners of the room. "The window, maybe?" he said. "Someone could've squeezed through the bars?"

Rowan stepped to the window and undid the latch. The iron bars outside, wet with rain, were streaked with rust. "No, they are spaced far too closely for that. These were meant to keep a young boy locked inside."

Walter shrugged. "A contortionist?"

"Even if someone had managed to get through the window, Irene would have heard it or seen it, and she would have screamed bloody murder."

"I know, but I can't think of anything else."

Rowan turned again, scanning the ceiling, the floorboards, the walls.

Nothing.

No gaps, no crevices. The closet stood ajar. The space beneath the bed was empty.

Rowan nodded. "I'm leaning toward our killer hiding inside this room before Ernie and Irene entered. The closet strikes me as the most reasonable place. It's large enough." He swung the door softly. "The door doesn't make much noise when it opens."

Walter shook his head. "But we checked right after the scream. There was no one else in here."

"That's right," Rowan murmured. "Ernie and Irene were the only people inside this room."

He dropped the cigarette into the floor and stamped it

out. He added quietly, "Of course, we didn't search the room until after Ernie opened the door—after the alarm bell rang." He moved to the window again, staring at the latch.

"Well, of course, Manory. We couldn't search the room before Ernie opened the door. I could have deduced that."

As he searched the floor and the curtains, he said, "You're not following my logic, Williams."

"I don't see any logic on display. And if you think—" Walter cocked his head. "What are you…*uh*… looking for over there, Manory?"

"This." Rowan bent down and picked up something so small that Walter had to cross the room to see it—a thin blackened remnant — almost invisible in the low light.

Rowan held it up triumphantly. "A tiny piece of string," he said. "Burnt."

Walter peered over his shoulder. "You mean... the killer opened the window with it? Like he had the string attached to the latch and unlocked it from the outside?"

Rowan smiled faintly. "No."

"Then what do you mean."

"The opposite."

"All right, enough of the detective act. Just tell me."

"The killer *locked* it from the outside."

"So, the window was unlocked?"

"No, it was locked. The killer unlocked it and tied a string on the latch. He escaped through the window and locked the latch from outside. After that, he burned the string. It dissolved into ashes, and the trick was complete. Sometimes it leaves a tiny bit of evidence." He squeezed the remnant of string between his finger. "A small piece can survive the fire."

Walter pointed at the window. "But the bars. There are five iron bars blocking the window. Even if the killer did this window trick, he wouldn't have been able to escape."

"I disagree." Rowan unlocked the right window and pulled it open. The cold wet air rushed in, carrying the scent of damp earth and old metal. He rapped his knuckles across the bars, one by one. They all rang with a hollow metallic note—except for the last two. They produced a dull, muted thud.

"Just as I suspected. He leaned forward and examined the base of the two end bars. "See here?" he pointed. "The tops and bottoms—someone smeared what looks to be asphalt putty around them. It's dried black, almost the same color as the bars. Easy to miss unless you're truly looking for it. I bet a good swift kick can knock them out."

Walter took the suggestion, hitting both of them with one swing of his leg. With a screech of old iron, the two bars snapped loose and clattered down the exterior wall to the muddy ground.

Rowan's face lit with joy. "And there we have it. The killer must have prepared the scene in advance," he said. "Sawed through two bars, left them hanging by a thread. Hid in the closet, waiting. When Ernie was hypnotized, the killer emerged and slit Irene's throat. Then, he kicked out the bars and escaped. My guess is that a jar of asphalt putty had already been planted inside the room. Once the killer escaped, he performed the string trick, affixed the bars with the putty, and left a perfectly rational scene of murder behind him. And…" All at once, Rowan's smile vanished.

"What's wrong, Manory?"

"That couldn't have been the killer's plan."

"Why not? I'd say it explains things pretty well."

"How would the killer have known Irene was going to hypnotize Ernie? If there were two witnesses, there'd be no time to kill them both. Unless... the killer *expected* them to be unconscious." Rowan's eyes scanned the room. He pointed to the water pitcher on the bedside table.

"Of course! Quick, give me your silver penknife."

Rowan flicked the blade open and dipped it into the water.

Walter frowned. "What are you doing now?"

Rowan laid the knife on the table. "The killer didn't touch Ernie—we can logically deduce that Irene was the only intended victim. The killer must have wanted to frame him for Irene's murder."

"That would have reset the will."

"That much is obvious, Williams. The question is—how did he plan to do it? The answer lies in the water inside this pitcher. The killer laced it with a sedative. When they were both safely unconscious, he could kill Irene and perform his little window trick. However, Irene hypnotized Ernie. She even announced when he would awaken from hypnosis. The killer had a literal clock that indicated the available time for his escape." He pointed at the knife. "Look."

The metal had begun to bloom with a dull gray film.

"Silver tarnishes in the presence of certain drugs. Barbiturates. Chloral hydrate. Things you'd slip into a drink if you wanted someone quiet."

Walter looked at the pitcher. "Well, I'll be. But which one of them—"

He was cut off by the last scream of the night. A shrill, gut-twisting sound from the foyer. It sounded like Beverly.

Thunder rolled through the house, like something vast turning in its sleep. Rain lashed the tall windows at the front, casting streaks of silver down the glass. When Rowan and Walter reached the foyer, they froze at the sight before them.

It was the woman. She was standing at the foot of the grand staircase, drenched and pale, with arms wrapped around Simon.

Her nails dug into his back like claws as if she feared he might vanish. Her soaked skirt clung to her legs, her hair matted to her face, eyes shining with feverish light.

Near the threshold of the hall, Beverly stood rigid, Timothy hovering beside her—tense, watchful, not daring to come closer.

"My son," the woman whispered. Lightning flashed, illuminating the trail of water she'd left in her wake. "I knew they had you—those evil Premingers."

Simon pulled back to get a good look at her face.

She cupped his cheek, trembling, laughing. "My name is Marie Lavasham."

His voice cracked like thin ice underfoot. "Why… why…" The word broke apart in his throat. He was too full of questions to form just one.

"I never abandoned you. Know that! It was your father that took you away from me."

"Was Cornelius my father?"

"Yes. He said he loved me. It was a lie. After I had you, he sent me away." Her eyes welled. "I never wanted to leave you, but he had me committed. I agonized over you—in my rooms, my stone-walled prisons, in all the asylums. So many years I was locked away, treated like a madwoman, forgotten. But I never stopped loving you."

Thunder cracked, loud and close, shaking the windows. Walter and Rowan stood back, waiting for the scene to play out.

"That's why I gave you the ring. It was your father's. I buried it long ago, a place no one would know. Now, he's dead and you deserve to have it. I left it in your room so you'd understand, so you'd know the truth. The music on the phonograph—it was your father's favorite."

Simon took the ring from his pocket with trembling fingers. His mouth parted as he turned it over, the engraved name catching a glint of light. His voice was a breath. "I always knew they were hiding something from me—Dolph and Sophie. I thought it was to protect me. But now…" He looked at the ring again. "Now I finally understand who I am."

He turned to Timothy and Beverly. "I'm a Preminger. Just as much as any of you. All those years, you treated me like an imposter. Now you know the truth!"

Timothy shook his head. "Simon... there's no way you could have been born from this woman. It's impossible."

"Lies!" Marie hissed.

"When you were a baby, your parents were murdered. A

drifter—some vagrant—took you and disappeared. I overheard mother and father discussing it once. They didn't lie to erase your past… They were trying to spare you the horror of it. So, this woman…it's impossible that she's your mother. I'm…I'm sorry."

The howling wind suddenly stilled, as if the storm were holding its breath.

Marie's hands fell away from Simon. "No..." she whispered.

Simon turned toward her, dazed. "He doesn't know what he's talking about. You can't believe him."

Marie took a step back, shaking her head. "How cruel." She stumbled back up the stairs, gripping the banister for support. "Where is my son? What did you bastards do with him?"

"I'm right here. Wait!" Simon called after her, starting up the steps.

She moved up the stairs faster now. Ten steps. Fifteen.

Simon's walk turned into a jog. "You have to be my mother. Don't you see? It all fits. He's trying to drive us apart and we've only just met! Please, Mother!"

With a sudden cry, she lunged at him—shoved him with a strength born of bottomless rage.

Simon fell—backward, twisting in the air like a broken puppet—then struck the marble with a sickening crunch. He didn't move as the group gathered around him.

A scream ripped from Marie's throat. "I will *never* know my child! This cursed family took him from me forever!"

Before Walter could run her down, she turned, climbed the last few steps, and hurled herself over the railing.

Her body struck the marble with a hollow thud—brutal, final.

The thunder stopped.

There was only the sound of rain, gentler now, tapping against the windows and dripping from the eaves.

Rowan stood outside the parlor door, frowning at Jasper's weak, pained groans. From the sound of it, he didn't have much time left.

Across the hall, Timothy shut the music-room door with quiet finality. His grey hair was frazzled, and heavy bags sagged under his eyes. But he was smiling.

"Well, Mr. Manory. It's a miracle. Simon is going to make it. He's not in great shape, and every movement causes him agony, but he'll live. I gave him an injection. He'll sleep like a baby. Nothing can wake him up."

Rowan lit a cigarette. "When he finally does wake up, he'll find himself handcuffed to his hospital bed. He's our killer."

Timothy paused. "You're quite sure about that?"

"Oh, yes. When we convened in the parlor, Simon stated he was going to bed. He made quite a show of retiring early. While the rest of us stayed put, he crept into Ernie's room and hid in the closet. No one liked him—he knew they wouldn't think to knock on his bedroom door to see how he was doing."

"And what was his plan exactly?"

"He'd already been here to prepare the bars outside the bedroom window. He laced the water on the bedside table with a sleeping agent. It just so happened that Irene put Ernie under hypnosis. It made his job faster and easier. He killed Irene and escaped outside. He reentered the house through the back door to the right-side hallway. Then, he knocked on the door to the study to establish an alibi with Jasper."

"Why didn't he kill Ernie too?"

"The longer he kept Ernie as a suspect, the longer he could get away with it." Rowan nodded into the parlor. "Jasper here was unlucky enough to be on the ground floor with him. Simon opened the billiard room door and untied Ernie to make it appear as if he were free to act through the house. Simon went through the secret passage, cut the power and then stabbed Jasper in the dark. He went back through the passage and exited the billiard room into the left hall. Once he locked the billiard-room door, the illusion was complete."

"I see. That's when he came out from the left hallway with a story about running into a killer in the dark."

"Exactly."

"Did...did Simon kill my parents and my brother?"

"Oh, yes. I have little doubt that an investigation as to Simon's whereabouts in the past few months will provide opportunities for him to have committed those crimes."

"And the arrival of Marie Lavasham?"

"I'm confident he had no idea she would be here. It was her appearance that stopped him."

"But what I said was true. Cornelius wasn't his father."

Rowan smiled. "Curses aren't real. It wasn't a curse that caused him to kill. Just hatred—and a lifetime of being treated like a stranger."

"I...wish I had been better to him."

Rowan shrugged. "Some men are born broken. Doesn't take much to push them over."

"Yes, well, I'd better get to bed. I'll see you in the morning. Good night and...thank you."

"Just doing my job, Mr. Preminger."

As Timothy went up the stairs, Walter, who'd been watching from the far end of the hall, approached Rowan. "I know that look, old boy."

"What look?"

He pointed at Rowan's face. "That look."

"You're very observant, Williams."

"So, what gives?"

"The murders are far from over."

"What?"

"You heard me. Simon is not our killer."

"First question—who is the killer? Second question—why did you tell Timothy it was Simon?"

"The answer to the first question will give you the answer to the second. I want Timothy Preminger to sleep soundly, certain we suspect nothing. I want him bold, unguarded, ready to act."

"Timothy? How do you know it was him?"

"There were many small clues. Do you recall how I described the cut on Irene's throat?"

Walter gasped. "Surgical. Yeah. And he has that doctor's bag with him. The sleeping agent in the water pitcher must have been his doing."

"Yes. And did you notice how quickly he offered up that story about Simon's real parents. It was a tense moment. One would hope a doctor would practice a bit of discretion in such a situation. His words led directly to the chaos that ensued."

"But how did he—"

"Hold that thought, Williams. I will explain everything after we are positioned upstairs. In a little while, Timothy Preminger is going to leave his room to pay his sister a murderous visit. When he does, you and I will be waiting to catch him in the act."

The house was dead. No wind rattled the windows. No footsteps echoed in the halls. Even the old pipes, prone to their nocturnal creaks and groans, stayed quiet.

Amid that quiet, the killer rose. He had hidden knives in various places throughout the mansion, so it was no trouble getting one. He opened a door.

Inside was a figure, motionless and covered with blankets. The air reeked of the fevered joy of murder. The killer breathed it in. It wasn't musty to him.

He approached the figure.

Slowly. Carefully.

He raised the knife high, the blade gleaming faintly in the moonlight.

Then he brought it down, sinking into flesh. He yanked it out and brought it down again, harder this time, deeper into the victim.

And still, miraculously, the victim did not stir. No screaming, No pain. No death.

A sudden burst of electric light filled the room.

Rowan Manory stood in the doorway, hand still on the

switch. Walter shadowed him.

The wound on the killer's side had opened from the strain of stabbing. He was slowly bleeding out where he stood.

"My apologies, Mr. Dunn, but your spree of murder is finished. Simon Preminger died instantly after falling down the stairs. Broke his neck."

Jasper froze, the knife suspended inches above Simon's chest, caught mid-scene, like an actor frozen in the spotlight. His expression flickered between shock and lingering rage. Finally, he doubled over in exhaustion, falling to his knees. "Why did you…say he was still alive?"

"Haven't you figured it out yet? I wanted to lay the bait for you. If you thought we would be upstairs watching Timothy and the chance for an easy murder was right across the hall…well, even with your injury, you couldn't resist the opportunity."

He huffed a laugh. "That's good. How did you know it was me?"

"Opportunity, motive, secrets. You had all the family paperwork, including the floor plans for the mansion. You could rig the bars outside the window. You knew about the secret passage. When Ernie and Irene went outside to get their luggage, you used the secret passage to get back to the left hallway undetected. It was easy to enter Ernie's bedroom and hide in the closet."

"How come your clothes didn't get wet?" asked Walter.

Jasper grinned. "I did it naked."

"Pardon?"

"I was naked when I went in the room. I slit her throat naked and I went out the window naked. I left towels and my clothes in the dining room. When I entered the back door to the right hallway, I dried off and got dressed and hurried back to the study. Simon came to see me. I'm lucky he didn't arrive earlier. He might have caught me coming down the hall."

Rowan nodded. "I knew it wasn't Simon because of the blood on Ernie's hand. How would Simon have planted the blood? You had to do it."

"That's right."

"While Simon was searching the left hall, you went upstairs and dispatched Robert quickly. He wouldn't put up much of a fight in his condition. Moreover, Beverly would never search a section of the house alone. Because she and Timothy were together, one wing of the upstairs would remain completely unwatched. When the filthy deed was done, you rushed back downstairs, went through the secret passage and cut Ernie's ligatures. You planted blood on Ernie's hands by cutting your own hand and using your own blood. The plan was to turn off the power and scream. When Simon came running to you, you'd kill him. When we found you, you could say you tried to fight Simon's killer off and he cut your hand. You heard him go into the library. We'd find the passage and an untied, bloody Ernie. No suspicion would fall on you. You'd be free to continue your murderous ways."

He lowered his head, exhausted. "It didn't work out that way. I overestimated my ability to operate in the dark. Simon ran into me and I…I fell on my own knife."

"You still did your best to throw us off the scent. It looked like Ernie was at fault, but certainly not the way you intended."

"Aren't you supposed to say why, detective? The motive?"

"You were a bit too vigorous when you defended Simon. The subject of adoption was obviously a sore spot for you. I also recall you mentioning the close friendship between Cornelius and your adoptive father. Tonight brought us murder, yes, but also a woman looking for her son. The son she had with Cornelius whose infidelity was also established this evening. It wasn't Simon. It was you. You were the illegitimate child of Cornelius and Marie. When did you learn the truth?"

"My adoptive father told me on his deathbed. That I was a Preminger. Instead of welcoming me, I was destined to be their servant. The family lawyer, never acknowledged, never loved. Sophie and Dolph never knew. Cornelius and my adoptive parents never told them. I was a dirty little secret."

"And the curse? Do you think it's real?"

Jasper used the last of his strength to lift his head. "I don't know if it is, but I wanted to make it come true. I wanted to kill every one of those miserable…those miserable…"

"Bastards?" offered Walter.

But Jasper never finished the thought. He died in front of Simon's corpse.

The rain had stopped sometime during the final hour of night. Now, as dawn broke over the soaked landscape, the clouds thinned into drifting veils of silver and rose. Water dripped from the bare tree branches like loose threads unraveling from the sky.

Rowan stood just beyond the porch. The front door was hanging crooked on its hinges behind him. He lit a cigarette with a practiced hand, the flame briefly flaring gold against the gentle gray. Smoke curled upward, mingling with the mist.

The Preminger house loomed at his back—still large, still broken—but no longer menacing. In the warm, forgiving light of morning, it resembled a structure that had simply run out of time.

Walter sighed. "I'd say it's all over for the Premingers now. Ernie's too far gone for fatherhood. Beverly is too old. And Timothy… let's just say I don't think he's the fathering type. Not unless there's a second immaculate conception."

"Yes," agreed Rowan. "I got the same impression."

"Probably for the best it ends this way. The Premingers don't have the greatest track record."

"No, they did not. Still, it's a pity. This family had potential for greatness."

Walter tilted his head, then grinned. "That's how the cookie bounces, I guess."

Rowan said nothing.

"Really?" asked Walter. "You're just going to let that go

uncorrected?"

Rowan nodded.

"You're getting soft, old boy."

5.

CUE, MURDER!

Atlee Burroughs swung open the door with the flourish of a stage curtain rising on a grand first act. He filled the doorway, broad-shouldered and expectant, a smile of delight poised on his lips.

"I thought you'd changed your mind."

At the sight of his guest's ragged appearance, Atlee's expression faltered, only for a moment, before the mask of warmth slipped back into place.

"My God." He reached for Paul's shoulder. "You look like you've been through the wringer, my dear boy."

Paul stood in the dim hallway, water trailing off his sleeves in slow, deliberate drips. His coat, too thin for the wet Chicago night, clung to him. His hands were shoved deep into his pockets, shoulders hunched. His face, still boyishly soft in the right light, was flushed from cold, his dark hair pasted to his forehead.

"I missed the bus, so I had to take the 'L' train. Long walk. It started hailing just as I got off."

"Well, you have to come in. You have to come in this instant." Atlee ushered him through the doorway with a gentle but insistent hand.

The apartment was a world away from the miserable cold outside—warm, dimly lit, rich with the scent of tobacco and the faintest trace of Atlee's lemon cologne. A heavy oriental rug covered the floor, deep red and intricate, like spilled wine drying on velvet. The furniture was worn but elegant—fainting couches, wingbacks, all collected from theater closeouts and estate sales, their history layered in fabric and fading grandeur.

"There," Atlee said, nudging Paul toward the radiator hissing in the corner. "You'll thaw in no time. Goodness, if I'd known you'd show up half-drowned, I'd have drawn a bath and left a robe out."

Paul grinned at the thought. He hunkered near a large pipe that ran from the floor to the ceiling, rubbing his hands together as the heat curled around his fingertips. "Thank you much, Mr. Burroughs."

Atlee *tsk-tsked* as he glided to the liquor cabinet. "Dispense with the formalities, my boy. This is not my classroom. You don't have to raise your hand to speak, you don't have to take notes, and you absolutely mustn't call me Mr. Burroughs. My friends call me Atlee. I insist you do the same." He shook his head with playful derision. "*Mr. Burroughs.*"

Paul let out a breath of laughter, half amusement, half nerves, as he slipped off his wet coat and draped it over the radiator. He turned back to see Atlee twisting the wire cage off a bottle of champagne, his movements unhurried, deliberate. The cork released with a subdued pop, and he poured, bubbles rising in narrow glasses like tiny golden ghosts.

"Champagne!"

Paul had already downed a few shots of rotgut earlier in the evening, and it wasn't sitting well on his stomach. At nineteen, he hadn't as of yet developed a strong constitution for alcohol. Champagne was new to him, so the consequences were unknown.

"Does that stuff muck up your guts?"

"You'll have to speak English, Paul. I'm practically an old man and I don't...*uh*...*swing* with the latest lingo. Isn't that what you kids say nowadays? Swing?"

"I mean, does champagne lay you out the next morning?

Do you wake up in agony?"

"Only if it's cheap," Atlee said, tilting the bottle to read the label. "And I am many things, but cheap is not one of them. See here—we are drinking Veuve Clicquot. I've been saving it for an occasion."

Paul's face turned its most innocent shade of curious. "Is this an occasion then? Is that what this is?"

Atlee's face relaxed, the slight wrinkles receding into a sincere smoothness. "We'll have to wait and see." He held the bottle at arm's length, trying to read the label. "Damn my eyes." He fetched a pair of reading glasses from his desk. "Don't ever get old, Paul. Let's see. It says, *Mis en bouteille dans nos caves à Reims.*"

"What does that mean?"

"You don't speak French."

"It's all Greek to me."

"What it says is unimportant. The only thing which concerns us is taste." Atlee handed him one of the glasses before holding up the other for a toast. "Here's to 1929. May it be a good year for both of us. Cheers."

"Cheers."

Clink.

Paul's first sip burned for a quick moment before turning sweet. "Oh, that's good."

With a knowing smile, Atlee said, "Pace yourself, my boy. It's dangerous."

"I can tell. Back home, we made applejack—it went down easy, too, but one sip too many and you'd wake up in the barn wondering how you got there."

"Ah, back on the farm, then?"

Paul stiffened, his fingers tightening around the delicate stem of his glass. Even if Atlee were only teasing him, the word *farm* landed wrong. Paul had spent every moment since leaving home trying to strip away anything that might mark him as unsophisticated. The reminder of his roots shook the image of what he was trying to become.

And he especially didn't want to hear it coming from Atlee

Burroughs.

Confidence and intelligence were just as attractive as good looks, and Atlee had all three in abundance. The signs of aging that might dull another man only suited him. The touch of silver at his temples, the slight paunch beneath his shirt—they lent him a warmth, a presence, rather than making him seem undesirable. He was just past fifty, still quite sexy.

Atlee noticed Paul's sudden reticence. "Did I say something wrong?"

"Mr. Burr…Atlee. I didn't ever have much to do with the farm. Or the people there—I never got along with 'em."

"So, you don't miss…what is it called again?"

"Hallidayboro," he said softly.

"You don't miss life back at Hallidayboro?"

"No. It never felt like my life. Not really. I'm meant to be other places, but my upbringing is holding me back. My classmates are all from here, or near here anyway. They all seem to fit right in. I mean, they know the places to go and they seem to be comfortable."

Atlee tilted his head, inviting him to continue, but Paul only took another sip of champagne. Finally, Atlee said, "I think I follow. Nobody back home is like you, but when you come to the city, you find that you're not like anyone else."

Paul nodded. "Exactly."

"That must be difficult for a young man." Atlee smiled softly. "I invited you to spend New Year's Eve with me because I understand you. At least, I think I do. I was lonely at your age, too. And I also wanted to be an actor. I didn't have what it took, so I turned to directing. I'm not half bad at that."

Paul swirled the champagne in his glass and lowered his eyes. "Do you think I have what it takes to be an actor?"

"Oh, there's no question about it. You need to be refined, sure, but you've already mastered the greatest tool an actor needs for success."

Paul looked upward. "Which is?"

Atlee tapped his ear. "You know how to listen, Paul. It's hard to teach listening. It isn't nearly as exciting as talking, but it is the secret of making drama a reality on stage. You have to listen and allow the words and actions of others to force you to action and deed. Trust me, Paul. I know what I'm talking about.

Not to beat my own drum, but I've shaped more than a few students into successful thespians. I can do the same for you."

"Like Jonathan Keltner?"

Atlee's cool demeanor dropped at the mention of the name. His voice wavered. "Jonathan?"

"Yes. You turned *him* into a successful actor, didn't you?"

"He's one success story of many, yes."

"Doesn't Jonathan live in this building? Doesn't he live in the apartment downstairs? That's what I heard from a few of the guys in the dormitory. You and he work together and practically live together."

Atlee nodded hesitantly. "Have you met Jonathan?"

"No, but I know about him. Heck, everybody knows about Jonathan Keltner. He's moving to Hollywood to be in a gangster movie for Paramount."

"Word travels fast." Atlee sipped his champagne. "I directed Jonathan in a few plays—*The Front Page*, *Chicago*, and *They Knew What They Wanted*—all had successful runs. Last season, we decided to do something a little coarser." He bit his bottom lip. "Something a little more fun."

Paul nodded. "*King of the Streets*."

"Oh, you know it?"

"Know it? I saw the darned thing three times. I was mulling over enrolling at the Goodman, and that show made it a done deal. I was tickled pink after finding out you'd be my teacher. If you were able to get a performance like that out of somebody, then I figured you were the man I should get to know."

"I'm honored. The agent from Paramount who saw the show agreed with your assessment. It was Jonathan's performance in *King of the Streets* that earned him an audition with Josef von Sternberg himself."

"I don't know who that is, but he sounds awful royal."

"Mr. Sternberg is one the cinema's most popular and successful directors."

"That don't surprise me. *King of the Streets* was the greatest thing I've ever seen. And I know Jonathan came from a small town just like I did. He didn't have many people supporting him, but he came to the city anyway. If he could do that…I have hope."

A flicker of something—annoyance?—crossed Atlee's face before he smiled again. "You seem to know an awful lot about Jonathan. Is that why you came here tonight? Did you come here to meet him? I thought you and I were going to get to know one another."

"No, Atlee. You're the reason I came. I just know that you were Jonathan's teacher and you worked together. Are you still… together?" Paul blushed and looked away.

Atlee set down his glass, the faint clink against the table lingering in the air. "We're still friendly, but he's moving away soon and I'm always looking for more friends—new friends. Do you need a friend too, Paul?"

Paul gulped the last of his champagne before he set the glass down. "Do you want me to sit on the couch? I'm still shivering a little."

Atlee shook his head. "You should stay there. I want you comfortable." Atlee knelt onto the floor beside Paul.

The heat from the radiator hummed against the quiet. The flickering lamplight caught in the sheen of Paul's curls as he turned toward Atlee.

"You should know something first. I've never—" Paul shook his head slightly.

"Never what?" cooed Atlee.

"I never—"

A clang erupted from the heating pipe, sharp and sudden, making them both jump. A nervous laugh passed between them.

Atlee took advantage of the moment. While they were both still laughing, he reached forward and brushed the side of Paul's hair, letting his fingers trail just a little longer than necessary as he traced the curve of his temple. "You're gorgeous, Paul. Do you know that?"

Paul's lips parted slightly, but instead of answering, he only gave a small shake of his head, his breath shallow.

"Gorgeous boys never seem to know how pretty they are." Atlee's thumb ghosted over Paul's cheek, the warmth of his skin like a quiet spark beneath his touch. "You're far better looking than I. You must think me a decrepit old man, old enough to be your father."

A faint *uh-uh* was all Paul could muster. He was lost now in the older man's eyes.

"I assure you that my spirit is…youthful."

The space between them narrowed, slow and deliberate, until Paul could feel Atlee's breath against his lips—warm, a little uneven, tasting of champagne and desire. The hesitation melted into a slow, soft kiss. Paul's fingers brushed Atlee's sleeve—hesitant at first, then firmer, grounding himself. The warmth of the room, the hush of the radiator, the lingering taste of champagne—it all folded around them as the moment stretched, unrushed, inevitable.

"I'm glad you came." The foreign, distant voice echoed, spectral and jangly from the heating pipe.

Paul turned from the kiss toward the pipe. "What was that sound?"

Atlee didn't move at first. His head remained tilted toward Paul and his eyes stayed fixed on him as though he hadn't heard anything at all. Then, with an almost languid slowness, he leaned back, exhaling through his nose.

"It's nothing, I'm sure. At least, nothing important—certainly not now—in this precious moment."

"No, I heard something." Paul scooted a few feet closer. "It came up the pipe from downstairs."

Atlee's fingers tapped once against his knee before he pushed himself upright with a measured ease, but there was the slightest tautness to his movements. He groaned a little.

"The pipes in this building carry noise. Perhaps Jonathan is speaking on the telephone." He ran a hand along the crease of his trouser leg before looking at Paul again, his voice light, offhand. "Is it really so important? Aren't you more interested in what's going on in this room right now?"

"I'm surprised you invited me, Jonathan, seeing how much I gall you."

"I don't hate you—on the contrary, I find you quite…useful. You scratch a certain itch I develop from time to time. Tonight, I thought you could scratch that itch for me."

"Come right off it! You look at me like I'm nothing. Like I'm some cheap whore—not worth the ticket price."

"Your opinion of me is just as low. What's more, you haven't been shy about expressing that opinion in the press and to my friends. By the way, I'd appreciate it if you stopped talking about me so much. The studio might get cold feet."

Paul pressed his ear close to the warm metal to get a better listen. The heat seeped into his skin, a low, steady burn against the lingering chill in his bones. He didn't pull away. Instead, he leaned in further, his fingers splayed on the floor for balance, his whole body drawn toward the muffled voices below.

"Someone is in the apartment with him. Another man. It sounds like an argument. Can you recognize the voice?"

Atlee moved next to him and listened.

"You're a bastard. Everyone thinks you're a swell fella, but I know the truth. You're crookeder than a dog's hind legs."

"Ease up on the insults, (inaudible). There's no reason we cannot be civil with one another. What's past is past, and I've been so generous to you. I suggest a truce. When I've gone off to California, you won't ever see me again…unless of course you (inaudible)."

"What did he say?" asked Paul. "Did he say that pasta is pasta??"

Atlee shook his head. "No, he said the past is the past."

"It sounded like pasta to me."

Atlee snapped back, annoyed. "What sense would that

make?"

"I don't know."

"Don't you dare smile at me, Jonathan."

"I thought you liked my smile."

"I hate it—snide, self-righteous, arrogant. Maybe, I better do the world a favor and wipe it off your beautiful face."

"What is that? What have you got there?"

"I'm sure you've seen a knife before. Let me show it to you real close up."

Paul gripped Atlee's sleeve. "Did he…did he say *a knife*?"

Atlee's mouth opened, but no words came out of it.

"You want to think about this before you do anything rash!"

"I've thought about it plenty. More than you can imagine. Hell, I've dreamed about this."

"They'll…they'll suspect you. Everyone knows you want me dead."

"Brother, half this town wants you dead! And they'll never catch me. Your killer will be a mystery forever. I've got the whole thing planned. When they find your corpse, the door will be locked and the key inside. I'll be long gone. I've thought of everything."

A series of crashes came next, followed by a horrible scream echoing in the wall.

Silence overtook the room. Even the pipe's usual clangs and coughs vanished.

Paul swallowed. "That was—" He hesitated, his eyes flicking to Atlee. "What happened…do you think?"

Atlee exhaled sharply. "It sounded awful. Didn't it?"

"It did."

"It sounded like…"

Paul looked at the pipe, as if expecting another voice to come through, but the only sound was a faint, empty hiss.

Atlee pushed himself up and strode toward the telephone. "I'll…*uh*…call the police."

Paul gasped. "Wait."

"What do you mean *wait*?" Atlee took a sudden step away from the phone. "You don't think I should? Why not?"

Paul wet his lips. "I—" He glanced at the phone, then at Atlee. "I just—"

Atlee watched him carefully. "What?"

Paul's fingers tensed into a fist. "If we call them…won't they come here?"

Atlee tilted his head. "Naturally. They can't investigate what happened downstairs over the telephone. They'll have to go inside the apartment."

"And won't they—" He exhaled, then forced the words out. "What if they ask what I'm doing here? What would I say? What could I say that didn't sound perverted?"

Atlee blinked.

"I mean, I'm—I'm a student," Paul went on. "I'm drinking. It's—it's New Year's, sure, but I—" He stopped again, glancing away. "Won't they think it's strange that we're together? Won't they ask questions?"

Atlee studied him for a long moment. When he responded, his voice was measured. "As far as the police are concerned, we're two friends sharing a quiet evening. They don't care about alcohol—not unless we're the ones selling the stuff." He gave a small, wry smile. "I am certain they will be far more interested in the argument downstairs than the coitus interruptus up here. For goodness sake, I didn't even get your shirt off of you."

Paul shifted. "But… but if they ask questions—" He exhaled. "What if they tell the school? Or—or contact my parents?" His voice lowered. "What if they think something's wrong about me being here?"

Atlee walked back and crouched beside him, his expression calm. "They're not going to care, and even if they do, it's none of their business. Unless…"

"Unless what?"

"Unless there's another reason you don't want them here?"

Paul shook his head right away. "No. No, of course not."

Atlee gave him another long look before standing again. "Good. Let's not waste any more time then."

Atlee picked up the telephone and dialed. His fingers drummed over the table as he spoke crisply and urgently.

"Yes, operator, connect me to the police." *Pause.* "Yes, I need to report an attack." *Pause.* "My neighbor, Jonathan Keltner." *Pause.* "Downstairs. I heard it happen through the heating pipe. There was shouting, an argument, and then a scream." *Pause.* "Because there was mention of a knife just before the scream." *Pause.* "Yes, I know him." *Pause.* "No, I didn't recognize the visitor's voice."

Paul kept his eyes on the carpet. His breathing was shallow, unsatisfying. "It sounded like a fight," he whispered. "Tell her it sounded like a fight."

"The address is 1129 Roscoe Street. First-floor apartment. I'm right above it. There are only three apartments in the building. There's one more above me—a Mr. Paul Kilgus, but he's out of town. You'll want to send someone quickly. It happened a few moments ago, but there hasn't been a sound since it ended." *Pause.* "Yes, we'll be here. What's that? Oh, my friend, Paul Chase, is here with me. He heard the argument too." *Pause.* "Thank you."

Atlee replaced the receiver with a firm click. "There. Now we wait."

Paul stood, rubbing his arms for warmth. "Shouldn't we go down and check on him?"

Atlee let out a short laugh. "Goodness gracious, no. I'm not the type to take on a violent man with a knife. Are you?"

"I just thought we could help."

"The best way we can help is to wait for the police to take charge and tell them everything we know."

Paul hesitated, clenching and unclenching his hands. "I don't know anything."

"I meant the conversation. We can tell them what we heard. I'm sure that will be very helpful. Let's not—"

A knock came at the door.

Paul sucked in a breath and took a step back, his eyes darting toward the entryway.

Atlee didn't move. His fingers remained curled against the table.

The knock came again, sharp and deliberate.

"Who is it?" asked Atlee.

"It's me, Buck. Could you open the door?"

Atlee approached the door and pulled it open.

"Buck?" He blinked, his expression smoothing into something unreadable. "What are you doing here?"

Buck Hollister filled the doorway, his shoulders nearly grazing the frame. His hat dripped with icy rain, and when he pushed it back, damp blond hair clung to his forehead. His jaw, rough with stubble, was set firm, but his pale grey eyes moved back and forth between Atlee and Paul. His heavy wool coat, dark with rain, hung open just enough to reveal a weathered shirt and the outline of a lean, muscular physique.

"Evening, Atlee." Buck's voice was steady, but the weight behind it made it clear he wasn't here for pleasantries. He looked to Paul with far more trepidation. "And you. I know we've already met, but I can't quite square the time and place."

Paul had backed nearly into the corner. He offered his name timidly. "I'm Paul. We met at Linda Veach's party a couple weeks back."

As Buck recalled the memory, he turned pale. The very sight of Paul Chase seemed to suddenly be distasteful to him. He exhaled sharply and turned to Atlee.

"I was supposed to meet Jonathan tonight, but he ain't answering. You know if he's coming back tonight?"

Atlee tilted his head. "We…that is…Paul and I just heard Jonathan talking with someone." He pointed to the wall. "Sound travels quite well through that pipe. Someone was in Jonathan's apartment and they were arguing."

Buck's eyes narrowed. "Someone? Who?"

"We couldn't tell. The voice was so distorted, really rather garbled in parts." He glanced at Paul. "Isn't that right, Paul?"

Paul glanced back at Atlee. "Whoever it was, it—it didn't sound good. It sounded… like…"

Buck let out a humorless chuckle. "Like what?"

"Like an argument that got out of control. It sounded like a murder."

Buck's smile faded. "You're shitting me." Without another word, he headed back down the stairs, boots striking the wood with purpose.

Atlee ran forward, but halted just at the turn of the staircase. He leaned over and shouted. "You shouldn't go down there. We called the police. They'll be here any minute."

Buck didn't so much as pause. He reached Jonathan's apartment and tried the knob. When it didn't give, he banged on the door.

He yelled up, "It's locked!"

His knuckles rapped hard against the wood, each knock ringing through the hallway. "Jonathan!" The hail outside rattled against the window panes, filling the silence between each unanswered call.

Atlee ran back inside his apartment. "Paul, come out and stand next to me."

Paul didn't move. "What if Buck was the guy with the knife? The voice was all mangled in the pipe. I can't tell if that was him or not. He could be pretending like he just arrived. You know, for an alibi."

"We can keep an eye on him together until the police come." He took Paul by the hand. "For God's sake, don't let me go down there alone with that gorilla. He could rip me apart with one hand."

Buck kept pounding on the door, each knock cracking sharply against the silence.

"Jonathan, I know you're home!"

His breath was audible now, uneven, his shoulders rising and falling with each word. He pressed his ear to the door. Rain drummed against the windows at the end of the hall, a steady, maddening rhythm.

"You asked me to come over. The least you can do is answer. Now, open the damn door!""

Atlee and Paul had stopped half-way down the stairs, perched far enough away for an escape back to the apartment.

Atlee rubbed nervously at his throat. "Buck, I don't think you understand the situation. The fight we heard sounded incredibly violent. Jonathan mentioned a knife."

"A knife?" Buck backed away from the door.

"At this point, there's no sense in getting ourselves killed."

"Did you hear the door open after the argument?" asked Buck.

Atlee shook his head.

"Well, then, if the door wasn't opened then the fella who attacked Jonathan must *still* be inside. I reckon that follows, don't it? There's no back door. We can help him. We can save him."

A scuffle of boots and a sharp bark of protest echoed from the vestibule. Two uniformed officers burst through the outer door. They were dragging a stout, red-cheeked man between them.

The man yanked against their grip, his voice dripping with indignation. "This is outrageous! You've got nothing better to do than harass law-abiding citizens?" He wrenched himself free and wiped at his forehead, his expression equal parts contemptuous and frightful. "I've never been treated with such disrespect."

Atlee recognized the man immediately. "Max? Why in God's name are you here?"

Buck knew him too. "Yeah, Max. What are you doing here?"

The officer nearest them, a lean man with a weathered face said, "Sorry to bother you folks. I'm Officer Burns" He nodded at his partner. "That's Officer Benedict. We caught this man lurking in the bushes outside. Thought we ought to ask if you knew him. I take it from your words that you do."

Atlee crossed his arms. "That's Max Medwick. He's the theatre critic for the Chicago Tribune."

"When he isn't busy spreading gossip," added Buck.

Max sniffed and straightened his sodden coat. "As I was explaining to these two numbskulls, I was not hiding in the bushes. I pulled my gloves out from inside my pockets and my keys went flying into the bush. I was merely trying to recover them. And I'm also the film critic for the Tribune."

"That tracks—you hiding in those bushes outside," Buck deadpanned. "It would take a whole hedgerow to hide your fat butt."

The second officer, Benedict, asked, "Say, what's going on here? Why are the three of you standing in the hallway?"

Atlee hesitated, then gestured toward the door to Jonathan's apartment. "Well, officers, I don't know why Max is here, but we have more pressing concerns. My name is Atlee Burrough. This is my student Paul Chase, and this is my former student Buck Hollister. We were upstairs when we heard a violent argument from inside this apartment—there was shouting, a scream, mention of a knife. We called the police immediately. The man who lives here is Jonathan Keltner and…and he doesn't seem to be answering the door."

"Right." Burns directed Buck to move and squared his shoulders, stepping toward the door. He rapped hard. "Mr. Keltner! Chicago Police! Open up!"

Silence.

He tried again, knocking louder. Still nothing. He motioned toward Benedict, who drew his revolver. Burns took a step back, setting his stance. The first blow of his shoulder sent a shudder through the frame.

"It's not strong and it isn't latched. This thing's coming down."

The second thrust broke it wide open.

The scene inside the room was instantly baffling. Just beyond the threshold lay a crumpled pile of celluloid strips tangled like discarded ribbons, their slick surface catching the dim light. Beside the pile lay an envelope.

The apartment was sparsely furnished: a rich leather chair positioned at a dark wooden desk. To the right, the radiator hissed beside the heating pipe. Its low, steady breath filled the silence. There was a large rectangular ghost print in the center of the room. The area rug that had once covered the spot was now wrapped up under the radiator. Inside was a body.

Burns announced aloud what everyone could see.

"Jesus Christ, there's a guy wrapped up in the rug." He called out. "Are you all right, sir?"

The man gave no answer.

The officer approached, crouching to tug back the edge of the rug. The dim light caught a ripple in the fabric—a sharp ridge above the chest. His fingers brushed the spot. Underneath, something solid. Something buried deep. The top of the head was cold to the touch. He folded the top corners down to reveal a dead man's face.

"Hoo boy." He exhaled, straightened, and walked back to the door. He reached out and flicked the light switch. A harsh glow flooded the room.

Atlee and Buck stood just outside the door. Max and Paul lingered behind them, catching glimpses over their shoulders.

Burns fixed them with a steady look. "Gentlemen, is that Jonathan Keltner wrapped up in the rug?"

They all nodded in unison.

The officer performed a quick search. No one else was in the apartment. When he returned to the door, he reached behind it and pulled the key from the keyhole.

"The door was locked from the inside." He stared at the key as if its dull brass would provide some sort of rational explanation for the problem.

He walked to the desk with a heavy sigh and picked up the telephone.

"Are you calling it in?" asked Benedict.

"No. These folks already did. I'm calling The Brown Bear Bar."

"Why?"

"I was there just before we started our shift. Rowan

Manory and his partner were having a drink. Maybe they're still there. Maybe they can make sense of this."

The detectives had gotten a slow start to their New Year's Eve celebration. A cup of coffee and the promise of a tantalizing puzzle sobered them up. Soon, they were at the crime scene.

The first clue, as in every murder case, was the corpse. The rug was now rolled open, revealing Jonathan Keltner's lifeless form beside the radiator. His skin was pale with the dull, waxy cast of death. He had been a handsome man not too long ago; that much was still evident from his bone structure. His final expression, however, was frightful, frozen in something just past agony.

The anguish on display was due, no doubt, to the knife embedded in the man's chest.

"It's an outdoor knife," said Rowan. "A trapper's blade."

Walter cocked his head. "Odd choice for a murder weapon. We usually see jackknives or stilettos."

Officer Burns stood behind them, trying not to interfere, but willing to offer any assistance. "We've got forensics on the way."

Rowan gave a soft, defeated sigh. "There will be no prints on the knife, Officer."

"How can you tell?"

"The handle is stag horn. Its porous nature causes oil and sweat to be absorbed."

Jonathan's clothing—elegant but casual—spoke of his short time in Hollywood. He wore a finely tailored, double-breasted vest over a soft silk shirt, the collar pinned down with a delicate gold bar. His trousers were high-waisted, sharply pressed, the cuffs breaking just right over his polished two-tone Oxford shoes. A well-cut overcoat, now askew from the struggle, lay open over him like a shroud.

The only item in the man's pockets was a piece of newspaper, an unwrinkled, finely-preserved clipping of a scathing review. Rowan was taken aback by the nastiness of the critique.

"My goodness."

Walter read it over Rowan's shoulder. "I guess he wasn't a fan."

Rowan slipped the paper into an evidence envelope. "Officer, didn't you tell me one of the individuals found at the scene was a critic."

Burns nodded. "Max Medwick. He works for the Chicago Tribune. Film and theatre."

Rowan stood from his crouched position and leaned back on his heels, studying the scene again. "Talk to me, Burns. What do you think about this scene? What questions do you have?"

He motioned to the rug. "My partner and I had an idea about why the killer wrapped him up in the rug."

"Don't be shy, Officer. Let's hear it."

"Most times a body's wrapped in a rug—it's for transport. The killer probably meant to move him, but something stopped him. Maybe he ran out of time."

Rowan considered this. He looked toward the back of the room. "There is no back door?"

Burns shook his head. "No."

"And the three windows in the apartment are all fixed?"

"Fixed?" asked Burns, confused by the term.

"I mean to say that they cannot be opened."

Burns nodded. "That's right. None of the three windows can be opened."

"So, the only way to transport the body is through that door," Rowan said, glancing toward the broken frame.

"Yes."

"The door which the killer somehow locked from the outside?"

Burns started to speak but stopped himself, his brow furrowing

Rowan continued. "Thereby locking the body inside as well. But you think the killer was interested in transporting the body."

As the logic seeped in, the officer turned red. "I'll…*uh* shut up now."

Walter clapped Burns on the shoulder. "Manory makes me look stupid all the time." He whispered loudly. *"I think he enjoys it."*

The only footprints that were readily visible belonged to Burns. Their damp outlines stretched from the doorway toward the body and through the kitchen, bedroom, and bathroom. The edges had begun to fade, drying unevenly, leaving behind a patchwork of footprints—some still slick, others reduced to a ghostly outline.

Rowan's attention turned to the mess of film strips scattered across the floor. Dozens—perhaps a hundred—lay in a tangle, each one folded in half and twisted into thin, warped ribbons. The glossy surface of the celluloid caught the light, but the usual flickers of shadow and image were absent.

Reaching down, Rowan plucked one from the heap. With careful fingers, he unfurled it, smoothing the crimped plastic between thumb and forefinger. There was a man's face on the frame.

"He looks familiar, doesn't he?"

Walter held up the strip to the light and let out a low whistle. "That's our stiff. Strange," he murmured. "Keltner was about to star in a picture, wasn't he? Do you think this is a message?"

Rowan straightened, brushing dust from his knees. "It seems to me that many of the elements in this room were meant to be messages, some of them painfully obvious."

Rowan's gaze drifted toward the doorway. The jamb was splintered, the brass strike plate bent outward where Officer Burns had forced entry. The latch bolt, now warped and misshapen, jutted at an awkward angle, half-embedded in the ruined wood of the frame. A rough break in the grain marked where the force of impact had driven it deeper before

twisting it out of place.

He tried to turn the doorknob. It didn't budge. Not from resistance, not from the catch of an interior lock—simply frozen in place. The damage had jammed the lock, rendering the latch bolt immovable.

Rowan smiled. *How convenient.* "Officer Burns, you are sure you found the key inside the keyhole."

"Hundred percent, yes."

"Is there any way that one of the persons of interest could have secretly replaced it after you knocked down the door?"

"No chance, Detective. They never crossed the threshold. My partner was watching them the whole time."

Walter looked up from his notebook. "Would that be Officer Bent-his-dick?"

"No. His name is Benedict."

"Yeah, I know."

"Oh. *Oh!*" Burns laughed helplessly. "That's a good one."

Walter nodded. "I know."

Rowan rolled himself a fast cigarette and lit it. "You mentioned an envelope."

"Yes. We found this letter inside. It's typed and without a signature." He handed Rowan the letter.

Rowan and Walter read it silently. Rowan clucked his tongue. "Officer Burns, I believe we are done with this portion of the investigation. Have you contacted the landlord?"

Burns nodded. "Yes, sir. He knows everything that happened here. We also got his spare set of keys."

Rowan tapped ash from his cigarette. "Good. I'll use the apartment on the third floor for my interrogations."

Burns frowned. "Interrogations?"

Rowan's gaze lingered on the body one last time before he turned for the stairs. "Yes. The killer is upstairs."

Rowan sat across from Atlee Burroughs at the small kitchen table in the vacant third-floor apartment. He exhaled a thin ribbon of smoke, watching it curl toward the ceiling. Walter stood by the refrigerator, his notebook at the ready.

Atlee puffed at his pipe, the embers briefly flaring before settling into a steady glow.

"I've read much about you, Mr. Rowan Manory. I dare say you are one of the great lions of Chicago. It would be impossible for one born and bred here to not know your name."

Rowan hummed with approval. "It isn't flattery if it's true."

"Of course, it isn't just Chicago. You're famous overseas."

"Is that so?"

"For the last two weeks, I've been hosting a workshop for a group of British students from the Royal Academy of Dramatic Art. They asked me if I had ever met you. A shame they're all leaving on a train for the coast tonight, I could have told them about this over breakfast."

"You are a teacher, Mr. Burroughs?"

"Primarily, I'm a director, but I am also a teacher." He looked away, the corners of his mouth turning rigid. "At the moment, I'm without work, so teaching is necessary." He shook his head. "Art is notorious for failing to pay the bills. I would say I am a struggling artist forced to teach."

"You do not enjoy it?"

"Oh, I wouldn't put it quite that negatively. Teaching has given me the opportunity to work with young people, to see talent in its rawest form." He gestured absently with his pipe. "My students keep me feeling young. Of course, the relationships I've had directing actors have been equally satisfying."

"Such as the one you had with Jonathan Keltner."

"A remarkable actor—one of the best I've ever had the privilege to direct." He frowned. "I suppose I must use the past tense when referring to him now."

"Was Mr. Keltner also a student of yours?"

Atlee chuckled. "At my age, I've taught most of the great actors working in Chicago. It's probably considered a rite of passage to sit in my class and listen to me pretending to know what I'm talking about."

"Were you and Jonathan friends? Did you spend time together away from the stage?"

Atlee smiled, but it didn't quite reach his eyes. "Our friendship had seen its better days. It turned into something casual—easygoing. We got on well enough. No expectations, no drama."

"You lived one floor apart. You must have seen him nearly every day."

"I introduced him to the landlord when the first-floor apartment became available. But that was only because I knew he would approve. The rates are quite reasonable. When Jonathan and I were working together regularly, it was quite convenient to live so close by. We could rehearse whenever we wanted…or enjoy one another's company." Atlee shifted in his chair. "And there's plenty of storage in the basement. The benefits are…are…many."

Walter looked up from his notepad. "So, were you guys still friends or…?"

"Yes. Yes, we were friendly. No bad blood. But he was moving to Hollywood and I wasn't about to go with him. I have no interest in the cinema."

"Did he invite you to join him?"

"No. Why would he?"

Rowan didn't answer. "Did Mr. Keltner have any enemies?"

Atlee gave a sharp nod. "Jonathan had no shortage of admirers, and, as is so often the case, admiration can curdle into something less pleasant. Two of them are sitting in my apartment at this very moment. That is to say they are one-time admirers who went on to harbor at least some measure of contempt for Jonathan."

"They are…" Rowan snapped his fingers.

Walter replied, "Buck Hollister and Max Medwick?"

"Correct," said Atlee. "Buck clearly had the stronger animus against Jonathan. That's my opinion of course you can take it with a grain or a truckload of salt. Buck was a troubled student with a bad attitude and even worse manners. Jonathan landed many of the roles Buck auditioned for—the kind tailor-made for a self-described tough guy like him."

"I take it Buck wasn't nearly as successful as Jonathan."

"That's quite true. It was a matter of attitude more than talent. Jonathan's genteel nature made him agreeable to direction. Buck despises direction. He is also far pointed in his assessments. Imagine criticizing the director during an audition. Buck was envious of Jonathan's success, and he felt himself far more deserving of Jonathan's accolades. When you speak with Buck, he'll deny it, I'm sure. He'll tell you that Jonathan was a phony, someone who sold out his talent. It's a smokescreen."

"Criticism often is. Speaking of that, what can you tell me about Max Medwick's relationship with Jonathan?"

"Complicated."

"How so?"

"Max has a habit of discovering talent just to tear it down. There are several artists he has buttered up only to later loathe with all his corpulence. Jonathan was but one of them. Max championed Jonathan's work early on. I believe they were even friendly. Atlee attempted to direct a film once and Jonathan agreed to star. Nothing ever came of it other than some raw footage. The project's failure only served to make Max bitter."

"Did he blame Jonathan for the film's failure?"

"He certainly wasn't going to blame himself. After that, Max wrote brutal notices of all Jonathan's work…" He paused, pressing his lips together. "All *our* work. Jonathan didn't care. He was quite immune to criticism."

Rowan's eyes dilated. "Are you quite sure of that?"

"Oh, yes. Jonathan believed in himself. It was one of his most attractive qualities." Atlee waggled his brows. "Confidence is moxie, don't you know?"

"Do you think Jonathan's recent foray into Hollywood might have angered Max even more?"

"I have no doubt about it. Max has dreams about success

in Hollywood."

"And you, Mr. Burroughs—were you jealous of Jonathan's success?"

"Everyone is jealous of success, Detective. But I'm rational about it. Jonathan was good looking and charming. It's only natural for good things to happen to him."

"I see." Rowan nodded in admittance. "Let's get a timeline down. Walk me through the evening."

Atlee leaned back, gathering his thoughts. "Paul Chase—the young man downstairs—and I had plans to celebrate New Year's together. The poor thing—he told me was all alone for the holiday, so I invited him."

"A very kind gesture. He's a student of yours?"

"Yes. He arrived at about ten after seven. The boy was completely soaked and shivering from the ice storm. I had him sit by the radiator to warm up. We were chatting over some good champagne, and not long after, we heard two voices travelling up the pipe."

Rowan pointed to the pipe in Mr. Kilgus's living room. "Are you certain the noise couldn't have come from above you—from this apartment?"

"Absolutely. The directionality of the noise was obvious. If you test the pipe, you'll see for yourself."

"Were the voices recognizable?"

"No, they were distorted. But most of the words were clear. The second voice—I mean to say the visitor—called the other man Jonathan. That's how I knew who was who. He said something about galling him—I remember that because I thought, *who says galled anymore*?"

"Who galled whom?"

"The visitor said that Jonathan was galled and Jonathan disagreed. They argued back and forth a bit about who hated whom more. It was quite the dramatic display of machismo. I distinctly recall the visitor saying that Jonathan was crookeder than a dog's hind legs." He snorted. "*Crookeder than a dog's hind legs.* That was a new one for me—I've heard plenty in my time, but never that. I tell you—"

"How did Jonathan react?"

"He turned snider, believe it or not. At one point, Jonathan said that the visitor was very useful to Jonathan. I'm not sure what that meant." Atlee's gaze drifted, as if he were suddenly listening to the conversation in the pipe once again. "And…I think Jonathan said that he'd been very generous to the visitor." Atlee paused, frowning slightly, as if the phrase perplexed him. "I suppose he meant financially? Maybe he helped the fellow get work? It struck me as odd at the time, but I didn't have long to dwell on it. Jonathan went on to say that the past was the past and he called for a truce. The visitor wasn't having any of it. He pulled a knife."

"How do you know he pulled a knife?"

"*'What have you got there?'* Jonathan asked, and then the man answered. *'A knife.'* Just like that. Cold. Final. Before the sound of the struggle, the visitor said he would never be caught and the police would find a dead body inside a locked room. Then came the scream, a dreadful noise, one I soon won't forget. I called the police. Buck arrived shortly after. When the police got there, they brought Max inside. I can't say anything definitive regarding their whereabouts before seeing them."

"Did you hear anything else after the conversation ended? Scurrying? Movement?"

"Nothing."

"How long between the voices and Buck's arrival?"

"Not long. A few minutes at most. Both Paul and I noticed how close it was to the murder. We didn't say it, but we felt it. Something about the timing—a little too convenient."

"I see." Rowan stamped out his half-smoked cigarette. "The last matter I wish to discuss with you is rather delicate. There was an envelope found in the apartment. It was lying just inside the door next to all those celluloid strips."

Atlee leaned forward. "I noticed that. What was inside?"

"An anonymous typed letter addressed to Jonathan."

Rowan set it on the kitchen table. "Please read it."

Atlee squinted at the paper. "Damn it," he whispered, plucking the glasses from his breast pocket. "Vision is the first thing to go."

"Take your time, sir." Rowan rolled another cigarette, his gaze never leaving Atlee. He noted the twisting of Atlee's face, how his expression slowly turned to horror as he moved down the page.

Atlee looked up at the detective. He whispered, "That's disgusting."

"Did you type it?"

"If you think I would blackmail anyone based on their… inclinations, then your deductive reasoning isn't worth a good God damn—pardon my French. I am not perfect. No one is." He tapped the note furiously. "But I would never stoop this low. And may I say that I do not care of your opinion of me, Mr. Manory."

"You mean of your inclinations?"

"That's right. You can keep your judgment to yourself."

"Were you in love with Jonathan?"

He stammered for a moment, but the previous burst of righteous indignation carried him over this particular hurdle. "At one point, yes. That's another reason I could not do this. I had far too much respect for the man. We may have lost our passion for one another, but we never lost respect."

Rowan watched him carefully. He lit his cigarette and took a slow drag. The ember flared and then dimmed. Finally, he exhaled and said, simply, "Okay."

Atlee blinked. "Okay? That's all you have to say?"

"Yes, Mr. Burroughs. I asked you a question, and I'm satisfied with your answer." Rowan waved a hand. "You can go downstairs and wait in your apartment. Please send up your young friend, Paul."

Atlee stood, adjusting his coat. "Good. I'm glad that's over with." Just as he reached for the doorknob, Rowan's voice stopped him.

"One more thing. Do you make a habit of hosting your

students? Giving them drinks and spending time with them alone."

Atlee's smile returned, lighter this time. "I have a nice apartment and I enjoy good company. It isn't a crime, is it? The boy is of age."

Rowan ignored the question. "You did the same with Jonathan, didn't you?"

Atlee nodded. "I'm sure I did."

Rowan smiled thinly. "Thank you, Mr. Burroughs."

Paul Chase looked like a rabbit in a snare—wide-eyed, pale, his hands gripping the edge of the table as though it might keep him from slinking to the floor.

"I don't know what I could possibly tell you that Atlee didn't. We heard the same exact thing and we were both together in his apartment."

Rowan kept his voice low and measured. "Witnesses often recall the same event differently. I can't tell you how many times three people have seen the same gunman and described completely different coat colors—one blue, one red, and one beige. Moreover, I don't want you to worry about what Atlee told me. Just tell me the facts as best you can." He narrowed his eyes. "Are you all right, Paul?"

Paul's lips sealed and jutted forward. He took a violent breath through his nose, then lurched to his feet, stumbling toward the sink. He didn't make it. The retching was violent, and the thin excuse for a meal he'd had earlier came up in an ugly mess on the kitchen floor.

"Jesus," Rowan muttered, pushing back from the table.

As Paul bolted for the toilet, Walter grabbed a kitchen towel. That, however, was the extent of his reaction. He stood, helplessly staring at the mess.

"This is not…not my job." He tossed the towel atop the mess. "Let's get the hell out of here." As the young man dry heaved for a few minutes, the detectives moved into the living room.

When Paul returned, he looked more mortified than ill.

"I'm sorry," he mumbled. "I drank some rotgut earlier. I think it finally caught up with me."

Walter chuckled. "Sounds like a drink that lives up to its name. Tell me, why would anybody drink something called rotgut?"

Rowan didn't find it amusing. "More importantly, why did you drink it before coming to Atlee's?"

Paul stuttered. "Someone offered, and I just… took it"

"Were you nervous about this evening? Did you have to steel your nerves before coming here?"

Paul gave a quick shake of his head, but his fingers tapped a frantic rhythm against his knee. "I wanted to try it. That's all."

Rowan looked him up and down. "Are you feeling better? Do you think you can continue?"

"I'll do my best."

"Very well. Did you know the victim, Jonathan Keltner?"

"Not personally, but I knew of him. He's an actor and he was going to star in a moving picture for Paramount. Atlee directed him in a few plays. I saw one of them. That's the long and short of it."

"And Buck Hollister?"

"I met him once at a party a few weeks back. We actually talked for more than a spell. He recognized me when he came to Atlee's tonight, but he didn't remember my name—no reason he should. I'm not famous or nothing."

"You're young. There's plenty of time."

Paul nodded. "Maybe."

"What did you discuss at the party?"

"Just small talk. He said the Goodman was a good program, and—um—oh yeah, his mother. He mentioned that she was a writer. He told me I might know her, but I didn't."

"That would be Victoria Hollister?"

"Yeah. She writes murder mysteries."

Rowan nodded softly. "I know."

"I picked up one of her books, just in case I ran into Buck

again. I figured it would…I don't know…impress him. No. That ain't the right word. I thought he would like me and…"

"You thought he could possibly open some doors for your budding career. Reading his mother's book would give you something to talk about."

"Yeah, that's it. I didn't expect anything to happen."

"Which book?"

"Huh?"

"Which book of hers did you purchase?"

"*The Glass Dagger*."

A small, subtle tension developed at the corners of Rowan's mouth. "And what did you think of it?"

"I haven't read it yet."

Walter said, "You're probably spending too much time drinking rotgut."

Paul grinned. "I only have that once in a while, Mr. Williams."

Rowan took a drag from his cigarette. "I thought tonight was the first time you tried it."

The grin vanished. "I meant… I meant that batch. The latest one. The guy who makes it keeps changing the recipe."

"And Max Medwick—had you met him before this evening?"

"Yeah. He was at that same party, but we never talked and I'm sure he doesn't remember me at all; he was drunker than a skunk. He kept going on and on about a script he wrote. The producer he sent it to didn't get back to him, and Max was sore about it. He said they don't know about real talent. He was really loud."

"Tell me about this evening—everything you remember."

Paul ran a hand through his hair, still damp from the ice storm.

"I got here a little late. Atlee told me to come at 7:00. He gave me the bus schedule, but I missed it, so I took the 'L'. The storm started right when I got off. The stop is about four blocks away. By the time I got here, I was soaked to the bone. Atlee left the front entrance unlocked. I ran up to the top floor as fast as I could, and he let me in." Paul shrugged. "I was getting warm by the radiator when I heard the voice."

"What was the conversation about?"

Paul's face tightened in concentration. "The sound was all brassy, hard to tell what they were saying exactly. The killer—at least, I assume it was him—said Jonathan had been bad-mouthing him. Jonathan accused the killer of the doing the same thing. To be honest, when I heard that, I thought of Max immediately because Max was saying bad things about Jonathan at the party. He said things that were close to what I heard in the pipe like how Jonathan was ungrateful and he was wasting his talent." He looked up. "I can't say it was definitely Max because the voice was distorted, but it wouldn't surprise me."

"We appreciate your opinion. Please continue."

"The killer said something…some insult, I think"

Rowan snapped his fingers and Walter flipped back in his notes. "*Crookeder than a dog's hind legs*?"

"That's it. I remember thinking that it was something my grandfather might say." He furrowed his brow in thought. "Didn't sound like Chicago talk to me. Then, Jonathan said something really strange. Something about *pasta*."

Rowan mirrored Paul's confusion. "*Pasta?* As in spaghetti or ravioli?"

"I think that's what he said. I thought maybe it was some kind of nickname or code… but it didn't make sense. In fact, he said it twice. And there was a point when Jonathan probably said the guy's name, I remember that clearly. Atlee and me couldn't hear it because the pipe clanged right when he said it. Atlee thought the guy said *the past is the* past, but I heard him. He said *pasta* two times."

"You seem quite sure of that."

"I am. Atlee heard it wrong." He nodded, as if trying to convince himself.

"All right. What happened after that?"

"The killer said he was going to wipe Jonathan's smile off his face. Jonathan asked him what he was holding, and the guy told him it was a knife. The killer gave a whole speech about the cops finding Jonathan's dead body in a locked room with the killer gone. Then…then it happened."

"*What* happened?"

"We heard a scream and Atlee called the cops." Paul thought for a moment. "Oh yeah, I forgot something. Jonathan said, *'Everybody knows you want me dead!'* The killer replied that everybody wanted Jonathan dead. It was like he was saying that no one would ever guess his identity because there would be too many suspects."

Rowan took his time thinking it over. "Who heard the voices first?"

"I did. It got my attention right away because Atlee and I were talking about Jonathan just before it all happened."

"Why were you discussing Jonathan?"

"I can't even remember."

"Try."

"Maybe Atlee brought him up as an example of a successful student he had. My memory's really fuzzy. Maybe I brought him up. I don't know."

"Too much rotgut?" asked Walter.

"Maybe, maybe."

Rowan asked, "Did Atlee invite you here tonight, or did you suggest coming over?"

"He invited me."

"Atlee told me you said you were alone, that you had nowhere to go for New Year's Eve. Is that the case?"

Paul nodded. "I haven't been in Chicago long. I'm from a farm down south. I know people, but none I'd call a good friend."

"Whereabouts down south?"

"Hallidayboro."

"Sounds like one of those places you pass through and don't even realize," said Walter. "What's your parents' telephone number?"

"Hallidayboro 237. Why? Do you need to call them?"

Walter barely shook his head. "Just in case."

"Just in case of what?"

Rowan answered. "Just in case we need to call them. I think those are all the questions we have at this time, Paul. When you return downstairs, please ask Buck to join us."

Buck's sleeves were rolled up, exposing thick, corded forearms, and now that his hair had dried, it was a sandy brown rather than the near-black it had appeared in the storm. His face, sun-creased and shadowed with stubble, had regained its color, though his pale gray eyes remained restless.

Rowan took in the scent of him—wet wool, stale cigarette smoke, and something sharp beneath it. Cologne. Strong. He made a note of that. He was a smoker himself, but his sense of smell was impeccable. As a detective, smell was just as important as the other senses. Years of practice let him separate scents like notes in a melody.

"Mr. Hollister—"

"Buck."

"Very well then—Buck. During my short time interviewing Atlee and Paul, I've grown quite intrigued by the relationships of you five men. I believe the solution to this murder lies somewhere within those relationships. Tell me—how do you know the others?"

Buck straightened up. His jaw flexed. "I'm not one of them. I want you to get that straight in your head right now. Let's not be confused, you and me."

"Pardon?"

"I'm not queer."

Walter, without looking up from his notes, muttered, "I just wrote it down. We will never be confused about it again."

Rowan tilted his head slightly. "Are you saying that the other three are?"

Buck huffed. "Queerer than a three-dollar bill."

"And Jonathan? Was he queer too?"

Buck hesitated…*too long*. It was barely a few seconds, but Rowan could have counted the spaces between heartbeats. The pause said more than any answer could.

At last, he muttered, "I don't know. I didn't know Jonathan well enough. Coulda been. Hell, I never asked, and he never told. Not my business."

It was so insincere it may as well have been a confession. Rowan let the ineffectual words sit between them for a moment before moving on. "Tell me about Paul."

Buck blinked as if caught off guard. "Paul?"

"Yes, Atlee's young friend. How well do you know him?"

"I don't." He rubbed his fingers along his jaw. "Met him once at a party. That's it. He never met Jonathan as far as I know."

"You recognized him when you arrived at Atlee's apartment, yet you didn't say anything. Why not?"

"Well, damn—I was surprised to see the kid. You see, I warned him to stay away from Atlee. I was awfully specific about it."

Rowan's expression didn't change. "Warned him?"

"Yeah." Buck leaned forward. "Atlee's a creep. He likes young guys—his students. Takes advantage of them. Gets 'em drunk, pretty soon he's got his hand in their pants. Even worse, he'll tell 'em what great talent they've got even if they ain't got any. Now, I never seen the kid act, maybe he's the cat's particulars and maybe he ain't, but I'm sure Atlee's spent plenty of time butterin' him up for dinner. If you follow my drift."

Rowan nodded. "I do." He remembered back to Paul's testimony.

The young man had been warned of Atlee's predatory nature. And what did he do? He told Atlee he was lonely and accepted an invitation to his home.

"And you?" Rowan asked. "Were you one of Atlee's students?"

Buck's mouth pulled tight. "Yeah." He said it without flavor, without color—like a man grimly pronouncing a death sentence.

"Did he make similar advances toward you?"

Buck's expression darkened even more. "He tried." He flexed his fingers. "I laid him out. So, he never tried again. He's hated me ever since. I bet he told you lots of nasty things about me, didn't he?"

Rowan smiled faintly, but he didn't answer the questions. "I take it then that you and Atlee are not on speaking terms."

"Not if I can help it. I only knocked on his door to see if he knew where Jonathan was. Believe me, I never wanted to go into that apartment again."

"What about Max?" Rowan continued.

Buck scoffed. "What about him?"

"What is your opinion of him?"

"He's a leech." Buck shrugged. "Doesn't create. He just tears down. Fancies himself an artist, but he ain't. Nobody likes him. He's got that fancy job with the paper because he's got a talent for cruelty—straight shooter with a crooked trail. If you know what I—"

"Yes, I follow. And Jonathan?"

Something about Buck's demeanor shifted again. The restlessness returned.

"We were friendly," he said carefully. "But he ran in circles higher than mine. He was successful and…and I wasn't. That changes things. We weren't equals. I couldn't help but feel he talked down to me even if he wasn't trying to do it."

"Why did you come to his apartment tonight?"

Buck's hand twitched before he rubbed his thumb along the bridge of his nose. "Dunno."

Walter arched a brow. "Not sure I can even write that down in my notebook without an explanation, Buck. It doesn't make much sense."

"Jonathan told me he wanted to talk. I didn't know what it

was about. He called me this morning."

That same tic again. The slight hesitation. The twitch at his nose. It was the same reaction he'd had when Rowan asked if Jonathan was queer. Buck Hollister was a terrible liar.

"And your timeline?" Rowan prompted.

Buck exhaled. "Had an audition for Randolph Cuyler at seven o'clock. He's a friend of Atlee's. Lots of folks didn't show up, so I was able to audition sooner than expected. Jonathan asked me to be here by seven forty-five. I got here early—about seven-twenty."

"How did you get here?"

"I walked. I walk everywhere I go. I was a little ornery I didn't take a cab on account of the ice storm. Walking's cheaper though."

"And then?"

"Then what?"

"What happened after you arrived?"

"You already know what happened." Buck exhaled sharply through his nose and shifted again. "I knocked on Jonathan's door. No answer. Door was locked. So, I went upstairs to Atlee's. He told me about the argument he heard. Then I went back down to…to check on him. That's then the cops came, and—well." He made a vague gesture. "The cops told you the rest."

Rowan took a long drag off his cigarette. He flicked at the frayed end with his thumb. "It seems to me, Buck, that you aren't being entirely truthful with me."

"About what?"

"Jonathan," said Rowan flatly.

"So that's it. You think I did it."

"I am far from naming you as the killer."

"Don't try to sell me vinegar for whiskey. I know how it looks. They hear him killed and I show up a few minutes later."

"Do you know anyone who wanted Jonathan dead?"

"No."

"Not even out of jealousy?"

"Look, he got certain roles that I—well, I shoulda got some of 'em. It's laughable. Jonathan was a pansy. I'm tougher than he ever was. You can be the best fighter in the room, but if you don't show it on stage, it don't matter. They just want you to be what they think you are. When I get cast, it's always the rube, the dumb hick who doesn't talk much. It's because I look the part and...and I don't talk much, I guess. Every director thinks I'm from some backwater town down south, that I'm stupider than shit. Does that make me angry? Yeah, it burns me up. But that don't make me a killer."

Rowan smiled faintly. "But you're not from the South. You're from Colorado."

Buck narrowed his eyes. "How'd you know that?"

"Your mother's a writer. A rather good one. I read her short biography on the about-the-author page of *The Glass Dagger*—that locked-room mystery she wrote. Your mother grew up on a ranch in Colorado. And so did you. You have two brothers. Your father's deceased."

"She wrote all that in there?"

Rowan nodded. "You haven't read the book?"

Buck grunted. "I've never read any of her books. I don't like murder mysteries."

"A shame. That one had a rather clever locked-room murder. Not so different from the one performed tonight." Rowan pretended to study his nails. "Do you own any knives, Buck?"

He shook his head in confusion, but answered in the affirmative. "A few. Why?"

"What kind?"

"Trapper knives...camp knives. Where I grew up they came with the territory."

"What kind of handle do you like?"

"Stag horn. They don't slip and they last forever."

"That's what I thought."

Max Medwick's sweat had suffused his collar. His ill-fitting suit clung to him in all the wrong places, and the stifling heat flushed his jowls, leaving them slick with moisture. Still, he smirked, radiating the same self-righteousness he carried in his reviews, as if every word he spoke was a decree from on high.

"I came here tonight to say goodbye to Jonathan. The news about the film was well-known. He had been out of town for several weeks. When I learned he was back in Chicago, I set aside some time to see him."

Just as he had done with the other interrogatees, Rowan let the silence stretch, inviting the other man to fill in the blank.

"Detective, you can play this game all you want. My story will not change."

Rowan reached into the evidence envelope, withdrew the newspaper clipping, and smoothed the sharp folds against his knee before reading aloud in a dry monotone.

"Keltner's performance was a hollow imitation of talent, his presence an offense to the stage he once graced with delicate characterization. The man should reconsider his profession before audiences are forced to endure another of his so-called performances."

He placed the article on the table and slid it toward Max. "That clipping was found inside Jonathan Keltner's pocket."

Max glanced down at the scrap, the smirk never leaving his lips.

"I'm flattered."

"How's that?"

"It's obvious that Jonathan felt highly of my opinion—enough to carry it with him wherever he went. Perhaps he intended to take the constructive criticism to heart."

Rowan's expression turned to stone. "I find it difficult to believe that his performance—the very one that got him an audition for a Hollywood film—was objectively this awful."

"There's no need for me to coddle anyone." Max scoffed. "I don't review elementary school plays. I work with artists striving for perfection. What you've got here," he said, tapping the clipping, "is pure honesty. That is the precise impression I had of his performance and I relayed that to my readers faithfully. If you take the time to read the rest of the review, you'll find that my main concern was the subject matter. Gangsterism is a disease, but Atlee's dreadful production treated it as heroism." He lifted his brows triumphantly. "I gave significant kudos to Arnie Campaneris, the production designer. His sets were outstanding, though certainly not enough to rescue this particular Titanic from sinking."

"When did you write this review?"

"June…July…I don't quite recall. Why is that important?"

"It isn't." Rowan refolded the crisp clipping, replaced it, and drummed his fingers against the tabletop before deciding to roll another cigarette. "You've got a certain reputation—lifting unknowns with your so-called 'raves' only to tear them down the moment they taste success."

Max inclined his head ever so slightly, feigning thoughtfulness. "Some artists let success spoil them. They forget what made them great in the first place. They lose focus."

"We found something else in his apartment. A letter. I believe it was slipped under the door."

Max ran his tongue over his lips. They glistened unpleasantly. "I'm sure I know nothing about that."

Rowan retrieved the letter from the evidence envelope and read it to him.

Jonathan—

Hollywood is a fragile dream, isn't it? One wrong step and it crumbles. I wonder if you ever lie awake at night thinking about that. I wonder if you sweat through the sheets imagining what would happen if someone whispered the right words in the right ears.

I know. About you. About your arrangements. About the woman they've given you to keep the cameras flashing and the papers clean. Clever, really. A pretty picture for the world. But pictures can burn, and I wonder what she'd do if she knew. More importantly, I wonder what she'd say.

Don't look for me. You won't find me. Don't ask around. You never know who might start asking questions of their own.

I have no intention of ruining you—not today. But then again, today isn't over yet.

Sleep well.

Max loosened his tie. His mouth opened, then shut. "I..."

Rowan cut him off with a warning tone. "You know, I once worked a case where a blackmailer used a Royal 10 typewriter to craft his threats. The t's were a little off—dropped lower than the other letters. Detectives get to know typewriters pretty well. The unique ones tend to pay off even more than fingerprint analysis. I remember the 't' detail of the Royal 10 like it was yesterday. Before you lie to me, know that I am perfectly willing to have the officers downstairs conduct a search of your home. I'd bet all the kolaczki from Maxwell Street to Milwaukee Avenue that there is a Royal 10 is sitting on your desk right now."

Walter said, "Max, don't you dare underestimate how much Manory loves pastry. He'll do it."

Max exhaled slowly, a bead of sweat tracing its way down his temple. Then, as if deciding there was no point in keeping up appearances, he leaned back, folding his arms across his chest.

"Fine," he muttered. "You want the truth?"

Rowan let out a short, humorless laugh. "This is an interrogation, Mr. Medwick. The truth is precisely what I've been asking for this entire time."

"Jonathan? An ungrateful hack."

"So, you hated him."

"Of course. He…" Max froze, realizing the implications of his own words. "Buck hated him more than I ever did. Go ask him. Ask anyone. Buck went to see his play and walked out before the second act. When I arrived here tonight, Buck was already on the scene. God only knows how long. I heard him upstairs talking to Atlee. I slipped my playful little note under the door and left."

"Playful?"

"And when I saw that the police were coming I tried to get out of their way."

"By jumping in the bushes."

He frowned. "Fine! God dammit, if you insist on every little detail. I realized my note might appear threatening to someone who…who…"

"Who would misunderstand its intentions?"

"Precisely! Thank you."

"You didn't want to kill him."

"No!"

"You only wished to psychologically torture him?"

"Don't put words in my mouth. Buck had a reason to want Jonathan dead."

"Which was?"

Max's expression twisted into something cruel, his upper lip curling over his barely-there mustache.

"Buck Hollister can't afford to live on those meager little theater scraps he got. He has to sell private performances. Jonathan wasn't a friend of Buck's. He was a client." Max continued, his voice lowering to a conspiratorial tone. "Now imagine what that must've done to a man like Buck. A big, strapping ranch boy from out west, forced to kneel for some two-bit stage pretty boy just to keep himself fed." Max laughed again, short and dry. "He can still look himself in the mirror and swear he's not queer. Just like a starving man can tell himself he's no thief."

"How do you know this?"

"I hired him…once or twice. Even a hard heart needs comfort." He looked toward Rowan as if searching for any hint of condemnation.

None was forthcoming. Rowan's voice remained steady. "And Atlee? Did he pay for Buck's services?"

"It wouldn't surprise me, but I do know that Mr. Burroughs likes them young, even younger than Buck. The *guest* in his apartment is certainly evidence of that."

Rowan lit yet another cigarette. Mr. Kilgus's ashtray was nearly full. "I've heard reports of you expressing your dislike of Jonathan's success. At a recent party."

Walter flipped back in his notes. "Thrown by one Linda Veach."

"I had a lot to drink that night. I could have said anything."

"Specifically, I've been told that you have ambitions for Hollywood." Rowan sat back, watching him. "And that Jonathan's move there bothered you greatly."

"It bothered everybody. My feelings on the matter certainly weren't unique."

"And yet, here you are. At the scene of his death."

The room was sweltering, thick with sweat and breath and the weight of words unspoken under the clang of the radiator.

"Mr. Medwick, did you ever make a film with Jonathan Keltner?"

"We shot some scenes. It wasn't meant for the public. I wanted something I could show potential producers."

"Just so I'm clear, did Jonathan act for you after your initial raves about him in the newspaper."

"Yes."

"He felt obligated to help you."

"I suppose. Where are you going with this?"

Rowan produced a celluloid strip from his pocket. Are these frames from the footage you shot?"

Max held it up to the light. "Yes, where did you get this?"

"This came from the cut-up strips inside Mr. Keltner's apartment. The footage looks as if it were taken from the same footage session."

"I kindly gave some of it to Jonathan. He must have…"

"What? Cut it up and spread it on his floor? Right next to your extortion letter?"

"That should prove my innocence. I could hardly have cut up the film and then taken the time to slip each individual piece under the door."

"I don't think you had to."

"What is that supposed to mean?"

"Thank you for your time and your honesty, Mr. Medwick. You can go back downstairs. I'll join you shortly."

Max lingered at the threshold. "So… can I go home now? Are we finished?"

Rowan didn't even look up. "As I said—wait downstairs."

Max sighed, resigned, and slipped into the hallway without another word.

Once he was gone, Rowan lit a cigarette, the tip flaring like a warning light in the dark.

Walter set down his notepad. "It's funny how not one of those people seems sorry that Jonathan Keltner is dead."

"An astute observation, Williams. In the right circumstances, they may have called Jonathan Keltner a friend or an object of admiration and affection and yet the difference between word and deed could scarcely be starker. The four men sitting in that room are each isolated—by distance or desire. All of them had a motive."

"What's next?"

Rowan took a thoughtful drag off his cigarette. "Let's have a look at that pipe."

The four persons of interest sat huddled at the table, surrounded by police and unable to take their eyes off Rowan as he stood next to the radiator. Walter had gone downstairs to Jonathan's apartment, while Burns had positioned himself in the top-floor unit.

Rowan called down to Walter through the pipe. "Say something, Williams."

His voice echoed up the pipe, warped and metallic. *"What do you want to hear, old boy? I could sing you my favorite. There she is! There she is! That's what keeps me up at night!"*

"Enough."

Though the pipe warped the voice into something ghostly and metallic, the direction was unmistakable—it came from directly below. Rowan recognized it as Walter's, but only because he knew him so well; to anyone else, it might have sounded like a stranger speaking through a mouthful of coins.

"Walk ten feet from the pipe," Rowan instructed, "and say something from there."

The thirty seconds of silence felt like an eternity. Walter's voice finally crackled through again. *"Did you hear that? I think it might have been my best performance."*

Rowan's brow furrowed. "No."

"I was standing ten feet away and singing very loudly."

"All right, Williams, now be quiet." He turned his attention upward. "Officer Burns, say something."

The cop's voice was faint. Rowan had to strain to hear it. "Speak up," he commanded.

"Hello, Mr. Manory!" Burns's voice came through louder this time. Again, it was fuzzy—not easily identifiable—but intelligible. The direction of his voice was easily apparent.

Walter responded from below. *"No need to be so formal, Burns. Just call him Manory."*

Rowan was about to tell Walter to keep quiet, but he stopped himself. His expression shifted, eyes widening slightly, back stiffening as though something had just *clicked* into place.

In the silence, Walter called up to him. *"Do you want us to do anything else, old boy?"*

Rowan's voice was sharp. "No! No, both of you come back to Atlee Burroughs's apartment."

When they arrived, Rowan wasted no time. He gestured to Walter. "I'm going downstairs. I want you to stand right next to the pipe and tell me what you hear."

Walter got into position and Rowan left the room. After a minute or so, Rowan's voice filtered through, weak and muffled.

Walter cupped a hand to his ear. "You have to speak louder!"

Rowan did. *"Can you hear me?"*

Walter nodded. "Yeah, it's a little clearer now. I wouldn't be able to tell it was you, though."

A moment later, Rowan returned, slightly winded. Walter smirked as Rowan caught his breath. "You need to lose a few pounds. One flight of stairs shouldn't do that to you."

Rowan didn't respond to the jab. Instead, he asked Walter and Atlee to join him in the hall.

The three men stood just outside the door.

"Mr. Burroughs, Williams is going to read you the basic reconstruction of the pipe conversation. It doesn't have to be precise. Just tell him if that's the gist or not. Go ahead, Williams."

Walter flipped open his notepad and cleared his throat.

"Good to see you."

"I'm surprised you invited me, Jonathan. I know I gall you."

"That's not true."

"You hate me."

"No, you're the one who hates me. You say it every chance you get. You think I'm not talented...blah, blah, blah. You can't keep your mouth shut."

"Bastard. You're crookeder than a dog's hind legs."

"Let's end this. What's past is past. After I go to California, we won't see each other again."

"Don't smile at me. I'll wipe that smile off your face."

"What have you got there?"

"A knife."

"Don't. Everyone knows you want me dead."

"Half this town wants you dead. I'm not going to get caught. When they find your body, the door will be locked and the key inside. I've planned everything."

Rowan turned to Atlee. "Is that it?"

"Basically, yes."

"Did either of them mention pasta?"

Atlee's brow furrowed. "Paul said he heard that word."

"He said he heard it twice."

"I know, but he was incorrect. Jonathan said the past was the past. I'm certain of it."

"Thank you, Mr. Burroughs. You can go sit down." When Atlee went back inside, Rowan told Walter, "Wait here, I'll be back shortly."

"Where are you going?

"Upstairs to make a few phone calls."

"Wait a minute, old boy—do you know whodunit? I don't want to presume, but...well, you have that look."

"This was a complex, well-plotted crime, but the clues are obvious and the nature of the killer transparent. You have heard and seen all the clues I have." He paused, tilting his head. "Except for one while you were downstairs. Regardless, I think anyone with an understanding of vowel sounds should be able to deduce the killer."

"Vowel sounds?"

"Yes, like the differences of the "a" vowel in *past* and *pasta.*"

"What does that have to do with the murder?"

Rowan gave a wide, satisfied grin.

It wasn't long before Rowan had returned. He stood in the center of Atlee Burroughs's apartment, rocking back on his heels with hands clasped firmly behind his back.

The air was thick with smoke—his own, mostly, curling from the cigarette currently smoldering between his lips. His suit, slightly rumpled from what had become a rather long night, stretched over his portly frame, the wide lapels casting small shadows under the dim lighting. He took a drag, exhaled through his nose, and gave the four suspects a slow, measured look.

An impossible crime," he began, his voice rolling through the apartment with the confidence of a man who'd cracked them before. "It's the sort of thing that sends the common policeman into a tailspin. A man found murdered in a locked room, the key placed inside the door, the time set by two aural witnesses, no method of escape for the killer. A paradox, a puzzle, a damned fine headache for the uninitiated."

He allowed the words to settle, adjusting the cigarette between his fingers, then pacing a few steps forward.

"But for me—" he gestured loosely with his free hand, "—this is familiar territory. I've made my name unraveling these little mysteries. And believe you me, I've seen it all. A man stabbed in a room dusted with flour, no footprints to be found. A woman shot in a bath, no gun and no murderer in sight. One time, I found a fellow strangled inside a closet. The damned thing had been nailed shut from the inside—not locked, *nailed.*" He smirked, shaking his head as if in admiration of past ingenuity.

"This one, though," he continued, letting the smoke drift from his lips, "this one was almost disappointingly simple. Too simple. Which was precisely why I knew there had to be more to it."

He turned, his dark eyes sweeping over the assembled suspects.

"Oh, gentlemen—this was not just an impossible crime. This was a trick within a trick." He tapped his cigarette into a nearby tray, then laced his fingers together. "The first was pure smokescreen. An easily solvable puzzle meant to send our dear friends in blue chasing shadows. But the second… ah, the second was meant to solidify the killer. This would be a solution for which the detective could pat himself on the back with satisfaction." He paused. A deliberate silence.

He wanted them to feel it. The weight of his words, the certainty in his voice. Then, ever so slightly, he smiled. "But unfortunately for our clever killer, the final layer of evidence tells an altogether different story."

He pointed at Max. "You, Mr. Medwick, were the only one who wasn't supposed to be here and yet your figurative fingerprints are strewn over the crime scene."

"I'm sorry," said Max. "What does that mean?"

"It means that your review was the only thing found in Mr. Keltner's pocket. It means the poison pen letter was found right next to the cut-up and twisted film strips that you shot. Why?"

"It's simple really. I slipped the letter under the door like I said, Jonathan must have used my review for motivation and carried it around on him, and I know nothing as to why our film was on the floor."

"Did Jonathan carry the review around with him for five months?"

"Pardon?"

"You told me that the review was published in June or July, but the newspaper was still crisp. It's almost as if the clipping had been purposefully planted."

"Why would it be planted?"

"To make the police suspect you as the killer. The filmstrips would do the same. A cursory glance would suggest that they were a message left by a failed filmmaker intent on revenge."

"And," said Max carefully. "—what would a careful second glance suggest?"

"It's laid on a bit thick, isn't it? This isn't a trail, it's a parade."

Rowan walked to Atlee's door and pulled it open. "This door was found shut, the latch engaged, and when tested, the handle would not turn. Is that correct, Officer Burns?"

"That's correct, Detective. I had to break it down by force."

"The key was in the keyhole and there was no alternate means of entry, no windows or other exits."

"That's right."

"The first instinct, naturally, was to assume the door had been locked from the inside. *But it wasn't locked at all.* It only appeared to be."

Burns protested. "I told you already. The knob wouldn't budge."

"I believe you, Officer." Rowan stepped forward, resting a hand on Atlee's door handle. "The doors in this building are fitted with a standard spring latch bolt—the sort you'd find in most apartments of the city. Unlike a deadbolt, which requires a key to retract, a spring latch can be withdrawn simply by turning the handle." He tapped at the extended latch bolt. "The door downstairs was broken. Luckily, we have an exact replica for demonstration."

As the cops gathered round the door, one of the suspects flinched ever so slightly. Rowan noticed, but he pretended not to.

"This crucial element of this trick is the mechanism of the latch. It must be extended fully into the strike plate before it can retract. If something obstructs it at just the right moment, the latch sticks in place, unable to proceed or recede. The handle won't turn, and the door, though technically unlocked, behaves as though it were sealed tight."

He demonstrated by releasing the handle and stopping the latch bolt from extending completely by holding it in place. Then he attempted to turn the handle. It wouldn't budge.

"Obviously, our killer couldn't hold the latch in place with his fingers. He needed an object to place there. It had to be thin and flexible, something that could in the small space between the bottom of the latch and the bottom hollow of the plate."

Walter's eyes grew wide. "The celluloid!"

"Correct. If positioned correctly, a folded strip of film would prevent the bolt from fully engaging when the door swings shut. The result? The latch is caught in place, unable to retract and unable to move forward. The handle won't turn, and to any casual observer, the door seems properly locked."

He straightened, smoothing the front of his coat. "Of course, this method presents two problems for the culprit. The first is that the door is unlocked. All the detective would have to do after breaking the door open is turn the handle. Immediately, he would realize that the door was never locked in the first place. In *The Glass Dagger*, the killer is able to surreptitiously lock the door after it had been broken down. In our case, the killer got lucky. The door panel housing the latch bolt was splintered, and the latch bolt itself was bent. There was no way to test the door and see that it was actually unlocked."

"The second and more important problem is that the film strip would be knocked to the floor when the door is broken in. That's how the trick was caught in *The Glass Dagger*. The detective in that story was able to piece the solution together because of the presence of a strip of film."

Walter scratched his head. "Why did our killer lay hundreds of film strips in front of the door?"

"To hide the trick. Naturally, we would believe that Max Medwick's film was a message from the disgruntled creator to his reluctant muse. It was a frame job."

Buck wrung his hands as he rocked back and forth on his kitchen stool. "You think I tried to frame Max and then hide my mother's trick? Is that the idea?"

Rowan turned his attention to Buck. "You must admit the crime fits you perfectly. The conversation, in particular, is a smoking gun. It obliquely refers to your…*um*…services that you provided Mr. Keltner. We both know you lied to me. Jonathan Keltner was as queer as a three-dollar bill and so are you. At least for the right price."

Buck smoldered, but he didn't deny the statement.

"Add in the low self-esteem, the jealousy, and the rather colorful phrases used by the killer—I'd say the conversation is quite damning. The knife being exactly as you described your own knives is the metaphorical cherry on top. Case closed."

"I guess I should talk to a lawyer then because I had nothing to do with—"

"Not so fast, Buck. That part about the latch bolt getting bent—that wasn't meant to happen. I said that the killer had gotten lucky, but I have the strangest feeling that the trick was meant to be discovered even if Chicago's greatest detective hadn't arrived on the scene. No, I think the evidence against you has the same problems as the evidence against Max. It's far too perfect."

Burns, who had been slowly steeling himself to move in

and arrest Buck, asked, "What do you mean by that, Detective?"

"First, the evidence points to Max—the review, the poison-pen letter, the film strips. But it's too neat. And then, another layer—Buck, with his history, his connection to Keltner. The locked room trick in particular is far too readily explained. If he had done it, surely he would know that his mother had used the exact same trick in a famous novel. And the knife—Buck wouldn't leave the same kind of knife he owns sticking out of the victim. The whole affair reeks of misdirection. Unless they are committing an unplanned murder of passion, killers spend a great deal of time thinking of ways not to get caught. This murder was well-planned. Buck didn't commit murder."

"Well, if those two didn't kill Jonathan Keltner, who did?"

Rowan pointed his cigarette toward Atlee and Paul. "I believe we should be looking in an altogether different direction."

Atlee, who had been leaning back with practiced ease, stiffened just enough to betray himself—a faint tightening of the shoulders, a moment's hesitation before reaching for his glass. Beside him, Paul went utterly still, his hand frozen around his own throat.

For a beat, neither spoke. The warmth of the room, the soft glow of the lamp—everything that had felt familiar only seconds ago—now pressed in like an interrogation light. Rowan hadn't even said their names, but the weight of his gaze did the work for him.

Atlee licked his teeth. "Don't you remember, Detective. Paul and I were right here, together when the murder happened. That is indisputable."

Rowan stamped out his cigarette. "We'll get to that. You have the strongest motive, Mr. Burroughs. All of your recent plays starred Mr. Keltner. It is obvious his departure is the reason you cannot find work. You alluded to that fact yourself."

"I was equally responsible for the play's success."

"Apparently your former producers disagree. They thought the box office draw was entirely due to Jonathan's popularity otherwise you would still be working. You must now teach rather than do. Of course, there are perks to teaching, youthful perks. But even those won't last much longer. A doddering old man, reading glasses permanently perched in his greying hair, is not an object of affection."

"Detective Manory, I have endured many things in my years in the theater—scathing reviews, backstage betrayals, artistic sabotage. But rarely have I been so insulted."

"You live in the same building as Jonathan. You would know his comings and goings. The physical aspects of committing this crime certainly make you a suspect, but it's the psychological factor that makes the idea so intriguing. You taught him. You were always there to help him."

"Our friendship was casual. I told you."

"That's a lie. You cannot direct someone in several plays with the span of a few years and then claim to be casual acquaintances. You can despise him or love him, but there is nothing casual about it. You built Jonathan's career. You made him what he became. When Hollywood came calling, he abandoned you. Isn't that what happened?"

Atlee said nothing.

In the silence, Rowan rolled up a pinch of tobacco into a paper, struck a match, and puffed the cigarette to life. A cloud of bilious smoke encased his visage. It slowly cleared away to reveal that the detective was now looking at someone else. "Funnily enough, it is you, Paul Chase, whom I find the most intriguing of suspects."

Paul's face had slowly turned ashen during Rowan's speech, as if every word made him appear more ghostly. His gaze turned to Atlee then Max, everyone else in the room one at a time before returning to Rowan. "Suspect? Mr…Detective…I…"

"During your interview, you tried your best to make it seem as if your appearance here was entirely Atlee's idea. The fact is you knew what Atlee wanted with you. Buck told you. What's more, you made sure to impress upon Atlee that you were lonely. He did not ensnare you, but rather *you* courted *him*."

"I am lonely," he blurted. "I wasn't lying."

"You liked that Atlee was interested in you. That was a good thing, was it not?"

Paul swallowed as if about to vomit again. "I want to go home."

Rowan exhaled a slow stream of smoke, his eyes settling on Paul with something between pity and amusement.

"Murder has been committed, my dear boy. That changes everything. Whatever propriety, whatever shame you may feel—it means nothing now. There are no secrets in a building where a man has been killed." He tapped his cigarette against the tray, watching the ash tumble.

"Pride, embarrassment, even desire—frivolous concerns in the face of death. The only thing that matters now is the truth."

"I said I want to go home."

"Hallidayboro or the dormitory?"

Paul stood. "I haven't done anything."

Burns quickly stepped forward and guided Paul back to his seat. "You get up again, I'm going to knock you on your ass, kid. Don't get brave now."

Paul slunk into his chair. "I think I'm going to be sick."

Rowan ignored the warning. "The facts are intriguing—the way they allow for you to know so much…*obliquely*. You don't seem directly involved. In a game of poker, you would be the wild card. Everyone else here, victim included, is a success, a professional. Except you. If Atlee gave Jonathan a career, he could do the same for you. All you'd have to do is allow him certain privileges over your body."

Atlee's face went blank. He scooted his stool back a few inches from Paul. "My God."

Rowan ignored the gesture. "Let's face it, Paul. You certainly knew enough to plot this murder. Max was at the party, drunkenly detailing his issues with Jonathan. You heard everything. Framing Buck wouldn't be hard. His extracurricular activities are not a secret and you admitted to owning the book his mother wrote."

"I told you I haven't read it." Paul was sobbing when he spoke now.

"Did you tell me the whole truth in your interview?"

"Yes!"

"Really. Did you tell me the truth about why you came here tonight?"

Paul's breath hitched. His lips quivered. He couldn't speak.

"I'll tell you what I think. I think you were terrified that the romance between Atlee and Jonathan might resume when Jonathan was back in Chicago. That wouldn't be good for you would it. You wanted to be Atlee's new protégé."

Atlee gasped. "He was very interested in Jonathan when we spoke tonight. He brought him up in conversation out of nowhere."

Paul shook his head. "Atlee, please—don't listen to him!"

"It's true, Detective!. He was far more interested in Jonathan than he was in me. I had a feeling about it."

Rowan nodded. "I thought that was the case."

Atlee asked, "But how did he do it. I swear to you that I heard the murder happen and he was sitting right next to me."

"We'll get to that in a moment. First, I'd like to ask Paul something."

Rowan took a slow step forward, his gaze locked on Paul like a predator closing in on its prey. His voice dropped, quiet but laced with a venom that cut deeper than any shout.

"What do you think your parents are going to say when they find out what you've been up to in the big city? What will your father think when he hears his boy—a boy raised under his own roof, with his name, his blood—has been whoring himself out to older men for the promise of success?"

"Oh my God," whispered Paul.

Rowan sneered, letting the words fester. "Your mother will probably convince herself it isn't true. But your father? He'll know. He'll see it clear as day, just like I do. Just like the jury will. He'll spit your name out like something rotten. He'll wipe his hands of you, Paul." Rowan's voice sharpened, the words twisting like a knife. "A filthy little degenerate."

Paul was crumpled on his stool now, knees drawn to his chest. "I'm sorry," he whispered. 'I didn't want to hurt anyone."

Just as the entire room thought Rowan was going to pounce on the boy, the detective pulled back. He took a stool in his hand and set it right in front of Atlee before sitting down.

"Look at him, Mr. Burroughs. He's the perfect patsy. Easy to manipulate. Easy to control. I just molded him into a heaping mess in seconds."

The color drained from Atlee's face—not all at once, but in increments, like a curtain being drawn back to let in the cold light of morning. His fingers, which had been loosely steepled in front of him, curled inward. His throat bobbed with a hard swallow. The nervous energy he'd been holding at bay—dissipated, gone—came roaring back with a vengeance. His breathing quickened, shallow but controlled, a man trying to keep pace with his own rising panic.

"Surely, I don't know what you mean."

"You understood perfectly that Paul would do anything you said. You must have seen the way he looked at you in front of the class. How he hung on every word and laughed at every joke."

"I have never forced myself onto anyone."

"No, I imagine you've never laid a hand on them. That's not your way. You don't shove—shoving is crude. You *guide*. You lay out the road, you light the lamps, you tell them how *lucky* they are to be walking it. And when they hesitate, when their conscience stirs or their stomach knots, you never demand. You just *wait*—wait for their own uncertainty, their own longing, to do the pushing for you."

Rowan tilted his head slightly, his eyes sharp as glass.

"No, you never force them. You just make sure they can't quite tell where *their* desire ends and *yours* begins. And by the time they do, it's too late, isn't it?"

"That's quite the self-righteous speech, Detective. If you have proof that I've broken some law, I suggest you present it."

"There were small hints on the scene, nothing airtight mind you, but some elements pointed in your direction. There were no footprints in Jonathan's apartment, yet everyone else—Max, Paul, and Buck—had walked through the ice storm and were soaked to the bone. They would have left something the same way Officer Burns did. And the way you were the one pushing Buck as the killer during your interview. It would have sweet revenge on the one student who violently rebuffed your advances."

Atlee summoned all the bluster he could. "Enough with the games. How did I do it when I was up here with Paul the entire time? Say it now, or admit you have nothing."

"I figured that out when I tested the pipe. You see, it was obvious that sound could carry one floor, but it was only when Williams communicated with Officer Burns that I realized sound could travel *two* floors. And *that's* when I remembered you had mentioned a basement."

"I don't understand."

"Of course you do, Mr. Burrough. The murder, at least aurally, was a performance, carefully staged. And the actors? Not on the scene of the crime, but in the basement below. Two performers in the basement acted the scene you had written. Paul was your unknowing alibi."

"That's…that's absurd."

"Not at all. I tested it out by speaking from the basement and Walter heard me perfectly well in this very apartment."

Walter raised a hand. "Who were the actors?"

"Just moment, Williams. We are almost there. Atlee knew Jonathan Keltner would be in town and more importantly, he knew that Buck had a scheduled...*appointment* with Jonathan."

Atlee breathed a little heavier. "When...when would I have the opportunity? I don't—"

"You killed Jonathan earlier, let's say sometime after six o'clock. The murder took place near the left side of his apartment. That was a problem because it was necessary for the murder to happen near the pipe."

"Why?" asked Burns.

"Because, as I discovered later, one must be speaking right next to the pipe in order for the sound to travel to the other floors. Naturally, Atlee couldn't drag the body to the pipe—the blood trail would prove the true location of the murder."

Burns gasped. "So, I was right! The body was placed inside the rug for transportation. But not out of the apartment. Just toward the pipe."

Walter patted him on the back. "Shame on Manory for trying to make you look foolish."

Rowan continued laying out the plot to Atlee. "You planted both the review and the film strips. In your elaborately staged murder, the red herring had his own red herring. You wanted the murder to appear as if Buck were trying to frame Max for the murder. The locked-room trick was the same one you had read in Victoria Hollister's book. Buck would naturally be the primary suspect. After you positioned the body near the pipe, you set up the celluloid strips, planted the review, and performed the locked-room trick. At around 6:45, your actors arrived. You paid them and led them into the basement. They were given a time to perform. 7:15 on the dot."

"How could you possibly know that?"

"Give me just another minute, Mr. Burroughs. I'll answer every desperate question you throw at me. The plan almost didn't work because Paul was late. Thankfully for you, he arrived just in time to hear the murder scene. You set him next to the radiator to get warm and you made sure he stayed there. After the actors in the basement finished their scene, they followed their instructions and left through the bulkhead. None of the apartments have a back door, but the basement has stairs leading directly to the back exit. Nobody would notice them leaving. The police, Max, Buck—they all entered through the front door."

"That's…" Atlee could barely bring himself to issue a denial. "That's all guesswork. Guesswork doesn't hold up in court."

"You were almost foiled again. Buck arrived much earlier than expected. You knew he had auditions because you're friends with the director. Because most of the actors didn't show, he finished his audition before 7:00. Had he arrived just a few minutes earlier, he might have ruined everything. Hell, he might have knocked on your door before the actors had a chance to play out the scene. That would have been awkward."

"Yes, but—how can you prove any of this?" said Atlee quickly. His voice carried an edge of forced steadiness, but his fingers, curled around the arms of his chair, had gone white at the knuckles. A bead of sweat traced a slow path down his temple, ignored, as he latched onto the one thing keeping him afloat—doubt.

"It's a great story, fine for the pages of *Detection Magazine.* But how could you get a jury to convict me?"

To this, Rowan quietly, confidently said one simple word. "Pasta."

"Pasta?"

"A major issue with you plan is keeping the actors quiet. The next day, they would read about Jonathan's murder in the newspaper. Knowing that they performed a scene involving the death of someone named Jonathan and it was performed at the apartment building you shared, they would no doubt call the police and report it."

Rowan turned away and blew a steady stream of smoke on the glowing ember of his cigarette. His gaze softened, as if staring into that fire brought him the gift of second sight.

"Then I remembered—you had told me about hosting a workshop for British students. These students had been staying in Chicago for two weeks. They were scheduled to board a train at 11:30 this evening to begin the first leg of their long, arduous trip back to London. If you managed to pay two of these students to perform the scene, they would be on a train and a boat for the next week. When they got back to England, they'd have no idea about the murder. Mr. Keltner wasn't quite world famous yet. I telephoned the Goodman dormitory master."

Rowan pulled out a slip of paper from his pocket and set it in front of Atlee.

"Andrew Finch and Hugh Dalrymple will not be joining their classmates on the trip back to London because they will have to give sworn statements to the Chicago police in the morning. They will swear that you told them you wanted to play a joke on a friend. You paid them ten American Dollars to perform your murder in the basement. Then, they left the scene quickly, just as they were instructed. They will also swear to the timetable I've laid out for you."

Walter asked, "What does that have to do with pasta, old boy? That's the explanation I've been waiting for."

"Hugh Dalrymple was the one playing Jonathan. When I spoke with him over the phone, I asked him the say the word *past*. He pronounced the vowel sound the same way Americans pronounce the vowel sound in pasta—the *paahhst* is the *paahhst*. When Paul heard the line, he thought he heard the word *pasta* twice. It's an obscure clue and I must say it was a great thrill for me to deduce. It kept bothering me and I couldn't stop thinking about it. And then it hit me. The actor had fallen out of his Chicago accent for a moment."

He stared down Atlee. "You were done in by a bad performance. In any event, we have the proof, we have the motive, and we have the killer. I suppose the confession is meaningless except for your own conscience, Mr. Burrough."

Atlee looked around the room. Every eye was glued to him now.

"Little did you know," said Rowan.

"What?" whispered Atlee.

"Little did you know when you woke up this morning that today would be the most important day of your life."

Silence overtook the room.

Atlee turned to the opened champagne bottle on the table. He poured himself a glass. The champagne dribbled down with a lifeless trickle. A few bubbles struggled to rise, popping weakly before they reached the top, leaving nothing but a dull, pale liquid that clung to the sides like it had given up. No effervescence, no sparkle—just the sad remains of something that had once been celebratory, now as flat and tired as the end of a long night.

He lifted the glass. "Happy New Year."

<u>THE END</u>

OTHER WORKS BY

JAMES SCOTT BYRNSIDE

Rowan Manory Mysteries

Goodnight Irene (2018)

The Opening Night Murders (2019)

The Strange Case of the Barrington Hills Vampire (2020)

Monkey See, Monkey Murder (2023)

Standalone Mysteries

The 5 False Suicides (2021)

www.ingramcontent.com/pod-product-compliance
Lightning Source LLC
Chambersburg PA
CBHW030655260626
47157CB00007B/2656

9798218688172